"Are you sure he's dead?"

"His axis vertebra is fractured," said the chiropractor.

"Oh."

Another siren wailed to the door, and a plump, middle-aged black man joined us in the waiting room. The friendly creases in his face were overridden by his current frown. Officer Terhanchi introduced him as Sergeant Green and attempted to explain Younger's injuries.

"Broken neck," summarized the chiropractor helpfully.

"There's a long metal bar with blood on it next to the chair in there. I picked it up," I said. Sooner or later they'd find out anyway . . .

Diamond Books by Jaqueline Girdner

ADJUSTED TO DEATH
THE LAST RESORT

ADJUSTED TO DEATH

JAQUELINE GIRDNER

DIAMOND BOOKS, NEW YORK

ADJUSTED TO DEATH

A Diamond Book / published by arrangement with
the author

PRINTING HISTORY
Diamond edition / January 1991

ISBN: 1-55773-453-4

Diamond Books are published by The Berkley Publishing Group,
200 Madison Avenue, New York, New York 10016.
The name ''DIAMOND'' and its logo are trademarks
belonging to Charter Communications, Inc.

PRINTED IN THE UNITED STATES OF AMERICA

10 9 8 7 6 5 4 3 2

For Greg

AUTHOR'S NOTE

The city and police department of Mill Valley as portrayed in *Adjusted to Death* are purely fictional, a product of the author's imagination, not to be confused with the real Mill Valley and its excellent police department in Marin County, California.

- One -

A VISIT TO the doctor's office always reminds me of death. Walking into the chiropractor's is no better, especially if you're there for a spinal adjustment. There's just something about being greeted by that sterile smell, the white paint and the false smile on the receptionist's face. But that morning the chiropractor's receptionist wasn't even pretending to smile. Renee's sturdy frame vibrated with displeasure. Every strand of her dark permed hair was coiled like a snake ready to strike. She pursed her lips and eyes, wrinkling the surrounding tan skin, as I came through the door.

The small waiting room was crowded and silent, none of the usual space music softly wafting in the background. Four of the eight Scandinavian-design chairs were occupied. I knew those inexpensive teak and beige upholstered chairs well. I had two just like them in that minuscule room I called my sales office. I had never seen more than two or three chairs filled at my chiropractor's before. I walked cautiously toward the receptionist's desk, also of Scandinavian-design teak.

"Kate Jasper," I told Renee. It was five years now since I'd been coming to Maggie for chiropractic treatment, but Renee still pretended she couldn't remember my name.

"You're early!" she said, aiming a sharpened red-nailed finger at me. Her accusation rang out in the silence.

I sighed. No gold star for punctuality here.

"And they're late," she continued, pointing in the general direction of a tall black woman sitting erectly with an expression of bliss on her face, and two white men, heads bent over their respective copies of *Rolling Stone* magazine. The black woman's eyes narrowed angrily for a moment before regaining serenity. The men ignored Renee.

"So how the hell am I supposed to get everyone in if they're late, Ted's on time"—I saw an older man with a crook in his neck. He waved at us. He must be Ted—"and you're early?"

I opened my mouth to answer, but was saved by the *whoosh* of a new victim coming through the door. I turned and watched the arrival of a wispy woman swathed in layers of purple. A young woman in jeans and an off-the-shoulder shirt clumped in behind her. I slunk over to the chair furthest from Renee, next to "on time" Ted, and sat down. It was cold there by the door, but in that position I could enjoy a clear view of everyone in the room.

"I'm early," the wispy woman announced in a hoarse but triumphant tone.

All heads in the waiting room moved simultaneously to better see and hear Renee's reaction. Would this timeliness provoke Renee to physical violence?

"Sit down!" she said. The words themselves were anticlimactic. But the delivery was so vehement that the wispy woman stepped back as if pushed, then winced at the pain the step had cost her. The younger woman took her by the hand and led her to a chair. But, before she sat down, one of the two men reading *Rolling Stone* rose to his feet.

"Aren't you Julie Moore?" he asked. The second man also stood up.

I remembered seeing these two guys in the office before. I had dubbed them Beauty and the Beast. The first man was classically good-looking, his pale triangular face nearly feminine with its small perfect mouth and bright blue eyes. His black hair was long in the back, but razor-cut short on the front and sides. The second man was one of the ugliest human beings I'd ever seen. His scarred face was dominated by a huge cauliflower nose and brows so low you had to be below him to see his eyes. His brown hair seemed incongruous as it curled softly over his pitted forehead. The only similarity between the two men was their stature. Both were tall and muscular.

The wispy woman seemed startled by the question.

"Yes, well, no, I . . ." She paused to breathe.

"Mom used to call herself that," said the young woman. "Now she calls herself Devi Moore."

Her mother was apparently incapable of further speech. Her skin was pale and I could hear her labored breathing from across the room. Whether her indisposition was occasioned by Renee, a cold, the first sight of the Beast, or Beauty's question I couldn't tell.

"Devi?" asked the man with a smirk.

"Yeah, you know, 'the ultimate reality in its feminine form,' " her daughter said in a singsong voice. She poked her mother lightly with an elbow.

"Well, I'm Scott Younger," the man said. "Your mother ought to remember me from her college days."

Before Devi or her daughter could respond, the black woman mouthed an obscenity, rose to her full six-foot height and moved to another chair across the room, for no obvious reason. She grimaced and clutched her lower back as she sat down in her new seat.

"And who are you?" Younger asked the girl, ignoring the interruption.

"I'm Tanya Moore," she said.

"That's enough," said Tanya's mother, finally recovering her faculty of speech. She grabbed her daughter's hand and dragged her to sit next to the black woman on the other side of the room.

"Nice meeting you, Tanya," Younger said, smiling across the room. "This is my friend, Wayne." He pointed at the Beast, who grunted softly.

Tanya opened her mouth to reply but was silenced by her mother's whispered "Don't talk to strangers."

"Mom, don't be weird. I'm fifteen years old, you know. What happened to universal openness and that kinda stuff?"

Younger's eyes widened with amusement at her response.

"You listen to your mama, girl. That man's a drug pusher, you hear, a drug pusher!" said the black woman.

Younger opened his mouth to object but then closed it again, shrugged his shoulders and sat down. Wayne sat down, too.

For an overcast November morning in upscale mellow Marin this was pretty heady stuff. I wasn't sure what was going on, but it was certainly the most exciting wait for the chiropractor that I had ever experienced. Even Renee's aggravation had passed. She now was staring, bug-eyed and slack-jawed at Scott Younger and Wayne. Was the man really a drug pusher? I wondered. And what was his relationship with Wayne? On the two occasions I had seen them here before it appeared that only Younger had been treated. Was Wayne his friend, lover, or keeper? He certainly didn't look like his brother. The two of them had buried themselves in the pages of their magazines again.

I took a better look at Devi and her daughter Tanya. Devi was thin and pale, her ash-blond hair as wispy as the rest of her. She was a symphony in purple, from the silk scarf wrapped around her neck to the suede boots on her feet. The only relief was the black of the yin-yang symbols embroidered on the ends of her scarf. Tanya was plumper, her short dark hair contrasting agreeably with her blue eyes and kewpie-doll mouth. The skin of her heart-shaped face had that clear, rose-petal soft quality that makes a middle-aged woman sigh with envy. I sighed.

"Has your mother ever told you the story of Saint Akkamahadevi, who loved Shiva?" asked the black woman. She sat erectly again, her strong features softened by the light shining from her large dark eyes.

"Oh my God, another teaching story," the girl responded. "Do you follow a guru or something?"

"Yes, Guru Illumananda. I have been blessed by her teachings. I'm Valerie Davis."

"Oh, I know Guru Illumananda," said Devi breathlessly. "Well, I don't *know* her, but I know her. Oh, let's see, two years ago maybe, I received Darshan from her. She tapped me on the shoulder and I felt her wisdom enter me, like—like I don't know, maybe electricity." She took some short breaths.

Devi's eyes sparkled like Valerie's. Their faces were luminous, like the old paintings of saints. Tanya groaned and rolled her eyes. Younger winked at her from across the room.

"Mom, I'm kinda hungry. Can I go to the 7-Eleven and, like, get something to eat?"

"No candy bars, honey."

"You know that guy?" came a question whispered in my ear. I jumped in my seat. I was so busy watching the others that I had forgotten I was sitting next to someone. I turned toward Ted, who had bent his crooked neck in my direction. He looked to be about sixty, with grey tangled eyebrows over lively brown eyes. His rabbity teeth were engulfed by a walrus mustache.

"Who? Scott Younger?"

He nodded, his mustache bobbing energetically.

"No, do you?" I returned the question.

"No, dunno much about him either. My wife knows him,

though. On some art committee with him. That'd sure get them riled up if they thought he was a dope pusher. Think he is?''

I looked at him. I hoped Scott Younger couldn't hear our whispers, or guess at their content.

"My name's Kate," I said, changing the subject.

"Sorry, heh, guess I forgot my manners. I'm Ted Reisner, Reisner's Hardware.'' He pulled out a business card and handed it to me. Silver ink spelled out the store's name in the shapes of various tools arranged against a royal blue background.

"Quite a work of art," I said, feeling the embossed pattern of the tools with my fingers.

"My wife made it. She's a real talented woman, heh, too talented to be wasted on an old coot like me. But I guess she doesn't know any better.'' He winked. ''What do you do?''

"I own my own business," I answered briefly. I was not exactly ashamed of the nature of my business, but I did find it slightly embarrassing. It is hard to talk about a gag-gift business with the same dignity associated with, say, a computer company, or a brokerage firm, or a hardware store for that matter.

"What kind of business, if you don't mind me asking?''

I did, but I told him anyway. "Jest Gifts. Spelled J-e-s-t. I design and sell novelty items by mail order, to professional people. Doctors, lawyers, chiropractors, people like that.''

"Sounds real interesting. What kind of items?''

This guy could have been an interrogator for the CIA. I pointed across the room to the coffee mug on the receptionist's desk. The mug's handle was formed into a curved skeletal spine. The lettering on the side read "chiropractors are well-adjusted people.''

"That's one," I said.

He jumped up out of his chair to take a better look. When he reached Renee's desk he picked it up. He laughed at the inscription, held it in the air and asked loudly, "Is this yours?'' I nodded, resisting the urge to bury my red face in a magazine.

"No it's not. It's mine!'' said Renee, grabbing it away from him.

Ted was saved from further attack by the entrance of Eileen Garza, Maggie's chiropractic assistant. She came gliding down the hall from one of the treatment rooms and put her arm around Ted's waist. Eileen was a small, dark-skinned woman with long black hair, whose gentle loveliness brought to mind Gauguin's paradise.

"Getting in trouble again, Ted?" she asked with a full, generous smile. I could almost feel the soft summer breeze in the palm trees.

"Heh, heh. Wouldn't mind getting in trouble with you, darling," he said.

"How about I put you face down on a table, put a hot-pack on your neck and let you think about your sins till Maggie comes in to play with your spine?"

"No manacles? Heh-heh. No spikes? You spoil me."

"But you'll have to sit down for a while until I get Mr. Younger set up." Her expression became more businesslike.

A heavyset woman erupted from the nearest treatment room, put on a pair of roller skates, waved, and skated out the door. Ted sat back down next to me.

"That woman's a stockbroker, you know," he said.

"Which woman?"

"The roller derby queen. Helluva nice woman, though."

Eileen turned to Scott Younger and asked him to follow her. Her tone, though not cool, was noticeably different from the warm voice she had used with Ted. Younger got up and followed her graceful form. Wayne did likewise. The parade disappeared down the hallway.

A few moments later Eileen came back and escorted Ted to the room which the roller skater had vacated. I could hear him chattering and chortling until the door slid shut. Devi walked down the hall toward the restroom. As soon as she was out of sight, Tanya slipped out the front door, presumably headed for the 7-Eleven.

I picked up a pamphlet titled "Restoring and Maintaining Health through Chiropractic Adjustment," and pretended to read. Valerie sat without moving, her dark face beatified. Renee quietly did paperwork. I was almost disappointed in the lull. It gave me time to imagine the chiropractic treatment to come, which ranked only above dental and gynecological exams on my list of favorite activities.

I knew that the pain in either my lower back or neck would ambush me if I didn't get my regular treatment. And Maggie was good. But there was always that inevitable moment when she would twist and snap my neck while commanding me to relax, listening for that satisfying spinal *pop*. And then she would start the whole process over again if my recalcitrant neck remained silent.

Before I had worked up a good sweat, Wayne came back down the hall and stood in the middle of the waiting room, his eyes focused on a spot on the wall above our heads. At that angle I could see the large melting brown eyes that were previously hidden under those brows.

"Nothing wrong with him. Just likes children. Doesn't have any of his own. The rest, it's all in the past," he said in a low, soft growl, and then returned to his seat and *Rolling Stone*.

As I considered his pronouncement Maggie came bounding into the waiting room like a golden retriever hoping for a Frisbee. My chiropractor was a big-boned woman, massively freckled, whose frizzy red hair was constantly escaping from the rubber band that held it away from her face. I could see a brown stain on one of the ducks on her sweat shirt as she crossed the room toward me.

"Kate, how are you?" she said. "I heard you and Craig are back together. That's so neat!"

"We were, but he moved out again," I said in the low voice I used in front of strangers while talking about my affairs, especially my affair with my almost ex-husband.

"Oh wow! But why?" she asked, her volume unmodulated.

"I should never have let him move back in, that's why. Things were fine when we were only dating."

"But you can't just 'date' your husband."

"That's what he kept saying. And after a while I believed him. So I finally asked him to come home." I could see Eileen taking Valerie to another treatment room. At least that was one less witness to the tale of my marital un-bliss.

"What happened?"

"The same as always. His business took precedence over his wife. We may both be fanatical vegetarians and enjoy bad puns, but beyond that . . . I don't think he actually likes me that much."

I knew that wasn't exactly true, but I couldn't explain it any better right there in her occupied waiting room. I averted my gaze from Maggie's moistly concerned eyes and watched Renee go through the connecting door into the business office. The only witness left in the reception area was Wayne. I hoped he wasn't listening. I couldn't tell from the top of his curly head, all that remained visible over his magazine. I turned my eyes back to Maggie. Her expression was still stricken.

"Maybe he'll go get himself a tall, voluptuous blonde this

time," I said in what I hoped was a nonchalant tone. "He's obviously had enough of short, dark, and A-line."

"But that doesn't sound like Craig at all," she said.

"Tall blondes? Probably not, unless she can cook vegetarian, dairyless meals. But he is gone, I assure you."

"But the last time I saw Craig he couldn't stop talking about how much he loved you, how glad he was you were back together."

"Please, Maggie, I know that. I . . . I've got to go to the bathroom."

I heard her say how sorry she was as I raced my tears down the hall to the restroom.

"Damn that man!" I said to the mirror above the sink, a few minutes later. I dabbed my eyes with a cold, wet, paper towel. The mirror was rusting on one edge and the bathroom had the same sterile smell as the waiting room, but the cold water felt good on my swollen eyes. I turned and memorized the bronze irises on the poster that was the only decoration in the white-walled room until I was in control again. Then I walked back down the hall toward the waiting room with studied dignity.

Maggie ambushed me as I passed the open door to her office.

"Jeez, Kate, I'm sorry I was so pushy. I, of all people, should know that sometimes even good, kind people just can't be married to each other. Will you forgive me?"

"Of course." I gave her hand a quick squeeze. I had forgotten that Maggie was divorced. I had never been that curious before about the details.

"What happened to you . . . ?" I began.

"Haven't you seen any of these patients yet?" Renee shouted from the waiting room, shattering the moment. "All the treatment rooms are full and we've got two more waiting. What the hell are you doing?"

"Sheesh, I'm going, I'm going," said Maggie. "Kate, do me a favor. Tell Scott Younger that I'll be about ten more minutes. He's in the last treatment room down, across from the restroom. I've got to see Ted first."

I nodded in agreement and wondered if this was her idea of occupational therapy. It was certainly a lot better than hanging around in the waiting room reading chiropractic propaganda.

I went back down the hallway and slid open the door of the last room. The walls of the room were mauve, the floor tiled with alternating blue and white diamonds of color. The only furnishings were two treatment tables and a chair. The first table was a multipurpose therapeutic couch on which patients were massaged by electrically operated rollers underneath the leather. It also had attachments for traction and other un-imaginable tortures. I tripped over one of those attachments as I entered the room, a long metal bar whose purpose I didn't want to think about. I picked it up gingerly and set it down on the lone chair.

The second table had a narrow padded surface with a hole at one end where your face could rest. On it Scott Younger lay face down, his arms dangling over the edges. I wished I could relax like that. His hot-pack had even slid off onto the floor, apparently unnoticed. When I lay on that table, I always clutched the handles on the sides during that endless stretch of time before Maggie arrived to pop my spine into place.

"Maggie says to tell you she'll see you in about ten minutes," I said.

He didn't answer. I figured he was asleep.

Sighing, I crossed the room and touched his shoulder softly to awaken him.

It was then that I noticed a small pool of blood on the back of his neck, just above the collar. I stopped breathing. The pool seemed to shimmer in psychedelic red clarity against the blackness of his hair. With icy hands I grabbed his shoulder and shook it hard; it was unnaturally heavy.

"Maggie!" I screamed.

- Two -

MAGGIE AND WAYNE were a close match running into the room, but Wayne sprinted ahead at the doorway. Maggie regained the lead quickly though once she saw my expression, shoving both of us aside to take Younger's pulse. She shouted over her shoulder at Renee to call an ambulance. When she couldn't find a pulse in Younger's wrist, she moved her hands up toward his carotid artery. Her eyes widened as she saw the blood. She felt the back of his neck with those large, strong hands, and her face lost all color under its freckles.

"Better make that the police," she said.

"The police?" asked Renee at the doorway.

"His neck is broken."

Wayne yelped and moved to approach Younger. Maggie gently intercepted him.

"He's dead. You can't do him any good," she said.

My upper torso floated selfishly toward the only chair in the room, dragging my weakened legs along unresisting. I flopped down onto that chair, only to pop back up again, goosed by the hard edges of the object beneath me. It was the metal bar. I picked it up and resumed my seat.

"Can't be dead," Wayne said, and then repeated himself softly.

Eileen came in and wrapped her dark arms around Maggie. Maggie's large form seemed to melt into the smaller woman. Wayne dropped to the floor next to my chair. I could see the tears oozing through his fingers, which he held pressed tightly over his eyes. My hand began moving of its own accord to stroke his hair, but my attention was arrested by the bar I still held. It was about a yard long, maybe half an inch thick and two inches wide. The edges were smoothly beveled. At the edge of the bar furthest from my hand I saw a red stain. I let go of the bar. It clanked loudly on the tile floor.

A collage of faces turned toward the sound. Valerie had entered the room, erect as ever, but mouth gaping. Ted followed her, looking unexpectedly frail. At the doorway I could see Devi pulling Tanya back out of the room and Renee looking in past them. Eileen and Maggie stared in my direction as one, still holding on to each other. Only Wayne seemed unaffected by the sound, isolated in the world contained by his fingers. The chiropractor's office no longer smelled sterile. It smelled of sweat and something else I didn't want to identify. I felt nausea rising.

"I think we should all sit in the waiting room until the police come," said Renee, her voice unexpectedly calm.

It seemed like a good idea. We all walked out slowly and silently, leaving Scott Younger and the metal bar behind. Only Wayne turned back at the doorway for a final look.

Once back in the waiting room I sat next to him. Belatedly, I realized mine was the chair last used by the late Scott Younger.

"Who would like some coffee?" Renee asked. Beaver Cleaver's mother couldn't have been more gracious under such stress.

"Do you have any herbal tea?" I replied.

Maggie laughed shrilly. "I can't believe you're worried about caffeine at a time like this," she said.

"Do I need to be jittery at a murder?"

The 'm' word was out of my mouth before I engaged my brain. The room became silent again, except for Devi's hoarse breathing.

"I'll have some herbal tea, too, if that's okay, I mean if it's no bother," said Devi finally. "Well, maybe you don't have any, but if you did . . ."

"That's okay," Renee cut her off. "We've got some."

"Oh, good, thank you. Maybe Tanya would like some too, or maybe . . ."

"It's all right, Mom," Tanya said. She put her arm around Devi's shoulder, brushing against the chandelier of sparkling crystals the woman wore around her neck. Healing crystals are considered more potent in Marin County than Vicks VapoRub. I felt a sudden surge of pity for Devi. Bad enough to be present at a murder, but miserable to have a cold at the same time.

"Sorry I flaked," said Wayne next to me. "Shock, I guess. Better now."

I felt better too. I was breathing evenly again, the colors around me were no longer dancing, and I hadn't thrown up. I could feel a hint of warmth returning to my hands. Then I remembered the metal bar I had picked up. The murder weapon, for God's sake. I was certain. I wondered who else's fingerprints were on it. My hands went icy again.

"Weren't you involved in a murder before, Kate?" Maggie piped up.

I felt eight faces turned toward me, a jury of my peers finding me guilty. Except for one, I thought. One of them knows I didn't kill Younger.

"I wasn't involved in that murder as the *murderer*," I explained, my voice sounding squeaky even to my own ears. "Nor this one," I added quickly.

"Of course not," said Wayne. "You couldn't be."

I turned toward his unhandsome face gratefully. What a kind man, I thought. Too bad he might be a murderer. But I couldn't actually imagine him as a killer. True, he was the only one of us who had appeared to know Scott Younger well, but the tears that had trickled between his fingers had been real. And why would he want to murder Younger so publicly anyway? I looked around me.

Maggie? Golden retrievers don't commit murder. They might knock over your lamp or track mud on your rug, but murder? Eileen sat next to her, her gentle dark eyes large with sadness. Hard to visualize those eyes filled with violence.

Renee came over to me with two steaming styrofoam cups. Now, she was a violent type. I could clearly picture her wielding the metal bar, her red-nailed fingers on one end matching the glistening red blood on the other. I shivered as I accepted one of the cups of tea from those fingers. The minty vapor floated up into my nostrils, and the heat of the cup warmed my hands.

She gave the other cup to Devi. Devi was out of the running as far as I was concerned. I doubted that a woman who couldn't ask for tea in less than five phrases was decisive enough to strike a death blow. And Tanya was just too young. At least I hoped this fifteen-year-old was too young to commit murder. I sipped the tea. It burned my tongue.

"I'll take a cup of that coffee now, if you don't mind," said Ted.

A hardware-store owner would certainly know how to swing a hammer. How about a metal bar?

"Valerie?" asked Renee. "Coffee for you?"

Valerie shook her head silently. Her strong features were now sculpted in fear. Perspiration dripped from her face. Why?

The shriek of a siren perforated the waiting room. Through the window I saw the arrival of a Mill Valley police car, theatrically spotlighted by a patch of sunlight showing through the low clouds. As the door to the police car opened, I felt that sinking sensation associated with getting a traffic ticket. But this was far worse than a ticket.

The uniformed woman who jumped out of the car had a classic model's face defined by high cheekbones and full, sensual lips. Her black hair was sleek in its long braid. She strode to the door, her dark eyes narrowing. As she entered the room her right hand traveled up to the gun on her belt.

"Officer Terhanchi," she announced. "I got a call about an emergency here."

"I called," said Renee. "There's a dead man in the last treatment room back."

"Are you sure he's dead?"

"His axis vertebra is fractured," said Maggie. "He's dead."

"Oh."

Another siren wailed to the door, and a plump middle-aged black man joined us in the waiting room. The friendly creases in his face were overridden by his current frown. Officer Terhanchi introduced him as Sergeant Green and attempted to explain the nature of Younger's injuries.

"Broken neck," summarized Maggie helpfully.

"There's a long metal bar with blood on it next to the chair in there. I picked it up," I said, not to be out done in helpfulness. Sooner or later they'd find out anyway.

The two police officers shot each other identical glances, characterized by raised eyebrows. Then Sergeant Green warned us not to talk among ourselves, and disappeared down the long hallway. When he came back his frown had deepened to a scowl.

"So which one of you hit the guy in the back room?" he asked.

His answer was silence.

"Any of you see who did it?"

More silence. He sighed.

"So who's in charge here?"

Maggie raised her hand uncertainly. "I guess I am. It's my office."

Two more middle-aged men entered the room from the street. Neither wore a uniform. The first man was tall, pale and slender with short dark hair and a pencil-thin black mustache. The second was short, blond and barrel-chested, with the red skin that comes from a sunburn, or prolonged exposure to large doses of beer.

"Glad this one's yours, buddy," said Sergeant Green to the taller man. "Luck of the rotation." He walked the two men back down the hallway.

Upon their return we were informed that Detective Sergeant Udel, the tall pale one, and Detective Inspector Parker, the short red one, would be taking charge of the investigation. We would be interviewed individually, and under no circumstances were we to enter the immediate crime scene, where Sergeant Green now baby-sat Younger's body, or to talk among ourselves. Officer Terhanchi would stay with us in the waiting room to enforce the latter edict.

They took Maggie first. Her shoulders slumped as they ushered her into her own business office. Poor Maggie. My eyes teared up as if her wretchedness was my own. It would be soon enough, I reminded myself.

I needed something to distract myself from the mass misery that surrounded me. Wayne was ineffectively stifling renewed sobs. Valerie's skin had turned an unattractive shade of grey. And Renee had taken to heaving large sighs in synchronization with the crossing and uncrossing of Ted's corduroy-clad legs. Internally, recurring nausea and tremors competed for control of my body, while my mind attempted to forget the sight of Younger. I wished for a good movie or even a religious experience, but decided a magazine would do. I got up to reach for one, and Officer Terhanchi's hand went to the gun on her hip.

I quickly sat back down and remained seated for an hour and fifteen minutes more, until Maggie came back out of her office with reddened eyes and a message. She told me it was my turn to be interviewed.

Detective Sergeant Udel sat behind Maggie's desk. He shifted his weight in the beige chair uneasily as I entered the room. His face was shiny with sweat. He had removed Maggie's stuffed animals and porcelain figures from her desk. I saw them piled unceremoniously in the far corner of the room. Inspector Parker sat in a side chair, notebook in hand.

After introducing himself, Sergeant Udel asked me to picture it all in my mind and tell him exactly what had happened.

I bobbed my head up and down energetically. I was ready to cooperate.

"Why did Dr. Lambrecht send you in to talk to the victim?" he asked suddenly, thrusting his head toward me.

It took me a moment to remember that Maggie's last name was Lambrecht, and a longer moment still to consider the feasibility of explaining how come it had all been my husband's fault. My hesitation couldn't have gone unnoticed. I looked up and saw his intent dark eyes, measuring me for the gas chamber.

"Everything was so busy," I stammered.

"Busy? What do you mean *busy*?"

I told him about the late people, the early people and on-time Ted. I described the conversations I had heard and engaged in: the roller skating stockbroker, Tanya's escape to the 7-Eleven, Ted's business card and everything else I could remember. I even told him about crying in the restroom. When I got to the part about picking up the metal bar and finding the body, Udel's questions flew at me like Alfred Hitchcock's birds. Why did I think he was dead? Why did I pick up the weapon the first time? Had anybody seen me pick up the bar? The first time? How about the second time? Why did I touch it the second time? What about the other door to the room? What else did I touch? How long had I known the victim?

Once I had explained in exhaustive detail every single thing I had done or observed that morning, the detective sergeant asked me the same questions again. Then again. I would never more be surprised by the stories of hardened criminals blurting out the truth under police questioning. If he had asked, I would have admitted: that I stabbed John Lee with the sharpened end of a pencil at age eight in a fit of ill-temper; that I had lied to my mother about where I went with my boyfriend one hot summer night in 1966; and that I still longed for the love of my almost ex-husband. Thankfully, his interrogation did not cover those areas.

Detective Sergeant Udel accompanied me back to the waiting room after Inspector Parker had searched my purse and found nothing that interested him, taken my fingerprints, examined my hands, and scraped the underside of my fingernails. The room was now filled with the buzz of police officials, both in and out of uniform, and the smell of food. Assorted sandwiches, bottled drinks, candy bars, and other goodies were lying on a folded 7-Eleven bag. My stomach growled, queasiness and hunger arguing. But, before I had a chance to root through the pile for a tofu burger, Udel told Officer Terhanchi to search me and remove my outer clothing for analysis.

"But I don't have any clothes to replace them," I objected. "I can't drive home in my underwear. It's cold out there."

"I'll drive you home and you can change there," offered Terhanchi. "Or we can go get you something at Nellie's," she said, pointing across the street to the "vintage clothing" store.

"All right," I said, reminding myself that it was a good idea to play ball with the police, even if it did mean paying Nellie's inflated prices. Nellie's was, after all, no ordinary thrift shop by self-definition, but an establishment dealing in the vintage apparel of the forties, fifties, sixties and seventies.

Terhanchi searched me in one of the treatment rooms and then we were ready to leave. I turned for one last look at the waiting room.

Only the police were talking. My murder mates were all silent, some of them eating. I could smell the tuna sandwich Maggie and Eileen were sharing. Tanya was gobbling a candy bar, while Devi sipped a mineral water absently. Had the police silenced Devi's objections to junk food? Ted's rabbity teeth were tearing into a turkey sandwich, and Wayne played with something on dark rye, his eyes downcast. Renee was rapidly alternating gulps of diet soda with bites of fruited yogurt. Only Valerie had nothing in her hands. She sat tall in her chair, with her eyes closed, pink palms up. I silently wished her luck in regaining her state of bliss.

I waved to the group as Officer Terhanchi ushered me out the door into the November chill. Only Maggie and Wayne waved back.

"I've always wanted to go to Nellie's," Terhanchi confided as we crossed the street. I was glad someone was enjoying this.

We stopped at the two-dollar bins on the sidewalk but these contained only belts and scarves and other accessories. I'd need more than that to cover my soon-to-be-stripped body. Inside, we found a thirty-dollar pantsuit, detailed in a white peace-pins design on a navy blue background. Terhanchi liked it. I did too. It looked just like one I had given to the Goodwill many lifestyles ago. I took off my comfortable shabby black sweater and corduroys and handed them over to Officer Terhanchi. She carefully placed them into a paper box. I left Nellie's in the pantsuit.

It wasn't until I was in the car driving home that I recognized the burn hole in the left knee. In my previous life, before health fanaticism, I had been a smoker. I had made that hole over fifteen years ago when I had dropped a cigarette while laughing uncontrollably at a Nixon impersonation.

Realizing that I had just bought back my own pantsuit for thirty dollars, I began to giggle. My giggles grew louder and louder as I guided my car carefully through the screen of tears that obscured my vision.

When I pulled into my driveway, my cat C.C. thumped across the redwood porch and down the four front stairs to greet me. I picked her up and passionately kissed her furry face. Impatiently, she jumped from my arms and led me to the front door.

I heard my telephone shrill.

- Three -

I SHOVED THE door open, threw my purse on top of one of the old pinball machines that littered the living room, and ran across the hall to beat my answering machine to the phone. C.C. was ahead of me all the way.

"Kate, is that really you? Or are you a machine?" asked Maggie.

I looked down and saw no metal, only quivering flesh. "It's me all right."

"Oh wow! I'm so glad. I need your help."

"What kind of help?" I asked cautiously, sinking into my old yellow naugahyde comfy chair. C.C. hopped into my lap and began to sniff my new pantsuit.

"With this murder thing. It's such a bummer, and I'm sure you can figure it out better than me. It was really neat the way you figured out that last one."

"Are you saying this in front of the police?" I asked.

"No, they sent me home. And once they've interviewed everyone, they're going to seal my office. Jeez, I mean, my office! Do you know what this is going to do to my business?"

"I hadn't thought about that," I answered honestly. I was glad for Maggie's sake that the police weren't listening. I had grown accustomed to her brand of artless insensitivity over the years, but I suspected that Sergeant Udel would find her selfish words more brutal than endearingly outspoken. They made me a little queasy myself, though Maggie did have a point. Who was going to go to a chiropractor whose patients came out with broken necks? Poor Maggie. But poorer Scott Younger.

"I thought maybe you could talk to people, see what you think," she continued.

"The police will take care of it," I said. But even as I said it an old feeling of dread arose. What if the police couldn't take care of it?

"I'm scared, Kate." Her voice was small and childlike. "The police are frantic. They don't know any more than us."

"Maybe they'll discover some physical evidence," I suggested.

"What if there isn't any?" she replied. "What then?"

"I don't know," I mumbled. What I wanted most of all at that moment was to obliterate all memory of my discovery of Younger's dead body, and of its aftermath. I felt sick and frightened.

"Please, Kate, help me. My business is going down the tubes if we can't solve this. They've already turned away most of my afternoon patients, and they're telling the rest to leave as they show up."

I looked at my watch. It was almost three.

"At least come over to my house, and talk to me about it," she said, her voice thick with tears.

I can be assertive, but only if I have prior warning. Dump a tearful request on me suddenly, and I fall for it as fast as sunglasses sliding down a tourist's nose and off the Golden Gate Bridge into the churning water below. "Please, Kate," she repeated. "It can't hurt to come over and talk about it."

I did need to talk. Anything to shake off the sick dread that was lodged in my stomach. I found myself agreeing, and wondered if I would regret it. She gave me directions to her home. I told her I'd be over in an hour or so.

After I hung up the phone, I sat huddled in my comfy chair while C.C. purred, clawed and shed ecstatically on my peace pants. I had tried to convince myself that I had no responsibility for her bad habits. She was, after all, a used cat.

Just before my husband, Craig, had come back home, my accountant had moved to a condo where no cats were allowed, leaving C.C. a potential orphan. So I adopted her, name and all. My accountant told me he had named the cat C.C. because of her markings. C.C. was a small black cat with white spots, one shaped like a goatee on her chin and another shaped like a beret rakishly balanced over her right ear. When she squinted her eyes just so, she looked ready to wail out the blues on a miniature saxophone, or at least smoke a tiny joint. Thus the name Cool Cat, or C.C. for short. At least C.C. had staying power, she was still with me. Craig was gone again, this time for good.

I considered hiding with my cat in that comfy naugahyde haven for eternity, or at least until she had completely shredded my pantsuit. But murder or no murder, I needed to eat, and so did C.C.

I got up and fed her some chunky kitty stew. C.C. was no vegetarian. Then I forced down a bowl of leftover brown rice before unenthusiastically approaching the telephone. I was late in making my daily call to the Jest Gifts warehouse.

November was not turkey-time for me. It was the season of mail-order madness for Jest Gifts. Everyone wanted a Christmas gag gift for their favorite professional, and Christmas ornaments too. For instance: Santa's stethoscope for the doctor; the tooth fairy to go on top of the dentist's tree (comes complete with tooth, only $7.95); festive shrunken heads for the psychotherapists; or our red and green shark sleighs for those members of the bar with a sense of humor.

I have two invaluable employees (actually I pay them nine dollars an hour), Jean and Judy, who fill the orders in my Oakland warehouse. I also had a couple of temporary part-timers to ease the seasonal crush. I do my sixty hours per week of designing, correspondence, promotion, payroll and bookkeeping from my home, and contract out the manufacturing. I only visit the warehouse to pick up paperwork, drop off paychecks and remedy disasters. It was Judy who picked up the phone when I called that day.

"Where have you been?" she demanded impatiently. I considered explaining, but she plowed ahead before I could. "Ed called from Ceramico. They still haven't finished the extra faw-law-law mugs. He promised he'll have them to us next week, though."

"Fine," I said, my mind on Scott Younger as he had been, alive in the waiting room. "I've already sent out back-order notices to the October customers."

"Wait a minute. Let me close the door," she said. I heard it slam, shutting her into the 9 by 9 sales office. "That new guy, Nate, you got from the employment office?"

"Yeah, what about him?" I remembered Valerie's words when she heard Younger's name.

"He doesn't think our stuff is funny!"

"That's his tough karma."

"Can I tell him that?"

"If you want to. He only has to pack the stuff. He doesn't have to appreciate it. Don't worry about it. Any other problems?" Wayne's scarred face appeared in my mind.

There were, of course, more problems. But all in all, it was a low disaster count for a November day at the Oakland warehouse. Better than in Mill Valley.

Once I had hung up, I sat staring down at the patch of beige rug between my Reeboks. Suddenly I could see Scott Younger's bloodied neck superimposed. I could even feel his limp shoulder in my hand.

A surge of brown rice and fear rose in my throat. I barely reached the bathroom in time to vomit. Then I shook and sweated for a few minutes more before picking myself up to brush my teeth and wash my face. It was time to visit Maggie. I needed to be with someone and it might as well be her.

The address that Maggie had given me was in one of the more affordable sections of Mill Valley, outside the city limits. I drove through the architectural hodgepodge of houses which characterizes the area. Modern, post-modern, and pre-modern cottages, mansions and apartment buildings nestled together democratically amid jungles and manicured gardens. Maggie's home was a modest white stucco box that looked as if it might have been built in the forties. Its simple shape was colorfully clothed in magenta bougainvillea and yellow roses.

Maggie opened the door when I was halfway up the brick walkway. I stopped in mid-stride. My chiropractor had turned into a bag lady. It wasn't just the undersized ratty orange sweater stretched over the baggy and tattered lavender jogging suit. It was her hair sticking out in frizzed red clumps, her crooked lipstick and her swollen eyes. Even her posture was cockeyed. One shoulder was pulled higher than the other.

"You look terrible," I blurted out.

"My back's out," she said. "Jeez, it hurts. I hope they finish questioning Eileen soon. She knows how to fix it. Anyway, come on in."

She led me into a living room that exploded in primary and secondary colors against a backdrop of white walls and a maroon carpet. I had never seen a bright green sofa before, nor shelves enameled red and blue with taxicab-yellow polka dots.

The posters on the walls looked right out of a Crayola box. Large orange and purple pillows were flung invitingly on the floor. I plopped down on a purple one. Maggie carefully lowered herself onto the green sofa.

"Where did you get the neat pantsuit?" she asked.

"At Nellie's. I forgot. I should have changed."

"No. I like it." I wasn't sure how to respond to fashion approval from a woman dressed in lavender and orange rags.

After an awkward silence, I asked her what had happened in the waiting room while I was being grilled. That wasn't what I wanted to talk about. I wanted to rant and rave about the shock of death, but I didn't know how to begin. "Oh boy, everyone in the world came. The chief, and the captain and a woman from the coroner's office, and a bunch of uniformed officers. They kept going in and out of the back room. They brought out the bar from the lumbar traction unit wrapped in paper."

"Was that the metal bar I picked up?"

"Yeah, why did you pick it up?" she asked.

"First, I tripped over it. Then, I sat on it."

"Oh." She lowered her glance.

"Yeah. 'Oh.' Speaking of 'oh,' what was that stain on your sweat shirt?"

"My sweat shirt?" Her swollen hazel eyes came back up, opening wide.

"There was a brown stain on your duck sweat shirt."

"Oh boy, the coffee." She hit her face with her hand and winced at the blow. "I spilled coffee on it. The police took it. They'll be able to tell it was just coffee, won't they?"

"Of course they will. Look Maggie, I've got to ask you two things. One, how come you don't think I killed Scott Younger. And two, why should I think you didn't either."

"I just know you didn't," she said vehemently. "And I know I didn't. Sheesh, Kate, I couldn't do something like that. And even if I could, there's no way I would jeopardize my chiropractic practice. It took too long for me to build it up. Even if I got away with the murder, my business would be ruined."

"All right," I said, considering. I understood full well the primacy of business survival. "You know these people. Who do you think killed Scott Younger?"

"Well, it wasn't me," she faltered. "Not you or Eileen . . ."

"How about Renee?"

She flinched. "Is it okay with you if I let Doc and Hound in?" she asked.

"Who the hell are Doc and Hound?"

"My dogs."

"You think it's Renee, don't you?" I said.

Instead of answering, she got up from the couch painfully and limped out of the room. I could hear her footsteps across a bare floor, and the opening of a door. Then the sound of yips and skittering nails. Two dachshunds danced around her feet as she returned slowly to the room. They spotted me and dove, squirming, sniffing and licking, onto my unprotected body. One lapped my face while the other shoved his nose in my armpit and then in my crotch.

"Doc, come to Mommy," Maggie said. The crotch-sniffer obediently trotted over and jumped in her lap. The licker settled down onto mine, rolling over on his back to stare at me with trusting brown eyes. Maggie finally spoke.

"I don't think it's Renee, but I guess I'm afraid it might be. She dated Scott for a while. But then she broke it off. She said dating him was just too weird."

"Weird how?" I asked.

"I'm not sure. You should ask her. That guy Wayne always went with them, I know that."

"That's pretty strange," I agreed slowly. Why would Wayne go with them? But I refused to let Maggie derail me from her receptionist. "Could Renee have done it, physically?"

"She's strong. And she gets so pissed off all the time." Maggie stopped and thought for a moment. "But it wouldn't take much strength anyway. About as much as swinging a baseball bat. Anyone could do it. But, Jeez, Renee really is an okay person. She works hard and sticks by me. . . ."

"How about opportunity?" I asked, cutting her employee recommendation short.

"The police asked me about that. I think all of us had the opportunity. All of the rooms, except for the bathroom, have connecting doors. Renee went back into the records office while you and I were talking. She could have gone out the other door into the hall, without our seeing her."

I nodded. I remembered that.

"Wayne always stays with Scott for a bit after Eileen gets him settled. Eileen and I were in and out. Devi and Tanya were wandering around."

"What about Ted and Valerie?"

"Valerie's room adjoined Scott's. All she had to do was walk through the door. And Ted could have gone through the connecting door from his room to the X-ray room, and from there into the hall. And you were there on the spot. Jeez, any of us could have done it." She nuzzled Doc sorrowfully. "It's hopeless. How can the police figure it out? And if they don't find the murderer, no one will ever come to my office again."

"Maggie, it's not hopeless. The police know what they're doing."

She just stared at me with swollen, disbelieving eyes.

"All right, how about motives?" I asked finally. I could feel a prickling of curiosity through the numbness of my shock over Younger's death. "You know these people, I don't."

"Eileen didn't particularly care for Scott, but she didn't know him outside of the office. Nor did I, for that matter. Wayne seemed to really like him."

"Why did Wayne stay with Scott all the time? What was their relationship?" I asked. The prickling was growing.

"Renee thought maybe he was a bodyguard. I know that sounds a little far-out, but that was the impression she had. Renee's kids actually liked Wayne. I don't know anything about him really. He's never been my patient. But he doesn't strike me as a killer any more than you do."

"Somehow I agree with you. But, besides Renee, he seems to be the only one who knew Scott well. Though Valerie seemed to know and hate Scott."

"Really?" Maggie said, raising her eyebrows.

"She accused him of being a drug pusher this morning."

Maggie's mouth fell open. "Wow!"

"And Devi wouldn't even let Scott talk to Tanya. Apparently Devi knew Scott in college. He must not have made a very good impression."

"See, Kate. You already know stuff I don't know. That's really neat."

"There is nothing 'neat' about it. I just heard them talking this morning in the waiting room. I am not a detective." I must have jerked my body when I spoke, because Hound slid off my lap and trotted across the rug to jump up on the green sofa. He began pushing Doc off Maggie's lap.

"You know," said Maggie, absently positioning one dog on

each thigh. "I guess it's okay to tell you. It's not a medical secret."

"What, for God's sake?"

"Valerie said something once about learning yoga in prison," she whispered, as if the dachshunds might overhear. "I wonder what she was in prison for?"

"You could ask her."

"Not me. I couldn't. But I could get everyone who was there together again at my office. Then you could ask them questions." She smiled at me with childlike confidence.

"Maggie, this is no game. We'd be dealing with a murderer. Anyway, how could you get them to come?"

"Jeez, Kate, this is Marin. I'll just tell them that we need to share our feelings to integrate the experience. I mean, it's really true. I feel awful about it. Not just the loss of business, but a death like that . . ." Her skin paled underneath her freckles. "Everyone must be traumatized. It'll do us good to get together and share."

"Except for the murderer."

"Even the murderer. God, the killer must feel just terrible."

I looked at her open face and saw only sincerity. She pitied the killer. Maybe she was right. Maybe whoever broke Younger's neck did feel terrible. I shuddered.

"Are you hungry?" she asked suddenly. "Because I am. Let's get something to eat."

She got up without waiting for an answer. Doc and Hound and I followed her into a sunny kitchen. She began flinging open lime-green and lemon-yellow cupboards, pulling out boxes, cans and jars.

"I've got some tuna, but you don't eat tuna, do you?" she said, closing that cupboard.

"Don't worry about me," I said.

"How about peanut butter?"

"Maggie, just feed yourself, all right?" I sat down at her orange-lacquer table.

"I've got it. Peanut butter on apple slices!"

I found I was hungry. The rich, crunchy apple slices were a feast, but getting more information out of Maggie was no picnic. Not that she wasn't wretchedly eager to help. But she refused to divulge any medical secrets and she just didn't know much else. She did tell me everyone's age. Ted was sixty-nine, as he was apparently fond of telling her with a wink and a leer. Tanya was fifteen and everyone else was in their thirties or forties. She also guiltily revealed that Devi was seriously ill, but refused to tell me the nature of her illness. Confidentiality. I was surprised Maggie knew the meaning of the word.

One thing became clear. Maggie had disliked Scott Younger. According to her, he was the only one of us capable of murder. When I pointed out that he couldn't have broken his own neck, she merely shrugged her shoulders and let Hound lick some more peanut butter off her fingers. Scott was cold and slimy, in her opinion, and rich too, as evidenced by the new bottle-green Jaguar he rode in to his appointments.

I also learned that Eileen's parents were Philippine immigrants, and that she was studying for her own doctorate in chiropractic. Renee was the divorced mother of a fourteen-year-old boy and a twelve-year-old girl. And Maggie thought Valerie had a daughter floating around somewhere too.

"So who do you think it was?" Maggie asked me hopefully when the last apple slice was swallowed and the last piece of information painfully elicited.

"I have absolutely no idea," I answered.

Maggie began to sob. She put her face into her hands and squeezed more tears out of her already swollen eyes. Doc and Hound rubbed against her legs and whined their concern. I put my arm around her. What could I say?

"Set up that meeting and I'll ask some questions," was what I did say. And, "I'll talk to Eileen and Renee. They must know something."

- Four -

DRIVING HOME, I berated myself for promising Maggie my help. It was too damn dangerous. I didn't even know Scott Younger. What did I care who killed him? But even as that thought came, I knew I did care. I remembered his dead body once more and shivered. No one should die like that.

As I waited impatiently at a stop sign, I considered the dexterity with which Maggie had manipulated my spine in the past. Had she just as skillfully been manipulating my mind with her sobs? Her childlike expectations invited fulfillment. She was a person others would always rally around to protect.

I told myself that I would leave this one to the police. Let them interview the suspects. Let them consider the evidence. Let them find the killer. There was probably evidence galore. Like . . . like my fingerprints on the murder weapon. Sweat turned my hands slippery on the steering wheel.

I worked all of that evening and deep into the night on the incredible bulk of paperwork generated by Jest Gifts. It went slowly. I was unable to focus. My mind was full of speculation and indecision. My body was full of dread and sadness.

Finally exhausted, I locked the cat-door, pulled on my red-and white-striped dropseat pajamas and lay down on my half of the king-size mattress, promising myself I would sleep in. I even broke my own rules and allowed C.C. to climb up onto the other half of the bed. After two hours of restless imaginings, I fell asleep, lulled by NatuRest, the ''natural'' sleeping pill, and C.C.'s purrs, which couldn't quite mask the sound of her claws shredding the comforter.

* * *

A ringing in my ears and a blow to my chest awakened me. I knew that I wasn't boxing when I heard the second ring. C.C. had just used my chest as a diving board on her way to the telephone. At the third ring I opened my eyes to the sunlight streaming down from the two skylights above my bed, and realized that I had forgotten to turn on the answering machine the night before. Cursing, I dragged myself up and lurched down the darkened hallway to the phone.

"It's Craig," said the telephone in my estranged husband's voice. I groaned and absently combed my hair with my fingers. Then I remembered that he couldn't see me over the telephone.

"Is it in the papers already?" I asked irritably.

"Is what in the papers?"

"Listen, I'll investigate if I want to! And, no, you can't move back in again," I asserted.

"Investigate what? Are you okay?" I could almost see his confused brown eyes.

I took a deep breath, sat down in the comfy chair and felt the shock of cold naugahyde through the open dropseat of my pajamas. It was time to begin the conversation over again.

"I just woke up. What time is it?" I asked.

"It's eleven thirty. What's going on, Kate?"

"I'm a little tired. I stayed up late last night doing paperwork. What did you call about?"

"I need to talk to you, face to face. I thought I could take you to dinner Friday night."

"I guess so," I said slowly. I was still sleepy. "You know we can't live together, don't you?"

"Yes, I know. That's why I need to talk to you," he said. I felt tears prickling my eyelids and self-disgust simultaneously prickling my awakening mind. The idiocy of my heart. He finally agreed with me, and I wanted to weep.

He told me he'd pick me up at seven. I hung up and nestled in my chair, ready to have that good cry I had been promising myself. The setting was right. The lights were off and the curtains closed in my cluttered home office. Desks, file cabinets and stacks of paperwork loomed ghoulishly in the dark. I looked for the cat to cuddle. But C.C. was nowhere to be found when I needed her. Maybe she was out finding another snake to bring me. Or was that just last week's sport? The doorbell rang, jarring me back to the reality of late Thursday morning.

When I pulled the front door open the glowing colors of daylight temporarily blinded me. But as my eyes adjusted I could see my friend, Ann Rivera, standing on my doorstep. Her grey-wool pinstripe suit and pink silk blouse dressed her tall elegant body for success, but her kind brown face was stretched into a goofy grin. She pointed at me and laughed loudly.

"God, those pajamas, feet in them and everything! And your hair. It looks just like Woodstock's, you know, the bird in *Peanuts*." I knew exactly what it looked like. When I slept with a pillow over my head, it flattened my hair from the sides into a lumpy Mohawk strip in the center.

"I'll have you know I've worked very hard at this effect," I told her, patting the lumps. "Why are you here in the middle of the day?"

"I'm here to tell you about Scott Younger, and to take you to lunch," she said. She quickly crossed over the threshold into the house and hugged me.

"Scott Younger?" I said, pulling back, suddenly fully awake. "What do you know about Scott Younger?"

"I knew him at Crocker University, almost twenty years ago."

"But why are you here? Do you know he's dead?"

"Of course," she said. She grabbed my shoulder and turned me in the direction of the hall. "Get dressed. I need to be back at the hospital by one thirty."

"I've got to take a shower first."

"Well, take it quickly. I'll talk to you while you do."

She followed me back down the hall, laughing even more loudly than before once she caught sight of the portion of my backside so inelegantly revealed by my dropseat. Then she gracefully perched on the toilet seat while I showered, yelling over the roar of the water.

As I soaped my hair and body, I heard that Eileen had called her the night before and told her about Scott Younger's murder. Eileen had been surprised to learn that Ann had known Younger years before, and had asked her to talk to Maggie. Maggie in turn had referred Ann to me as "the detective," instructing her to tell me everything she knew about Scott. Maggie had not realized that Ann and I were already acquainted.

"Where do you know Eileen from?" I shouted, rinsing in the warm water.

"ACA meetings. Eileen said it was okay to tell you."

"What's ACA?"

"Adult Children of Alcoholics. They're like Alcoholics Anonymous meetings, but for people who grew up with alcoholic parents."

"Why do you go?"

"ACA's have similar sets of problems," she hollered, articulate even at that volume. "A sense of worthlessness, confusion, despair, and anger. And a tendency to take care of everyone but ourselves. We share and learn."

I got out of the shower and dried off while Ann spoke in softer tones about her ACA experiences. I was putting on my corduroys and sweater when the phone rang.

"I've got it all set up for tomorrow," said Maggie eagerly. "You can talk to Eileen and Renee in the morning. And all of the suspects have agreed to an afternoon meeting."

I didn't even ask her how she had managed this. I had experienced her manipulation first-hand.

"Has Ann Rivera called you yet?" she asked.

"She's here now," I said, nodding at Ann coming down the hall.

"Oh neat! And Wayne wants to visit you tonight. I told him to call you."

"Maggie, he might be a murderer!"

"Oh, he couldn't be," she blithely assured me. "And he knows I know he's visiting you, so you're safe in any case. I told him you might want to look over some of his short stories."

"You told him what?" I squawked. Ann's eyebrows went up inquiringly.

"Wow, Kate. Don't get upset. He's a writer. I told him you'd be interested. It gives you an excuse to talk to him."

"Great. And who is going to be running Jest Gifts while I'm reading Wayne's stories, and interviewing everyone else?"

"Jeez, be glad you have a business to run," Maggie said. I shriveled with guilt, just as she had probably intended.

"All right, I'll talk to him. But please don't set anything else up for me without asking." I needed to curb Maggie's enthusiasm, and soon.

Ann teased me about my capitulation as we drove to Miranda's Restaurant in downtown Mill Valley.

"You ought to come to an ACA meeting. You're obviously a born caretaker," she said. I ignored her.

"Tell me everything you know about Scott Younger," I ordered.

"Yes, ma'am." She aimed a crisp salute in my direction. "It's strange to think he's dead after all these years. I met Scott in 1970 at Crocker University. You know Crocker, don't you?"

I nodded. Crocker is one of those small private universities where parents with money send their kids, if the kids don't have the grades for the most prestigious schools like Stanford and Berkeley. Its campus is an architectural jewel set in the rolling hills of Sonoma County, just over the county line from Marin. Plenty of Marin movers and shakers got their degrees from Crocker University.

"Scott was in one of my classes. He was tall and gorgeous, a P.E. major, but not a jock." I glanced over when I heard her voice soften, and saw that her eyes had gone out of focus and into memory. "He had long black hair tied back in a leather thong in those days. And he wore handmade embroidered linen shirts with gathered sleeves and open necks. Robin Hood in a Volkswagen van. Only he didn't steal from the rich. They paid him for drugs.

"His father was a judge in Monterey. I met him once, a pleasant man. His mother was dead. I think she died giving birth to Scott.

"All the women at school wanted him, including me. I was up for anything exciting and new then. New roles, new ideas, new politics, new experiences." She looked my way as if for approval. I nodded my understanding.

"I knew him for a year before he asked me out. What I didn't know was that he had spent that year building up a very profitable drug business. He was not your average student, selling a little to support his own habit. He was a real dealer."

"What did he sell?"

She shrugged her shoulders. "Marijuana, LSD, mescaline, the hallucinogens, mostly. Some speed too, I think. Student stuff."

"How did you find out?"

"My sister's boyfriend told me, after I was already involved with Scott. But I had wondered. He wasn't living in a dormitory, or in his hippie van. He was living on an estate, his estate—five acres in the hills. A two-story house complete with a maid and two bodyguards. And the loudest stereo system I'd ever heard."

"Bodyguards?"

"I didn't know they were bodyguards at first. I thought they were his friends. But they wouldn't talk to me. Two silent, nasty-looking, big men." She shivered, but then smiled, her face soft once more.

"My first night with Scott was like a magic carpet ride. Those men chauffeured us everywhere. Scott and I lay in the back of his van on a mattress-sized velvet cushion, listening to the Moody Blues and smoking dope. It was laced with a little something extra, I think. When the van stopped, he lifted me out into a formal rose garden. I've never found out where that rose garden was. We sat there on a stone bench, surrounded by the fragrance of flowers and looked up at the stars. Then they drove us back to his house to make love."

I pulled into Miranda's parking lot. I didn't get out of the car. "And . . ." I prompted, lost in her story.

Her eyes refocused. "And, a lot more. Let's go in and I'll tell you over lunch." She was back to the present, a brisk mental-hospital administrator on her lunch break.

Miranda's Restaurant precariously combined nouvelle cuisine and health food. Too often, this meant a minuscule scoop of brown rice surrounded by a handful of artfully arranged vegetable bits. The decor was tasteful, however. Pastel colors, original art, fresh flowers and classical music. We were seated in a mauve booth by an ethereal-looking waitress dressed in Chinese silk pajamas. A bowl of iceland poppies and fairy primroses sat on our table.

Ann ordered the plum soup and Greek salad from the "creative menu." I asked for the Indonesian tofu and vegetables. And we both requested hot herbal tea to ward off the November cold. When the waitress left I turned back to Ann.

"You were making love to Scott," I reminded her.

"Ah, yes." She smiled. "The man was strange, in and out of bed."

"Just for starters, tell me how he was strange in bed."

"This is kind of embarrassing," she said, looking at me intently across the table. "Remember, times were different then. Sex, drugs and rock 'n' roll."

"Yes." I sighed nostalgically. "And now it's fantasy, mineral water and New Age music. Go on with the story. Your *coitus interruptus* is killing me."

She laughed, and then stopped abruptly. "I can't believe he was murdered. How awful."

I nodded. Of course it was awful. Flippancy was my antidote to the awfulness of finding his body, a memory that rode on my shoulders constantly now, like an uninvited hitchhiker. I wiggled my shoulders impatiently, shaking it off. Ann began to speak again, her face now serious.

"First off, while we made love, his bodyguards stood right outside the door, which was actually left open."

"How bizarre. Did they listen?" I asked.

"No, I don't think so. At least they pretended to be totally disinterested. And considering the number of women Scott was probably seeing, maybe they really were. Scott was quite a Lothario. And talked as if he wanted to get someone pregnant. I heard he did once, after my time. But apparently the woman ran away and got an abortion."

Our waitress floated to our table and served us tea. I sipped mine absently, hoping the tea would soothe the queasiness I felt. For all of my flippancy, something about discussing the sex life of a man I had last seen brutally dead was not sitting well on my empty stomach. But I didn't change the subject.

"And that wasn't the strangest thing," Ann said.

"What was?"

She bent toward me and whispered. "He cried when he made love. Sobbed like a baby. It was so spooky. I've never forgotten it."

The waitress brought us our food. Ann's plum soup was an unappetizing shade of purple, but her salad glistened attractively with olive oil and feta cheese. On my plate thin slices of red, green, and yellow peppers were spread out like chrysanthemum petals from a doughnut-shaped mound of brown rice, tofu and broccoli. In the doughnut's center was a small dish of dipping sauce. I dipped and tasted. The sauce was spicy peanut butter.

"Why did he cry? Did he ever say?" I needed to know.

"Never. And I never asked. I wasn't very experienced at the time, and I thought maybe crying during lovemaking was normal for men." She slurped a spoonful of purple soup. I tried to imagine her eighteen years ago, without her grey suit or the self-assurance that went with it.

"Scott rarely spoke at all," she said. "And stranger than that, I didn't notice the absence of dialogue for months. He had this presence. He gave an impression of intelligence, of being involved in a conversation without actually opening his mouth.

"He just watched and listened, like an observer from another galaxy. God, he was cold. I think that's why I finally broke it off. He was a good lover in spite of the kinks. A gifted photographer, too. And a shrewd businessman. But after a while I realized that I never knew who he really was.''

''Maybe that was just as well,'' I said.

Ann looked thoughtful for a moment and then nodded. Raising her teacup in a toast, she proclaimed: ''To our health and unending naiveté.''

When I returned home, there were two messages on my answering machine. One was from my warehousewoman Judy.

The other was from Wayne Caruso, requesting an evening interview. As I listened to his gentle husky voice I wondered if he had ever listened to Scott Younger making love. But I doubted that I'd ever ask him.

- Five -

I CALLED JUDY back at the warehouse. First off, she wanted to remind me that Friday was payday. I couldn't fault her priorities. And second, the salesman from Softisculp had been around. He wanted to know if I liked the models and how soon he could expect my order.

My brain churned. Who the hell was Softisculp? Guiltily, I remembered; they were rubber-toy manufacturers. Softisculp had been kind enough to make some prototypes of my latest design ideas. I had brought those models home and put them . . . Where had I put them? I assured Judy I wouldn't forget payday, and began a search for the models.

My search was ended on the top of Hayburners, one of the pinball machines that had survived our short-lived home-amusements business. Living under a pile of old magazines and newspapers were: Advo-cat, a lawyerly feline complete with briefcase and red tie; Accountant, a calculating-insect holding an adding machine in one feeler, and various other creatures come to rubbery life from my pun-ish imagination. I cleared them off of the unused machine and considered my next move.

I had a truckload of paperwork to cope with. I had to make a decision about Softisculp. I needed to call Wayne Caruso back. And I could have used a nap. But, most of all, I wanted to escape all thoughts of Scott Younger's death. My hands decided to play pinball.

I reached under Hayburners and flipped a switch. The machine was bathed in a pink glow. A push of the red reset button brought the joyous *kerchunk* of the backboard metal racehorses assuming their starting positions. I shot the first ball and worked the flipper buttons on the sides of the machine. The ball rolled toward my right flipper. Slapping its button, I propelled it toward the back targets on the playfield. It rolled lazily up to the top of the machine and down a side lane, rewarding me with the sound of a bell and fifty points, and then came rolling back toward the center drain.

Another bell rang as my ball went down the drain. It was the doorbell.

Sergeant Feiffer of the Marin County Sheriff's Department was on my doorstep. So was C.C.. She shot through the open door like a cat out of hell. Much more fun than entering through her laboriously installed fifty-nine-dollar cat-door. Feiffer was slightly more polite, and much more attractive. He stood there, six feet of masculinity under curly blond hair, and twinkled his clear blue eyes at me.

"Neil Udel tells me you've got yourself tangled up in another murder," he said.

"I didn't get myself tangled up. I didn't even know the guy," I objected. My voice sounded shrill, even to my own ears.

"The Mill Valley police have called us in to help. Seeing as we're old buddies from the last case you 'didn't' get yourself tangled up in, I thought I'd stop by." He glanced over my shoulder and his eyes widened. "Hayburners," he said in a hungry whisper.

"Like to play a few games?" I asked, feeling the balance of power shift to myself as owner of the alluring Hayburners. I could see the struggle in his face. He bobbed his head from side to side. His lips tightened and relaxed. Finally, he followed me into the room.

"Only in the line of duty," he said. "Set her up for double play, and I'll ask you a few questions while I beat your . . ." I could have finished his sentence, but he wouldn't. His face flushed.

"Yes?" I said inquiringly. Then, "We'll see about that." I hit the reset button twice.

"Ladies first," he said, smiling.

"Oh, no. Cops first," I replied demurely. We both knew full well that the second player had an advantage.

Hayburners was an unusual machine. It had no thumper bumpers. Instead, there were side bumpers and high-point side lanes, jellyfish rollovers in the center, and upright targets on the sides and back of the green, orange, yellow, and red playfield. Multicolored metal horses raced to a finish line in the pinkly illuminated backboard, when the ball hit various targets. As each horse came in, the corresponding jellyfish bumper and backboard target increased in value from ten to a hundred points. The side lanes randomly alternated from fifty to five hundred points. Hayburners also sported a double set of flippers, top and bottom, and a moving ball launcher.

Feiffer launched his first ball. It was a good pitch. It darted up the upper side lane and won him fifty points. It would have been five hundred if the lane had been lit. The ball drifted over the top and back down the playfield, gaining speed. It was almost to his right flipper when I spoke.

"So who do the Mill Valley police think did it?" I asked. His fingers hesitated a fraction too long on the flipper button. The ball skated on the flipper and then slid off its tip and down the drain hole. But he didn't answer my question.

"Your turn," he said sweetly, between clenched teeth.

I stepped up to the machine and fondled the flippers. Then I poised my hand over the launch button, ready to shoot.

"They don't suspect anyone in particular," he said as my hand came down. "But I can tell you whose two sets of prints are on the murder weapon."

My shot went wild. It careened off the side bumper and came hurtling toward my left flipper.

"Detective Udel says to be down at the police station for a little get-together at three o'clock," he continued.

Three o'clock? I thought it was near to three then, but I couldn't look at my watch. I was too busy trying to control the ball. I desperately bobbled it on my flipper while completing my anxiety attack. When the ball rolled toward the inside joint of the flipper I released the button slowly, edging the ball to the flipper's center. Then I slammed it. The ball sailed up the playfield toward the back targets, bouncing over jellyfish bumpers on the way. The game was in play again. Bells began to ring and the score reels spun.

"Nice save," Feiffer said grudgingly. "What did you think of Scott Younger?"

"I didn't know the man personally," I replied, slapping a flipper. I was in stride now. The ball danced up the playfield. One of the horses reached the finish line. Now there were two one-hundred point targets lit.

"How about before?" he asked. The ball went down the lighted side lane. Five hundred points.

"Before what?" I passed the ball from the right to left flipper with a surgeon's precision, and shot.

"Didn't you know him before you met him at your chiropractor's?" he asked slyly.

"Nope." The ball hit one of the lighted targets and rolled back down the playfield over two jellyfish bumpers, bringing in another horse. Then it began its lazy descent, heading for the tip of my left flipper. It would be a difficult shot.

Feiffer moved in closer to me. I could feel his body heat and smell his scent, made up of spicy aftershave and a more primal strong, clean sweat. An unexpected surge of carnal desire temporarily immobilized my body. The ball kissed the tip of my rigid flipper before plummeting down the center drain.

"Tough luck," he said, with a sincere smile this time. "But you've racked up a good score for your first ball."

He stepped up to the machine. I peppered him with questions as he played. Had Younger still been a drug dealer? Not anymore, as far as they knew. Not that Younger was ever convicted. A perfect side lane shot. Who inherited? None of my business. Another horse in. Who was Wayne Caruso? Chauffeur, cook, nanny, bodyguard, take your pick. Hundred-point bells were ringing as the ball skittered over the jellyfish bumpers. But even Feiffer couldn't stop the ball as it dived down a side drain.

Four more turns and a few hundred questions later, I had won. But barely. My score was 6441, to his 6296.

"Best two out of three?" he proposed. I looked at my watch. Two o'clock. I set up another game. He won that one. I won the next.

I expected him to suggest the best three out of five, but he didn't.

"Do you ever stop and wonder why you always end up involved in these things?" he asked instead.

"Yes," I answered. "But I haven't figured it out yet. Isn't that a pretty metaphysical question for a County Sheriff?"

"Ah, but I am a Marin County Sheriff, ma'am. With the emphasis on Marin. It's been a pleasure, Ms. Jasper."

He turned and marched his gorgeous body out my door.

I turned off Hayburners and called Wayne Caruso back. Maggie had asked him to speak to me about Scott. He was willing to tell me all he knew, at my convenience. His voice was low and unassuming.

"Don't really have to look at my stories," he added, his voice sinking and barely audible. "Pretty sure Maggie made that up, your being interested." In my mind I saw his homely face burdened by dejection.

"No, I am interested," I heard myself say. "Not that I know anything about writing."

"That'll make two of us, then," he said with a soft laugh. "We can share the experience."

I chuckled, pleased by his unexpected lightness. I told him to come by the house at six o'clock, and rushed out the door to my appointment with Detective Sergeant Udel.

Midway to the Mill Valley Police Department I slowed down. I didn't want to get a speeding ticket on the way to my murder interrogation. I arrived at nine minutes after three. I wondered whether my tardiness would be construed as evidence of guilt, or possibly as an innocent's nonchalance.

Pushing a glass door open, I entered a large waiting room furnished simply with two brown-and-white plaid couches. I told the uniformed officer at the desk that I was here to see Sergeant Udel. He smiled and asked me to take a seat. Sitting comfortably on one of the couches, I took a moment to enjoy the November sunlight that filtered warmly through the glass door, and remembered the words of Oscar Wilde's *Ballad of Reading Gaol*, "that little tent of blue which prisoners call the sky."

My reverie was interrupted by the sound of a door being buzzed open. Renee came briskly through the door with a smug smile on her face. She didn't even glance at me as she sailed past.

Inspector Parker escorted me into an interrogation room where Sergeant Udel sat at a bare table. This room was not warm and sunny. Nor was Sergeant Udel. His pale, distressed face looked even thinner than it had the day before. And his eyes were round and staring. Was this Renee's work? He chewed viciously on a pen and gestured for me to sit down.

I was busy feeling sorry for him, when he began to question me. Then I started feeling sorry for myself. He asked me all the same questions he had asked the previous afternoon, prodding me here and battering me there, helter-skelter. Inspector Parker took notes, his red face set impassively. Then Udel shifted to new questions. What did I know about Renee, Maggie, and Eileen? He tapped his fingers on the table and chewed his pen. And how about Devi, Valerie, and Ted? Tap, tap. Chew, chew.

"Do you take drugs, Ms. Jasper?" Udel asked in another rapid shift, his eyes searing into me.

"No! Well, I used to take tryptophan before it was recalled, but it's an amino acid, not a drug really."

"Acid, like LSD?" he demanded eagerly. Even Parker's eyes opened up.

"No, *amino* acid, like in protein. You used to be able to get it in a health food store," I answered desperately. "Over the counter."

"And what other drugs do you take?" he asked, chewing on his pen once more.

I decided not to tell him about my herbal sleeping pills. "Sometimes aspirin," I replied. "Though I try not to very often. No coffee or sugar or alcohol. Or meat or dairy products for that matter. I'm a strict vegetarian. . . ."

"What about Dr. Lambrecht?" he interrupted.

"Maggie?"

"Yes. You must know what kind of drugs she uses."

"Coffee," I revealed triumphantly. "I keep telling her it's poison, but she won't listen. And she puts sugar and cream in it, too. Triple poison . . ."

"I'm not interested in coffee, Ms. Jasper. Coffee is not a drug."

Damn me if I couldn't resist correcting him, even though I could see the styrofoam cups on the table, filled with the dregs of the insidious drug in question.

"But it is a drug. Do you know what it does to your body? Did you know that people go through withdrawal symptoms when they stop drinking coffee?"

"*Illegal* drugs!" he shouted. Then there was a cracking sound as he bit through his pen.

I stared as a trickle of blue ink spilled over his lower lip. He looked like an improperly painted vampire. He burst out of his chair, gagging and spitting. Then he stormed through the door, shouting at Inspector Parker to take over, and slamming it behind him.

Inspector Parker had a different approach. He plodded through a list of illegal drugs, one by one (marijuana, cocaine . . .) and asked if I was taking any of them. Then he asked if I had taken any of those drugs in the past. I lied and said I hadn't. I didn't feel too guilty about the lie. I wasn't up for a Supreme Court nomination or anything. Then he asked the same questions about each of the other suspects. I honestly told him that I knew absolutely nothing about their illegal drug habits, if they had any at all.

"Anything else you can tell us?" he asked finally.

"No," I said, with some reservation. But I wasn't about to get Ann Rivera involved with the police.

"Then you're free to go. Call us if you think of something new. I'll buzz you out."

Midway through the door he stopped and turned to me.

"You hafta excuse the sergeant," he whispered. "He's under a lot of stress. Never handled a murder before."

I was back into the large sunlit room once more, sucking in the sweet air of freedom. Closing my eyes, I breathed deeply and straightened my posture. A series of clenched muscles let go. My jaw, neck, shoulders and stomach relaxed. Then I opened my eyes and headed for the door to the outside.

Valerie Davis was sitting, rigid as ever, on the far end of the couch nearest the door. There were circles under her eyes and her skin still had an unhealthy greyish cast.

I nodded hello and smiled. I wanted to say something comforting, but I couldn't think of the appropriate words. A simple "good luck" seemed inadequate, especially if she was a murderer.

I pushed out through the glass door. Once in the womb of my aged brown Toyota, I sat gratefully savoring my escape. But unease swept over me as I considered Inspector Parker's parting words. I turned the key in the ignition. Sergeant Udel had never handled a murder case before, much less solved one. Could he solve this one?

Pulling out of the lot, I assured myself that I had a friend in Sergeant Feiffer, fingerprints or no fingerprints. Or did I? Maybe I should have let him win the last game of pinball. And I was probably Detective Sergeant Udel's favorite for the electric chair right now. Would he be so unfair as to let the absurd results of my coffee fanaticism influence his view of my criminal guilt or innocence? Only if he was human, I answered myself unhappily. Damn my self-righteousness!

I turned onto East Blithedale and told myself to quit whining and to think positively. Of course the police weren't telling me all they knew. They probably already had a good idea who had killed Scott Younger. They were just gathering evidence to prepare their case.

By the time I turned onto my street, I had restored my own confidence in the Mill Valley Police Department.

When I pulled into my driveway there was already a car there. Felix Byrne, reporter for the *Marin Mind*, recently appointed western correspondent for the *Philadelphia Globe*, and my best friend Barbara's current sweetheart, was sitting comfortably on my front porch in a peeling white lawn chair. As I walked up the stairs he stood and waved. He wore a snug-fitting pair of jeans and a turquoise sweater over his lean, small-boned body.

"Howdy, hi," he said. "I hear you got yourself mixed up in another one." His shaggy mustache moved as he spoke, the only indication that there was actually a mouth underneath it. He winked one large brown eye at me.

"You're not going to get your story from me," I warned him. "This time, the police are taking care of the murder investigation."

He emphatically shook his head no. "I've talked to my source at the police department. They don't have a clue."

- Six -

"THEY HAVE DIDDLY for physical evidence," Felix continued as
I opened the door. "Anyone could have struck the blow. No
particular strength necessary. And with Scott Younger lying down
the way he was, they can't even tell the height of the person who
bashed him. All they've really got are . . ."

"My fingerprints on the weapon?" I finished for him. He
turned his eyes away from mine. I felt sick.

I dropped my purse on top of Hayburners and plunged into
the depths of my naugahyde chair.

"Want some tea?" Felix asked. He was always good for tea
and sympathy, especially when he sniffed a good story.

I nodded and he went into the kitchen. He knew where to find
the kettle.

Felix had sought me out as a source when researching another
murder, last year. His inside story of that murder had resulted
in his assignment as Western correspondent for the *Philadelphia
Globe*. His friendship with me had also led to his romance with
Barbara.

Barbara, my best friend. Barbara, who was lying somewhere
in the sun on the coast of Maui during the time of my need. My
thoughts traveled back across the Pacific to my estranged husband. And then to the disappearing C.C. Abandoned by all, I
felt a bad case of the suspected-of-murder, no-one-loves-me blues
coming on.

"Tea will be served in a moment, madam," said Felix with
a bow as he returned from the kitchen. He pulled up a rolling
office chair and sat down across from me.

"Felix, do you think there's something about me that brings these things on?" I asked softly.

"No, you are not creating murder out of your bad vibes! Get that crap out of your mind." I was surprised by his vehemence. Did the man protest too much?

"Let's put it this way. How many murders have there been in Marin recently?"

"Two," he answered.

"And how many have I been involved in?" I stuck two fingers up in the air to coach him. He remained silent. "And," I added, "this time I found the body."

"That must have been a real bummer. Tell me about it," he said, a reporter's gleam in his eye.

The teakettle whistled. We both jumped in our chairs.

"What's with the police, anyway?" I asked, when he had returned with a cup of mint tea. "Are they incompetent or what?"

"No, they're not incompetent. How are they supposed to know who did it? No witnesses. No condemning physical evidence. No confession." He threw up his hands. "One of the cops told me about the last murder she could remember in Mill Valley. A wife shot her hubby in the Safeway parking lot. Six people saw it happen. There was a smoking gun in her hand, and she immediately confessed to the cop who arrested her. This one isn't like that."

"So what are they doing to solve it?" I asked, blowing on my tea and sipping cautiously. I had burned my tongue, among other things, a little too often lately.

"Digging. Looking for leads. Wayne Caruso inherits, so he looks pretty good."

"That guy couldn't have done it. You'd know that if you met him. He's too . . . too gentle," I said.

"He's a friggin' black belt in karate," said Felix.

"So? Younger wasn't killed by karate, for God's sake. He was killed with a metal bar!" I could feel my face getting hot.

"Okay, okay," said Felix, raising a hand in front of his face as if to shield himself from my wrath. "They're interested in Valerie Davis too. She's got a record."

"What did she do?" I asked, remembering her pitifully frightened face.

"I couldn't find out."

"I'm surprised there was something you couldn't find out,"

I said snidely. "Your friendly female officer wouldn't divulge all the police secrets?" Felix blushed.

"Finish your tea," he said. "I'll come back when you're in a better mood."

I slurped up the remaining few drops. He took the cup from my hand. "I'll stay if you need me," he offered in a softer tone.

I shook my head. I had work to do. He flung a "take care" over his shoulder on the way out the door. The score was three men down so far that day. And one more to go. I hoped my social skills improved by the time Wayne Caruso arrived.

For the next hour I frantically did paperwork, trying to make up for lost time. I started with employee paychecks. Why hadn't I received a raise when everyone else had? Sighing, I reminded myself that the owner's salary is dependent upon profit.

I was looking out my window when the bottle-green Jaguar glided up my driveway. It was exactly six o'clock. I had just enough time to put away the company checkbook and drop the paychecks in my purse before I heard footsteps clatter up the stairs.

Wayne Caruso stood at the door. He looked handsome, at least up to his thick neck. He was comfortably dressed in loose corduroy pants and a tweed shawl-neck sweater. This cozy outfit failed to disguise the muscular contours it covered. His misshapen head looked for a moment like a lion's, bizarrely mated with human form. A strangely erotic vision.

Guiltily, I shook the vision out of my head. Craig was only gone two weeks and I was sexually attracted to every man I saw. Not every man, I corrected myself. I hadn't been attracted to Sergeant Udel or Felix, or Inspector Parker, for that matter.

"Flowers," Wayne said and extended a muscular arm in my direction. A dozen gently blushing white rosebuds were clutched in his massive hand.

I felt a hot flush rising in my face as I stood staring, momentarily stunned by his gesture. When I saw that flush reflected in Wayne's scarred cheeks, I came to, and used my gaping mouth to thank him.

Flustered, I donned my gracious hostess persona. I showed Wayne into the living room, where he lowered himself into one of the beige canvas chairs that hung on long heavy ropes from the rafters. An adventurous type. Most people studiously avoided sitting in those chairs. And then they asked if I had children.

I opened up the curtains and let the sunshine filter into the little-used room. It sparkled on the pinball machines, and on the pinball backglasses that decorated the walls. Once I had put the flowers in water, I brought out brown-rice crackers in a basket, and asked if he'd like tea. He shook his head. I stood uncertainly. The transition from gracious hostess to interrogator is a difficult one. "A seat?" suggested Wayne with a tentative smile, motioning to the chair hanging across from his. I put the basket of crackers on the table, then plumped down gratefully and pushed off with my feet so that my chair moved gently forward and backward. Wayne matched my movements. We swung in time with one another.

"Ask your questions," he said. "I'll answer them."

"Were you Scott's bodyguard?" I began.

"I was hired as a bodyguard twelve years ago. Over the years, though . . ." He stopped to think and swung slowly. "I provided cooking, driving, housework, friendship. The job description changed. There was no more need for a bodyguard. Or so I thought." His hands clutched the ropes, disturbing the path of his chair. "I was wrong. Dead wrong."

"It wasn't your fault," I said. He looked across at me. I caught the glint of his eyes beneath the heavy brows.

"Thanks. Should have been more careful, though. I thought it had become an affectation."

"What? His needing a bodyguard?" I asked. He nodded, his chair moving rhythmically once more.

"But why did he need a bodyguard in the first place?" I asked.

"Did business with nasty people. There were threats made. He had two bodyguards originally, brothers. One quit to get married. Scott hired me."

I took a big breath and asked, "Did Scott sell drugs?"

Wayne's face colored, the network of scars on his cheeks standing out in angry purple relief against his skin.

"Not for a long time. Made his money and got out. He was not a monster, no matter what they say." His eyes glinted at me again. "A photographer. Promoted artists and musicians. Got into the restaurant business to give artists a place to hang their work and musicians a place to play."

"He owned restaurants?" I asked.

"All over California," he answered, nodding. "And art galleries, music clubs."

"Do you inherit them?"

"Yes, I'm the only one left. His father died two years ago. I'm the primary beneficiary, executor of his will. Got to establish a trust fund to encourage starving artists, though. And a few bequests. To the local art committee, his college, art schools."

"Do you need the money?"

"No. Scott's been generous over the years. I could live off the dividends of my own investments. Or practice law," he said in the tone of voice that said he'd rather not.

"Law?" I said, stopping my chair in surprise.

"Got a law degree going to school part time. Interesting, at least in an academic setting." He smiled wryly. "Never took the bar. Too many lawyers in the Bay Area. Half of them don't practice anyway. Too much competition."

From behind me came a demanding meow. The missing C.C. had arrived. Ignoring me, she crossed the room and leapt gracefully into Wayne's lap mid-swing.

"Like to be useful, though," he said as C.C. settled in on his well-muscled thigh and began to claw.

He took her paw in his hand and held it. "No," he said firmly, looking her straight in the eye. I chuckled at his innocence, expecting to win over C.C. with a simple "no." C.C. moved to the center of his lap, lay on her back and purred. I stopped chuckling.

C.C. continued to purr, her claws at rest, while I questioned Wayne about Scott's relationship with Renee. He explained in his sad low voice that Scott had been a solitary man who longed for a family and had been afraid he couldn't father one. Scott had hoped for a built-in family with Renee. But Renee's children hadn't taken to him. Nor had Renee, for that matter.

C.C. was asleep in Wayne's lap by the time I had asked him all the questions I could think of. He didn't understand any better than I the hostility that Scott had sparked in Valerie and Devi, much less why Scott was killed. But he wanted to understand.

"Not for justice, or vengeance," he said, "but because it was my job to protect him. I've got to know how I failed." His hands gripped the chair's ropes tightly again. His eyes gazed downward, invisible under the thick curly brows, then suddenly lifted to me, glistening.

"We'll find out," my voice said softly. My stomach was tight with tension.

Suddenly I wanted it to be true. I wanted to find the killer for him. I wanted . . . vivid sexual images flooded my brain. What would happen if I walked over there and touched him, sat with him, held him? A lion surprised. Pathos and eros danced together for a moment in the space separating us.

"Would you like a cracker?" I asked, motioning toward the long-forgotten basket. Pathos and eros dropped onto the beige rug and shattered.

Wayne laughed as if he had heard the sound. C.C. woke up, glowered in my direction and jumped off his lap.

"No, thank you," he said, lowering his eyes once more. "But one of Scott's restaurants, in San Francisco. We could eat dinner there."

"I need to drop off some checks at my warehouse tonight," I mumbled. Fantasy was better left alone, untested. I was afraid to spend any more intimate time with this man.

"Where is your warehouse?" he asked.

"Oakland."

"Could drive you," he offered. "Then go to dinner."

I hesitated. His chair stopped moving.

"Didn't mean to pressure you. I'll leave you to your work," he said, standing up.

"No," I said. "I mean, yes. I'd like to go. But I have a couple more things to do first."

I left him in the living room and went to my office. In that millisecond after agreeing to dinner, I had remembered that Wayne was a prime murder suspect.

I found a yellow pad and wrote, "Dear Felix: Just in case something should happen, this is to let you know that I am going out with Wayne Caruso tonight (warehouse and dinner)." I dated the note and stuffed it in an envelope addressed to my friendly reporter, Felix.

As we walked down the front stairs I noticed a new black Cadillac parked across the street, in front of my neighbor's house. An unusual sight. Her visitors habitually arrived in beat-up, significantly less impressive means of transportation. A new, wealthy man in her life perhaps.

Wayne opened the passenger's side of the Jaguar for me. I sank into a leather seat with a sigh of sensual delight. A step up from naugahyde. The leather even smelled of luxury. But a step down for some poor cow. I shook off that thought, only to wonder if I was sitting in Scott Younger's seat.

Wayne guided the car smoothly through the tide of homecoming traffic, stopping at a mailbox upon my request. As I got out to mail my letter to Felix, I noticed a black Cadillac parked down the block. Briefly I wondered if it was the same one I had seen across from my house. There couldn't be that many in Marin. It was not a yuppie car.

Then we were moving again, our words flowing less smoothly than the Jaguar. Talk of my practice of tai chi, a soft martial arts form; his long years of practice of the harder karate form; the health crisis which had precipitated my vegetarianism, and his decision to cut down on red meat took us over the Richmond Bridge in fits and starts. A burst of incomplete sentences expressing his sense of lost purpose upon Scott's death took us down Highway 17. And my self-conscious warnings about the tackiness of my business pulled us into the parking lot by my warehouse.

I could have skipped the warnings. Wayne appreciated Jest Gifts with the enthusiasm of the closet punster. He chuckled at Chiro-crackers, hollow-tooth cups and "uh-huh" ties for therapists. Then we glided across the Bay Bridge to San Francisco for dinner.

"La Fête à L'oie" announced a discreet sign somewhere in the chilly grey financial district. Wayne pushed open the door to the warm lobby and I froze mid-step. I was still wearing the same corduroys and sweater that I had put on that morning. Silk dresses, wool suits, high heels, Rolexes and jewels turned to stare, if staring is the right word for intense, quick glances and subsequently averted eyes. I might as well have worn my drop-seat pajamas.

"Monsieur Caruso," came a voice through the crowd. "And a young lady. We are so pleased." Following the voice came a tall tuxedoed form with a handsome Mediterranean countenance. Now, heads turned back with interest. Rich eccentrics? Casually dressed celebrities? I could almost hear the silent speculation.

"Have you been to La Fête before?" asked the tuxedo. I shook my head. "Of course not, I should have remembered such a striking young lady."

I looked down at my worn Reeboks and tried to smother my giggles. Striking, indeed! And still a young lady at thirty-eight. I did not want to betray my class (middle) with unseemly behavior. But when I raised my eyes and saw the grin stretched across Wayne's ugly puss, I could hold it in no longer. Raucous laughter exploded out of my mouth like popcorn.

"Perhaps a viewing of the gallery first before dinner?" asked the tuxedo, as if I had merely tittered.

"Thanks, Henri," answered Wayne, escorting me through the door into the thoroughbred gathering. "We'll look. Need a non-dairy vegetarian dinner for two, no sugar, no white flour." He turned to look at me. "Right?" he asked.

I nodded, impressed that he had actually caught the details of my diet. Most people pretended to and then suggested cake and ice cream for dessert.

The foyer was filled with works of art, and with low murmurs of appreciation from those viewing them. One wall displayed eight large squares of solidly colored canvas, each with a single shimmering line through its center. "Ah," sighed the crowd. I preferred my shark ties. Another held frames bursting with layered scraps of paper, wood and cloth. "Ooh." I could relate to these. They reminded me of my desk.

I liked the photographs best. One especially. A view beginning in a grey drab interior and ending in a doorway bursting with flowers, leaves and light.

"Scott's," said Wayne in a voice so tight that the woman standing next to us flinched.

"Your table is ready," announced Henri seconds later. We were led to a simple linen-draped table, gleaming with silver, china and glassware, its only decoration a single magnolia blossom floating fragrantly in a glass bowl.

A matched pair of tuxedoed waiters served us with rapt attention. Had they already heard that Wayne had inherited the restaurant? I followed Wayne's lead and ate with silent and serious concentration.

I sampled eggplant caviar and vegetable pâtés, then savored a spicy watercress soup. A small green salad was next, followed by a teaspoon of sorbet to refresh the palate. I forgave the sorbet its sugar content and loosened my waistband unobtrusively. Wayne smiled across the table at me gluttonously.

Then a second series of gold-rimmed dishes appeared. Rectangular thin slices of potato fanned out like cards in a deck. Marinated asparagus spears. Lemon-flavored rice, mushroom and artichoke-heart dolmas. Rosettes of beet, squash and avocado purées that looked as if they belonged on top of a wedding cake. A feast for the eyes and for the mouth, but a heavy burden for the stomach.

A pristine bowl of fresh strawberries ended the meal.

"Had enough?" Wayne asked. Was he serious?

"Yes, thank you," I replied, my voice sounding strange after the uninterrupted quiet of my feeding frenzy.

As I waddled out the door, I wondered aloud why there were no women serving the tables. Henri's face shifted uncomfortably.

"Will be soon," Wayne predicted, with what looked like a wink under his low brow.

It was ten o'clock by the time Wayne left me at my door with a quick goodbye. No kiss, no hug, no handshake. I wondered if I had read him wrong. Was he gay? Had he been Scott's lover after all? I turned to enter my house then remembered, and turned back. He had already reached his car.

"What about your stories?" I shouted to him.

"That's okay," he responded.

"I want to read them," I insisted.

He rummaged in the trunk of the Jaguar and pulled out a pile of large manila envelopes. He brought them up the stairs and handed them to me under the porch light.

"Thank you," I said and squeezed his hand. He turned around and headed down the stairs. The back of his neck was flushed pink.

I watched him as he drove off. I heard another car start and then saw its black shape moving away from the curb; it was a black Cadillac.

- Seven -

I PLOPPED DOWN in my comfy chair to consider whether or not I had been on a date. The evening had borne all of the classic earmarks. Invitation, dinner, awkward conversation. But I still wasn't sure.

And what if I had been on a date? I had become accustomed to Wayne's disfigured face. In fact, his features seemed perversely attractive to me when combined with his well-proportioned body. He was intelligent, centered and attentive. He laughed at my jokes. And his combination of strength and gentleness was seductive. But I recognized the undertow of despair in him all too well. It was the same despair that I kept at bay in myself, by sheer willpower. And it frightened me to see it reflected in Wayne.

C.C. thumped through her cat-door and into my reverie. When she reached my chair I bent down to pick her up. Simultaneously I was pierced by two separate barbs of pain. One at each end of my spine, lower back and upper neck. Damn! I had never received my preventative chiropractic treatment.

Wincing, I collected my roses and limped to the bedroom. After changing into my dropseat pajamas, I took the last two NatuRest and lay my tortured body down on the bed. C.C. jumped lightly onto my chest, extended two paws around my neck and gave me a whiskery Eskimo kiss good night.

By eight-thirty the next morning I was at Maggie's door for repair. The police had unsealed her office and she was back in business. I had figured I could sneak in without an appointment at that hour, but I was wrong. There were three unfamiliar patients ahead of me in the white waiting room. A square young man in a flannel shirt and a round middle-aged woman in a cashmere sweater held magazines in front of their respective faces. The white-haired old woman in magenta velour wasn't as introverted. She waved her cane at me in greeting as I entered.

The celestial tones of Constance Demby floated on the sterile air, inviting relaxation. But Renee's harsh tones bulldozed the harmony.

"You here to ask me questions?" she asked. The sour expression on her tan face indicated her probable attitude regarding such an imposition.

I moved closer to her desk in an effort at privacy. The old woman's bright eyes followed me all the way.

"I'd like to talk to both you and Eileen," I said. "But I'd also like a treatment, if Maggie can fit me in."

"Are you kidding? You aren't even in the appointment book." Her sharp nails tapped the open page of that book as irrefutable evidence.

"But my back . . ."

"Kate, how are you?" Maggie danced into the room, her red hair virtually vibrating with exuberance. "Have you talked to the police again?" I opened my mouth to answer, but not fast enough. "They questioned me for two more hours. But guess what! I've got a bunch of new patients. It's really neat!"

"Maggie, maybe we could talk in your office," I suggested. I could feel eyes burning into my neck alongside my pinched nerve.

"Okay," she said, and led me into the next room.

As I lowered myself carefully onto the visitor's chair, I could see that her office was back to normal. Stuffed animals, paperwork and junk were all jumbled together in her unkempt ecosystem. It was hard to imagine that Sergeant Udel had been behind that desk two days ago.

"Can you work on me this morning?" I asked. First things first. "My back and neck are killing me."

"Of course I can. You look terrible. See what happens when you don't get your regular adjustment?"

"A little murder got in the way, remember?" Her eyebrows shot up. "Didn't seem to hurt your business any, though," I added.

"No, that's the strange thing. All these new people called up for treatment. Jeez, I guess there really is no such thing as bad publicity.'' She shook her head.

''Maggie, do you still want to know who killed Scott Younger?''

Her eyes widened. ''Of course I do. I can't just let this go by, business or no business. I have to know.''

''Thanks,'' I said, feeling my stomach muscles relax.

''Oh, wow, I should thank you! In fact I'll give you your treatment free. You can talk to Eileen and Renee in a minute. And at four o'clock I've got everyone who was here Wednesday coming in for a talk—except for Tanya—Devi thought it would be too much for her. But Ted and Valerie—Wayne and Devi—and the rest of us will all be here.'' She was wiggling in her chair with anticipation. If she had had a tail she would have wagged it.

''Maggie!'' came Renee's yell.

Maggie jumped up.

''Have a seat in the waiting room,'' she said rushing out the door. ''I'll get to you soon.''

I returned to the waiting room, which was now empty except for the white-haired woman. The sound of George Winston's piano had replaced Constance Demby. I sat down in the nearest Scandinavian-design chair and closed my eyes to enjoy it.

''My name's Ida. What's yours?'' asked a rasping voice. I opened my eyes and saw the old woman regarding me intently, her chin on top of her hands, on top of her cane.

''Kate,'' I answered cautiously.

''So who's gonna take the fall for the Younger job?'' she asked, squinting her eyes and pulling her chin up.

''Take the fall?'' I repeated.

''Aw, come on. You must know who looks good to the cops. Who iced Younger? That's the question. I heard he was a dope-dealer.'' She tilted her head as if requesting confirmation.

''Who are you?'' I blurted.

''Ida Morris. I write under the name Dick Fury. You heard of him?''

''No.''

''I've published seventeen Dick Fury's, and you never heard of him?'' Her raspy voice was raised in disbelief. Should I claim illiteracy? The opening of the front door saved me from the deception. A familiar, slightly built man limped in, his steps accented by operatic groans. "Hey, Felix," I greeted him enthusiastically. "Your back giving you some trouble?"

He straightened up his posture when he heard me, then quickly slumped back into his previous pose. A pink blush crept up his neck and into his cheeks.

"He another suspect?" asked Ida eagerly.

I shook my head. Ida put her chin back onto her hands.

Felix hobbled over to sit next to me. "I threw my back out last night. I thought I'd give your chiropractor a try."

"Where does it hurt?" I asked.

"Oh, around the lower back." He gestured vaguely. His eyes asked me to let it go at that.

"Felix, this is Ida," I said, pointing. "Ida writes the Dick Fury stories. Felix writes for the *Philadelphia Globe*."

The two were eyeing each other speculatively when Eileen called my name from the hallway.

"Please walk this way," she said, leading me back to Maggie's office. I walked behind her, but there was no way I could duplicate her graceful relaxed stride. As we went through the door I heard Ida asking Felix about the murder. I wondered how many of Maggie's new patients were reporters, crime writers or undercover police.

Eileen sat looking serene behind Maggie's desk.

"What do you need to know?" she asked, smiling the encouraging smile of a psychotherapist.

"Who killed Scott Younger," I answered.

A frown banished the serenity from her features, but not the loveliness. "I'd like to know too, for Maggie's sake."

"Business doesn't seem to be suffering."

"It's not the right kind of business, though. You have to touch people in this profession. And when they're thrill-seekers, vultures, it feels nasty to touch them." She paused, her large brown eyes distant. "I didn't like to touch Scott Younger either."

I kept quiet, hoping she would go on. She did.

"There was a coldness about him that I couldn't get past. Like a snake. He rarely spoke. He didn't even move. You know how most people move a lot, even when they're at rest?" I nodded. "Well, he didn't."

"That's spooky," I said, and squirmed in my chair. The pinched nerve in my back protested. "Why do you think he was like that?"

"He was probably depressed, but most of the time he struck

me as just plain evil.'' She shuddered. "I always had to wash my hands after touching him.''

"Why did you guys even keep him on as a patient?''

Her laughter was a lilt amid the gloom that her words had evoked. "If we only treated people with clean spirits we wouldn't be in business very long.''

"Do you think he was evil enough to die for it?'' I asked.

"No,'' she said, serious once more. "I just said he felt evil to me. I own that feeling, not him. He was probably a perfectly decent human being. And even if he was evil, that's not something you kill for. I can't really believe someone killed him.'' She raised her palms in the air. "Or imagine it was any of the people that were here Wednesday.''

"That's what I wanted to ask,'' I said. "Is there anything about any of us that feels wrong to you, like Scott Younger felt wrong?''

"No.'' She shook her head. "Everyone has their troubles. You with Craig, for instance.'' My skin flushed. "Or Devi with her health. Ted afraid of getting old. Valerie obsessed with her guru. And Wayne seems painfully shy. But all good people.'' Her hands went up again.

"Did you notice anything that day? Something out of place? Someone somewhere they shouldn't have been?'' She shook her head. "Anything?'' I asked again, an unintended whine creeping into my voice.

"Nothing.''

I sighed deeply. The movement set off the nerve alarms at both ends of my spine.

"Where do you hurt?'' asked Eileen, compassion flowing once more from her brown eyes.

"Neck and back.''

She came around the desk and put her hands gently on my shoulders. I hoped she wouldn't have to wash them afterwards.

"Thanks for trying,'' she said. "We really do appreciate it.'' She gave my shoulders a quick squeeze before leading me out the door.

In a matter of minutes Eileen had laid me out on a therapeutic couch and switched on its invisible rollers. I sank into the comfort of the mechanical massage. Unfortunately, this couch was located in the mauve room where I had last seen Younger's dead body. As the rollers moved back and forth they seemed to drone "so what?'' with each stroke.

When the timer buzzed, Eileen transferred me to the narrow padded table where Younger had lain. I lay face down as he had, to wait for Maggie, hot pads on my neck and lower back. Perhaps someone else could have taken that quiet time for spiritual contemplation. I embraced anxiety and dread. There was plenty of fuel. Flashes of Younger's bloody body in this very room, Craig's desertion, lonely old age, imminent early death, a life sentence for murder, and the torturous chiropractic treatment to come kindled the flames of my agitation.

The mental din was so loud that I barely heard the softly approaching footsteps, footsteps that did not sound like Maggie's or Eileen's. I could see nothing through the hole in the leather where my face rested. Pain gripped my neck and back as I tensed my muscles. It redoubled as I rashly pushed off the table and leapt to a standing position. I found myself face to face with Renee.

"You shouldn't get up like that," she said, and bent over to pick up the scattered hot-packs.

"You're probably right," I agreed. The jolt had done my spine no favors. But had that leap saved me from a deadlier blow? I looked closely at Renee. She didn't appear to be carrying a weapon.

"It just screws up your back worse," she said, shaking her pointy finger in my face.

"Right," I agreed once more.

"I suppose you think I'm a total bitch," she said.

I shrugged my shoulders. If the muzzle fits, I thought uncharitably, wear it.

"Well, I'd like to see you take care of Maggie sometime!" She shook her finger at me again. "Before I took over here, she spent all her time talking instead of giving treatments. She was making zip. I turned that around. But does anyone give me credit?" She thrust her sullen face nearer to mine.

"No," I ventured.

"That's right. No way! People tell her she should get rid of me because I'm hostile. Bullshit! Without me this business would go to hell in a handbasket."

I nodded my understanding. I could imagine how demoralizing it would be to keep Maggie on track by playing the perpetual bad guy. The nod seemed to satisfy her.

"So what did you want to know about Scott?" she asked. She

sat down on the one and only chair in the room. I leaned awkwardly against the padded table.

"I heard that you went out with him for a while."

"I guess so. If you call going to a few gallery openings and weird plays going out. That's all we ever did together without my kids." She crossed her arms angrily.

"What did you do with your kids?"

"Whatever they damn well wanted, that's what! He would ask them what they wanted to do. Not me. Them! We even chauffeured John to this god-awful punk music concert because John thought The Bloody Spikes were really 'rad.' John didn't want us sitting near him, of course. So we huddled on the sidelines until it was over, and took him home. Great date." She twirled her finger. "And where do you think Kimberly wanted to go?" she continued.

I shrugged my shoulders.

"I'll give you a clue. She's twelve years old."

"The zoo?" I guessed.

"The zoo." A harsh laugh came from her throat. "It's easy to see you don't have kids. No, the mall. Shopping. Her idea of paradise is unlimited credit at The Village.

"So we all went shopping. Me and John and Kimberly, and Scott and his creepy sidekick. Scott bought all this crap for her. Fifty-dollar Mickey Mouse sweat shirts, pink leather purse and matching Reeboks, and a five-foot plush bear, just for starters. Do you believe it?

"I suppose I shouldn't have let him. I didn't let him buy anything for me. But if he was foolish enough to waste all that money on her, why not?" Her voice rose defensively.

"Sounds right to me," I said. I wasn't going to judge her actions.

"And then John got wise. He got a leather jacket, some forty-dollar sunglasses and a cassette player before I put my foot down. He wanted a dirt bike next.

"But the funny thing was it didn't work. Scott spent more money on those two kids in one afternoon than my ex has on child support in a year. And they still didn't like him.

"And then, Kimberly wanted sushi for dinner. A twelve-year-old kid and she wants sushi, no McDonald's please. So we go to the city to this sushi place Scott says is the best. The bill was over a hundred dollars." She shook her head.

"Why did he try so hard with your kids?"

"I think the kids were the main attraction. Nothing kinky though." She shook her finger at me as though I had suggested it. "He just wanted a prefab family."

"I know what I look like. Even if I lost weight I wouldn't be pretty." She shifted her sturdy body impatiently.

"That's not true," I said. "You're an attractive woman." And she was, in her own way. Strong and vital, if a little dictatorial.

"Maybe to a bus driver like my ex, but not to a guy like Scott Younger. I mean, his house was incredible." Her eyes changed focus, recalling it. "And his clothes, his car, everything. He could land Miss America if he tried. No, he wanted a family. He wasn't particular about the wife."

"Why did you split up with him?"

"You think I shouldn't have passed up the chance, don't you?" she accused, her eyes flashing. My protestations were drowned by her tirade. "Just because I'm a poor single mom, you think I'll never get another chance like that. Well, the guy was god-damn weird. He wasn't happy. He barely talked. I may not be that educated but at least I can talk. No, he just sat there with that weird-ass smile, looking superior. No wonder the kids couldn't stand him.

"And he took that creepy guy Wayne with him wherever we went." I flinched at the description but held my tongue. "The kids liked Wayne better than Scott, for God's sake. The whole thing was just too weird, so I broke it off," she finished. Her shoulders slumped.

"How did he react to that?"

"He was okay. I think he realized the deal wouldn't have worked since the kids didn't like him anyhow."

"He didn't quit Maggie as a chiropractor?"

"No. Maggie did a good job on him. And he was cool about me. No hard feelings on either side."

"Did he talk about his dope-dealing days?" I asked.

"I told you, he hardly talked about anything, much less his past. I had no idea. Not that it would have made any difference. I still would have given it a shot." She looked straight at me. "The only reason he asked me out in the first place was because he met me here, and I talked about my kids. I don't think he saw very many other people. He didn't hang out. Like at the gallery openings, people would come up to talk to him and he'd just shine them on. Kinda sad really." Her tone softened.

I nodded. Scott Younger's life was beginning to sound as sad as his death.

"What else did you want to know?" she asked, straightening her shoulders.

"Do you remember anything important from the day he was killed? Maybe something you didn't tell the police?" I asked hopefully.

"No," she answered, suddenly succinct.

"Any secrets, motives, anything?" I tried.

"No," she said. Then she looked up. "Except for Maggie and Eileen. But that doesn't have anything to do with murder."

"What about them?" I was on the scent.

"No. You don't need to know."

Renee remained adamant on this. In fact, I suspected she had only hinted at a secret in order to torture me. Didn't she have to be a sadist to work for a chiropractor in the first place?

In due time Maggie came in to snap, crackle and pop my spine back into shape. Painful as it was, it worked. I got off the table and moved without agony. Maggie's business sense may have been wanting, but she was a damn good chiropractor.

After my treatment I decided it was my turn to manipulate Maggie. My logic was as follows. If I pretended to already know her secret, Maggie would blurt out all of the juicy details in defense.

"Renee told me about you and Eileen," I lied.

"Oh, neat," she responded, looking back at me with friendly eyes. That was it. So much for trickery.

She bounced alongside of me as I walked carefully back to the reception area.

"Kate's treatment is free of charge," she said to Renee, waving her hand in my direction grandly.

"Maggie!" began Renee and turned on her with pointed finger.

I slipped out the door as quietly as possible.

- Eight -

I COULD FEEL the dark rain clouds weighing upon the roof of my Toyota as I drove home. The funereal pressure was apt, if a little late. Nature just waking up to the violent demise of one of its creatures.

Once I had pulled into my driveway and parked, I walked over to retrieve my mail from the overstuffed box on the street. Orders, bills, charitable requests and advertisements spilled out into my reluctant hands. I'd have to get a bigger box soon.

I was leafing through the mass of paper when an explosion of hisses and yowls burst into the air, followed by a small flash of black and a larger flash of orange, both heading underneath my parked Toyota. I recognized the orange as the bullying ginger tom who lived next door and the black as my own cat, C.C.

By the time the moaning growl which C.C. reserved for serious distress reached my ears I was sprinting toward the car, carried by the adrenalin pumping through my body. Suddenly C.C. was not the cat who had shredded the laps of all of my pants, but the trusting little bundle of fluff that curled in my arms purring, waited at my bedroom door in the morning, and had stuck her head shyly under my arm when I had brought her home for the first time.

I crawled under the car on my belly, bumping my knees and scraping my hands on the gravel. C.C. cowered under the tom's glare. I threw my bundle of mail toward his orange body. It hit the undercarriage of the car and scattered on the ground uselessly. He stood firm, eyeing me with silent menace. If I had had a gun I would have shot him. I picked up a handful of gravel and flung it in his direction. But, again, my cramped position caused my aim to go wild. My target merely moved a few steps back.

I pulled myself out from under the car, thinking of water. But before I could reach my hose the ginger tom loped out from under the car nonchalantly, to disappear through the wooden slats that fenced off his owner's property. C.C. raced up the stairs, across the porch and through her cat-door to safety. I followed her, shaking with thwarted rage. I spent the next half hour stroking C.C. back to purring and clawing normalcy.

I was on my belly beneath the Toyota again, painfully gathering my mail, when Felix drove up. He was full of questions but scant on information, until he got to Valerie Davis. By that time, he had made and poured us both tea.

"I found out what she went to prison for," he said. He paused and sipped his tea with a great show of unconcern. I resisted the urge to grab his slight shoulders and shake the information out of him.

"Really," I said, matching his tone of indifference. "Are you planning on sharing the details with me?"

"It would serve you right if I didn't, the way you sicced that crazy old woman on me." He bent forward, glaring at me. It took me a moment to realize he meant Ida Morris, a.k.a. Dick Fury. I strangled the laugh that was gurgling up in my throat when I realized he was actually annoyed. I changed strategies.

"She'd make a great story, wouldn't she?" I said.

"Maybe." His eyes moved upward as he considered. Then he smiled. "Okay, you win. Valerie got sent up on an armed robbery charge."

"Armed robbery?" It didn't square with the woman I had seen in Maggie's office.

"In 1970. She and two other women. It was a political robbery, according to them. They were all militants. Valerie was an honors student in her second year of college, when she got radicalized, and pregnant, at the same time. She and the other two women decided to put their political beliefs into action by subsidizing a group of poor single mothers with a large involuntary contribution from the Bank of America. The cops caught up with them within a few hours of the robbery. Valerie gave birth to her child, Hope, while she was in custody, awaiting trial. The trial was a political circus. The only defense the three women offered was the failure of the American system to deal with the oppressed.''

''God, Felix. Criminal or idealist, how could anyone risk something like that?'' I felt a mixture of awe, fear and guilt, considering Valerie's crime and punishment.

''Maybe she didn't think they'd be caught. Maybe she believed in what she was doing so much, the risk seemed worth it.'' He shrugged his shoulders. ''She certainly paid the price, going to prison. Her parents raised her baby.''

''No wonder she's scared. The police have to be looking at her. Do they think she killed Younger?''

''They still don't have a firm suspect. But she's up there in the running. They're not considering you as seriously now.'' I let out a large breath. ''Actually, they're leaning more and more towards Wayne.''

My stomach sank. I was convinced Wayne hadn't killed Scott. And I hope Valerie hadn't. Why couldn't there be a suspect in the case that I would have liked to see in prison?

Felix left. I spent the next four hours doing paperwork, my thoughts never far from the murder.

I walked into my chiropractor's office for the third time in three days, and stopped short. Renee was glowering from behind her desk. Wayne was holding a copy of *Rolling Stone* in front of his face. And Valerie sat as blissfully erect as she had two days ago. Ted smiled at me and waved. Everyone was seated where they had been Wednesday morning. Everyone except Scott Younger. My feet exercised the kind of caution my reckless mind could learn from. They refused to move forward.

The spell was broken by the sound of hoarse breathing and scurrying footsteps behind me. I stepped through the doorway before Devi could run me over. She was dressed in layers of turquoise that day, including a turquoise scarf splashed with white and purple. Tanya was not with her.

''I hope I'm not late,'' she said, breathless as usual. ''Our clocks were an hour and a half behind. I wouldn't have known, but I heard the MacNeil Lehrer report on the radio and they don't come on . . .''

''It's okay,'' Renee said curtly. ''Sit down.''

Devi chose the chair between Valerie and Wayne, where Younger had last sat. Did she realize? Wayne lowered his magazine and studied the occupants of the room. I sat down next to

Ted by the door, to do the same. I could feel Wayne's intense gaze upon my face before I saw it. He smiled and then looked away quickly when Valerie spoke to Devi, breaking the silence in the room.

"Beautiful scarf," Valerie said. Her large eyes were luminous once more. Studying her face, I saw only a deep peace, underlined by sadness and fear. I certainly didn't see a bank robber, much less a murderer.

"Oh, this?" asked Devi, glancing down at her scarf as if surprised to find it there. "I made it. I make all my scarfs."

"Do you sell them?" asked Valerie. "I would love one in greens."

"No, but I could make you one if you'd like," she offered. "It's about the only art work I do these days."

"How are you doing, little lady?" asked a voice in my ear. I jumped in my seat. Once more, I had forgotten that Ted existed.

"Fine," I answered, turning to face him. He had recovered from Wednesday's events, if his face was any clue. Again, he looked younger than his sixty-nine years, his brown eyes lively with interest and curiosity, his mustache twitching with energy above his buck teeth.

"Maggie tells me you're going to unmask the murderer," he said.

I groaned. What was wrong with that woman? Even if I were going to investigate, it wouldn't help to put each and every suspect on notice.

"First of all, I'm not a detective, and I don't plan to detect . . ." I began.

Maggie bounced into the room before I had time to finish my declaration. I glared at her fiercely. She didn't seem to notice.

"Oh wow, everyone's here," she said, smiling. "Eileen will be out in a sec. I'm so glad you all came."

"Just what are we supposed to be doing?" asked Renee, making no attempt to disguise the irritation in her harsh voice.

"Well, let's see. First, let's bring our chairs into a circle," Maggie answered. She pulled two teak chairs into formation. The rest of us followed suit, with varying degrees of efficiency. Renee sighed, but came out from behind her desk, dragging her rolling office chair with her. By the time Eileen's languid steps brought her into the room, we were all arranged in a circle that brought an encounter group to mind. Only no one was doing any encountering.

Maggie sat with a large, expectant smile on her face. Wayne stared at the floor. Devi twitched and breathed loudly. Ted was squirming in his chair. I realized I was squirming as well, and made an effort to still my body. Only Eileen and Valerie seemed relaxed. Renee was the first to speak.

"Yeah, now what?" she said. I appreciate her directness. I was also beginning to sympathize with her perpetual irritation. We turned toward Maggie.

"Well," she said brightly, her head tilted to one side. "Does anyone have anything they want to share about Scott Younger?"

Wayne pulled his curly head up and took a deep breath.

"He was a good man," he said in a low growl. "Know most of you don't realize it, but it's true. Lots of stuff in the past. Who doesn't have stuff in the past?" His voice was stronger now. I felt a tug of guilt. I had cared very little about the dead man as a human being. From the lowered gazes of most of our group, I guessed that there was a lot of guilt going around.

"Wanted to help. Helped artists, musicians, sculptors. Wanted to love, be loved. Just didn't know how," Wayne continued, shaking his head. Moisture glistened in his eyes. At least one person genuinely mourned Scott Younger's passing. "That's all," he ended gruffly.

I reached across Ted, who sat between us, to pat Wayne's hand. Ted looked old again. Eileen put her arm around Wayne's shoulders.

"Let's have a moment of silence for Scott," she said, her voice sweet and gentle. "Offer our thoughts, prayers, whatever feels appropriate." Wayne nodded.

We sat in silence for some time. I closed my eyes and offered up my agnostic hope that Scott Younger might find love wherever he was, and peace. I heard Devi's hoarse sobs as I did. My own eyes had teared up but declined to spill over. Sadness and loss filled the waiting room. I opened my eyes when I heard a mass clearing of throats. The faces around me were drained but peaceful.

"Does anyone have something to add aloud?" asked Eileen. Ted raised his hand as if he were in school. Eileen nodded. He moved his head around to face Wayne.

"I feel real bad about your friend," he said. "He was too young to die. Here, I'm an old coot, terrified that death is waiting around the corner and then, some young guy gets it, just like that. Doesn't seem right to me."

"Don't be scared," said Devi, her eyes lighted from within. "Death is just going home really. This"—she glanced downward—"is only a shell." She waved her thin white hands in the air as if this would help us to comprehend her words. Or prove them to be true. Ted looked unconvinced.

"Just as a long-caged bird hesitates to leave when the door is opened," Valerie added. The words sounded like a quotation. She sat tall in her chair, with her eyes momentarily closed. Was she thinking of death or the cage of prison?

"Thank you," said Wayne. The words seemed to have comforted him. His head was held high enough that I could see directly into his brown eyes, and the muscles in his face had relaxed. The whole group seemed to be more relaxed.

"Kate has some questions to ask," Maggie broke in. I could almost hear their hearts zipping up. Fear and suspicion returned to the room.

"Not really," I snapped. I needed to clear the air. I let my eyes travel around the group, and continued in what I hoped was a calm and forceful voice. "Contrary to what you might have heard, I am not investigating this death. I want to know what happened. I think we all do, but I don't have any special status."

"I—I would like to say something, since you're getting this sorted out," said Devi, her eyes on me, asking my permission. So much for clearing the air. I nodded. "The reason that I pulled Tanya away—I'm sorry now—but I pulled Tanya away because I had heard bad things about Scott at Crocker." She took a few breaths. "I knew Scott at Crocker. Maybe he changed. But I didn't want Tanya talking to someone who—well—someone with that reputation."

"I just talked to someone else from Crocker," I said, lightening my tone in an effort at normal conversation. "Maybe you know her. Ann Rivera?"

"No." Devi shook her head violently, as if accused. "I don't think so, not that I remember." She turned her face away and began to cough.

After the coughing wound down, Valerie looked at Wayne with troubled eyes, and spoke. "I'd like to apologize for my words about Scott. I didn't know the man had found a new path. Anyway, I should have forgiven him. Forgiveness clears the mind and holds us together in the universe. Will you accept my apologies in his place?"

Wayne nodded. Valerie's eyes cleared.

"Is there anything more?" asked Renee impatiently. She tapped her red nails on the arm of her chair.

All eyes looked in my direction. They still believed I was running an investigation. Maybe I should have asked some probing questions. But my mind was immobilized by the grief and guilt still lingering in the room. And, even if I could have formed the questions, I didn't want to encourage Maggie's expectations any further.

"Not as far as I'm concerned," I said. "Wayne?"

"No, just thank you. Appreciate it."

Renee got up first. She went behind her desk, retrieved her purse and sailed out the door wordlessly.

This seemed to signal the end of the meeting. The whole thing had lasted all of twenty minutes. Eileen squeezed Wayne's shoulder and left, telling Maggie she'd see her later. Ted stood up and handed Wayne a business card. "Come down to the store some time," he said. He stood for a moment looking uncertain, and then followed in Eileen's wake.

Devi stopped on her way to the door and turned toward me. Then she turned toward the door again, and finally turned back to face me. I was getting dizzy just watching her. She scribbled her address and phone number on a torn piece of lavender stationery and handed it to me.

"Call me if you need to," she said and departed.

Valerie came up to me next. "Maggie says you're interested in Guru Illumananda's teachings." I silently cursed Maggie for yet another fabrication. I was not interested in Guru Illumananda. Gurus made me nervous. I plastered a tight smile on my face as Valerie continued. "I wanted to invite you to visit the ashram where I live. Perhaps you could come to one of our evening programs. You, too, Wayne. Or for a meal. We are blessed with a wonderful vegetarian cafeteria."

She gave us each a small, beautifully printed pamphlet with her phone number penciled in above the peach and aqua border. Then she strode, ever erect, out the door. Only Maggie and Wayne remained. They both stood up as I turned to them.

I moved toward Maggie with violence on my mind. Sometimes she went too far. "Interested in the teachings of Guru Illumananda? Ready to unmask the murderer? What else have you told people about me?" I asked when my nose had arrived six inches from hers.

"Sheesh, Kate. Don't be mad," she said, stepping back and

then from side to side nervously. "I was just trying to make things easier for you."

She tugged at her frizzy red hair. I wanted to help her pull it out by the roots, but there was a witness present. And he seemed to be smiling.

"Okay?" she asked, her eyes round and innocent.

"I guess so," I snarled. She grabbed me and hugged me quickly. Then she bounced off in the direction of her business office, humming an unidentifiable tune.

Wayne and I were left alone in the waiting room. Wayne held his muscular body straight and tall, his marred face expressionless. He was broadcasting an intensity of emotion that could have heated a stadium. But I couldn't identify the exact nature of that emotion. Lust, sorrow, fear? or something else entirely? With a little nerve, I could test for the first possibility.

I advanced on him before he had a chance to move, then threw my arms around him in what might be interpreted as merely a friendly Marin hug. But most Marin hugs end above the waist. I put my full torso into it. I felt his body stiffen, in all the right places. His arms came around me hesitantly at first, then strengthened into an incendiary embrace. Just for a moment he pressed his lips to mine, firm sweet-tasting lips unencumbered by mustache. I felt in that moment the heat of his body and the rhythms of his accelerated breathing and heartbeat. My bones melted. Then he broke away.

"Sorry," he growled. Sweat was beaded on his flushed forehead. The force of his gaze fried my already scrambled brains.

"Sorry?" I panted blankly. Sorry for the kiss, or sorry for breaking away?

"Big sister is watching," he whispered.

- Nine -

I WAS TRYING, unsuccessfully, to decipher the meaning of "big sister" when I saw Maggie peering out of the doorway of her office. Her neck was stretched so long she looked like a cartoon goose.

"Jeez, you guys. What are you doing?" she asked once she realized our eyes were upon her. Her body followed her head out of the doorway.

"Talking," I answered briefly.

I heard a muffled snort from Wayne's direction.

"Did you guys know each other before?" she asked in an overly casual manner. Her usually wide-open eyes were squinting, her head pushed forward like a retriever on a scent.

"Before?" I repeated. I had not yet regained my full powers of speech. My mind was still mush. And my legs felt rubbery.

"No," answered Wayne firmly. "I've seen Kate here in your office before. But nothing more. We're not conspirators in Scott's death. So please, get that idea out of your head."

"Oh, God, is that what you think?" I asked aloud.

"Sheesh, Kate. What am I supposed to think? You don't want to investigate . . ."

"Maggie, I never promised to investigate. I said I'd ask some questions, and I've asked them! I don't know any more than I did before. And I don't want you telling everyone I'm a detective."

"Might be dangerous," Wayne contributed.

"But if someone tries to kill Kate," said Maggie wriggling in place eagerly, "then we'll know who did it. See?"

" 'Kill Kate,' " repeated Wayne, his growl no longer soft and gentle. "Do you realize what you're saying?" He quickly stepped into the space separating me from Maggie. There he loomed over her in a stance of barely contained violence. She flinched and stepped back. I didn't blame her. He was scaring me too. Why had I believed that I had known this man?

"That's all right," I said, using the calming voice I had developed in my two years of working in a mental hospital. "I haven't learned anything. No one's going to try and kill me." I tugged at his arm. At the touch, he whirled around toward me. I backstepped a little more quickly than Maggie had. My whole system was on alert, my body automatically converting to a tai chi posture.

"Sorry," he said, his stance softening along with his tone. "Just concerned. None of my business." He lowered his head.

"Jeez," said Maggie. Her repetition of that particular word was wearing on my nerves. She was looking in my direction now, avoiding the possibility of Wayne's gaze. "I'll stop telling people you're investigating. It was just an idea. You're not mad, are you?"

"I'm all right now, Maggie. You're forgiven," I answered. But that wasn't enough for her.

"And we can still get together and talk about it, can't we? I really think we can solve this between the four of us," she continued, eagerness creeping back into her voice.

"What four?" I asked.

"You and Wayne, and Eileen and me," she said.

"Eliminating about half the suspects, aren't you?" asked Wayne. His voice was soft again, with a hint of amusement.

"Jeez, I know none of us could have done it," she said. Then her brow wrinkled. "But then, I can't figure out exactly who could have . . ."

"Enough already, Maggie," I said. "I'm leaving. I'll talk to you later." I added a quick goodbye in Wayne's direction. His eyes were once more invisible under lowered brows.

I was in my car, turning the key in the ignition, when he startled me with a gentle rap on the window.

"Sorry," he said as I rolled down the window. He squatted so that his bushy eyebrows were eye level with me. "Always seem to be saying 'sorry.' Wanted to apologize for pushing you."

"Pushing me?" I asked. "Sorry, I always seem to be repeating your words. When did you push me?"

He cleared his throat. His skin turned a dark plum shade.

"Oh, that." Now I was embarrassed. If anyone had pushed it had been me. I giggled inanely for a moment. I couldn't believe I was thirty-eight years old and giggling over a kiss.

"Okay to call you?" he asked.

"Of course," came out of my mouth.

He mouthed a brusque "thanks," and walked away swiftly.

I shivered while driving home under dark clouds. The glimpse of the violent underpinnings of Wayne's kind and gentle nature had frightened me. And then, there was the intensity of his sexuality. That intensity had lessened my doubts concerning his intentions. But I was disturbed by the mixture of feelings that our short kiss had churned up in me.

I gripped the steering wheel tighter as I considered my own behavior. The face of death had apparently brought Devi and Valerie closer to God. Not me. I was horny. My face burned in memory of my attack on Wayne. Somehow, lust didn't seem to me an acceptable response to murder. But something about Scott Younger's lonely death had made my need for a lover compelling. Not only to make love, but to love and be loved. I shook off my thoughts in irritation. I told myself the mood would pass. Fat chance.

Once home, I sat down to my cluttered desk and looked at my calendar to see what tasks were left to overflow my afternoon and evening hours. The last entry for the day read: "7:00 / Craig / dinner." I stared at the entry with the growing realization that for the entire day I had forgotten to worry about my date with my estranged husband. A burst of energy flooded my body, tingling in my hands and brain. It lifted me out of my chair and carried me around the room in an exuberant jig.

For the past two years of arguments, separation, reconciliation, moving out and in and out, tears, pain and anger, I had never failed to think of Craig at least once a day. But today, my mind had relegated our date to secondary status. I had learned to forget. I settled down to my inevitable pile of paperwork cheerfully, the taste of triumph sweet in my mouth.

I hugged that triumph around me as a shield when Craig rang my doorbell two hours later. I opened the door and essayed a dispassionate survey of the man I had been married to for thirteen years. He was handsome, no doubt about it. His tall, well-proportioned body was perfectly dressed for success in a navy blue suit and red tie. The features framed by his razor-cut hair were regular: straight nose, large dark eyes, high cheekbones and sensual lips under a clipped mustache. As I looked at Craig's mustache the memory of Wayne's mustacheless kiss sparkled in my mind. I smiled.

Craig smiled back. The smile lit up his face. Of course he assumed my smile was for him, I realized with a pang of guilt.

"Hello, Kate. Short time, no see," he said. "I thought we could go to Mushrooms."

"Sounds fine," I replied.

"You might want to change your clothes," he suggested with a pointed look at my corduroys and sweat shirt.

I bristled. Was he doing this on purpose? His insistence, and my refusal, to dress tastefully had incited our arguments for years. I had failed to make the transition to yuppie as gracefully as he had, and this incompatibility had plagued our relationship. I willed myself not to respond to this outdated bait, to transcend. Anger can be as entangling an emotion as love, and I wanted to sever my connections with Craig.

I asked him to wait in the living room, and changed into my best outfit, a periwinkle-blue mohair sweater my mother had given me for Christmas, and charcoal-grey woolen pants. For the first time in years I felt free in my decision to wear my finest clothing. My sloppy outfits were no longer to be a weapon in my war with Craig. Maybe I would even buy a dress one of these days, or that gorgeous velvet jumpsuit I had seen at Nordstrom's.

Mushrooms was crowded when we arrived. I was glad that Craig had made reservations. Hordes of people waited in the lobby, their faces eerie in the restaurant's unique illumination. Mushrooms had no windows. The only light came from scattered rosy shell-shaped light fixtures and a series of backlit fish tanks set randomly into the walls. The sound of whale music completed the illusion of being underwater. I had never figured out what, if anything, the decor had to do with mushrooms. But they did serve tasty mushroom-based dishes, many of which were vegetarian.

Soon we were seated and had ordered the mushroom platter for two. Would Craig spend the evening in jokes and charming pleasantries or would he come to the point? He came to the point.

"You were right all along. We can't live together. We should get a divorce." The words tumbled out of his mouth quickly. His eyes were on my face, hurt puppy-dog eyes, waiting to be whipped for a mess on the carpet. The eyes I had loved and looked into for years.

Tears welled up. My throat felt raw. I couldn't speak. I tried to call up my earlier feeling of triumph but it was gone. My body was frozen in misery.

"You know I love you," he continued, his eyes still on mine. "I can't seem to stop loving you. But I can't afford a grand passion. It gets me off track."

"Business." I forced the word out of my sore throat.

"Yes, business. I can't run my business and love someone like you at the same time. The cost of loving you is too high in emotional energy."

"Too much hassle, you mean."

The waiter delivered our salads, performed his ritual pepper offering and left. I forced a bite of romaine lettuce into my mouth and began to chew slowly. I wasn't sure how I was going to get it down my throat.

"Maybe there was too much hassle," Craig said, without touching his salad. "Always having to plan my time, telling you when I'd be home. Entertaining you. It drained me." I swallowed the bite of lettuce painfully. The remembered hurt of knowing he begrudged our time together came welling up. He looked down at his lap. "Suzanne lets me be. When I see her, I see her. No demands."

It took a while for the name "Suzanne" to slither into my consciousness. Who the hell was Suzanne? I had never heard of her. When I realized he was probably speaking of the "other woman" I felt adrenalin pumping into my body, banishing the tears and cauterizing the sore throat.

"Suzanne?" I asked sharply. He flinched at my tone.

"She's an attorney, a woman I know. She can do the divorce." His voice was high and defensive, his eyes now directed away from mine.

"Are you trying to tell me she's your lover?"

He sighed. "Yes, I guess I am. I met her at the Marin Business Exchange. She'd just started working at a law firm in Novato. She's on her way up now."

"A good recommendation for a lover," I remarked snidely,

and instantly regretted my pettiness. I speared another piece of lettuce and chewed fiercely.

"But for me, it *is* a good recommendation. She's ambitious. She understands my goals. She's not bound by conventional ideas about marriage." Monogamy, another old argument.

A new thought slithered into my consciousness alongside Suzanne's name.

"How long have you known this woman?" I asked. His red face gave me an estimate, if not the actual dates.

"A year and a half," he said.

"Let me see if I have this right. You knew her before we split up the first time. Were you her lover then?" He shrugged his shoulders. "So we've had an open marriage for all this time and I didn't even know it." My anger was healing me. I could feel the strength in my limbs, the focus of my mind. Suddenly, I was ravenously hungry. "And when you begged to come back and live with me, told me there was no one like me, you were still seeing her." I shoveled salad down my throat.

"Kate, I was telling the truth. Suzanne is not you. I don't love her like I love you. She and I get along. I like her. She likes me. The passionate kind of love I had for you didn't cure our problems, it created them."

"Maybe we would have had a better chance if you had been honest with me."

He bent forward and looked at me. "I wouldn't have had a chance with you at all, if I had told you about Suzanne, would I?" It was my turn to shrug my shoulders. "I wanted that last chance. I didn't make love to her while we were together this last time. I tried to make it work between you and me. I gave it my all. It just didn't work."

I knew he was telling the truth. He usually did. And he really had tried. But I didn't want to acknowledge all of that. I wanted a simple bad guy. I wanted the clarity of my anger back.

"What does Suzanne look like?" I asked.

"Why do you want to know?" he replied, focusing his large brown eyes on mine. Something he saw there must have frightened him. "Never mind," he said, waving his hand. "You don't need to answer that. She's tall, with long blond hair."

Just as I had predicted to Maggie. I began to laugh, my tension dissipating as I did. I knew it would return, but for the time being I felt only release. Before Craig could ask me what was so funny, our waiter brought our mushroom platters. The stuffed mushrooms were great, the teriyaki and lemon mushrooms divine.

Over the last of the food he mentioned that the police had asked him about me. Tension returned to my body.

"They wanted to know if you knew Younger outside of Maggie's. You didn't, did you?" he asked.

"No." I considered telling him I had picked up the murder weapon but decided against it.

"Good," he said. "I called Maggie. She said you were sleuthing for her."

"Maggie told everyone that, including everyone who might have murdered Younger. You know her better than me. What is wrong with that woman?"

"Ask Eileen."

"Why Eileen?"

"They're lovers. Didn't you know?"

I didn't know, and Maggie had never told me. How could the open and honest Maggie have harbored a secret like that? Probably in the same way that the open and honest Craig could have hidden a year and a half affair. But was Maggie's secret "the" secret, the motive for Younger's murder somehow? Is that why she had kept it from me?

"Why did she tell you? Why not me?" I asked Craig angrily. His face reddened.

"I asked her for a date," he finally said.

"Before, during or after myself and/or Suzanne?" I snapped.

He didn't answer. I can't say as I blamed him. It was a complicated question.

He dropped me off at my door after dinner. I didn't ask him in. When I closed the door I realized something was missing. It was the cord that had tied me to my husband for thirteen years. His revelations had severed it finally. I was free.

- Ten -

FREEDOM HAD ITS advantages, but sleeping well was not among them. Not for me that night. I lay writhing under the covers in my dropseat pajamas, C.C. clawing happily next to me. My brain was stubbornly awake. It had been taken hostage by a mad projectionist who showed movies of the last three days' events over and over, with and without sound tracks.

I wanted a new reel. I trudged into the living room to look for a book, but found instead the manila envelopes that Wayne had given me the night before, still sitting on the pinball machine where I had left them. I emptied each of the envelopes onto the machine's glass top, until there was a stack of fourteen stories, all typed neatly on white bond paper. Then I bent my head closer and caught a whiff of Wayne's scent.

I took the stack back to my cold bed and dived into the stories, hoping for some light entertainment. The first one chronicled the last years of a self-made millionaire, friendless except for his servants, to whom he could never allow himself to be a friend. The second told the tale of a man so shy that he visited prostitutes, not for his own satisfaction, but to learn to make love properly. The third story was about a boy raised by a mad but magical mother. The boy loved her without reservation, endlessly fought the other kids who called her crazy, and won a university scholarship. The day he left for college, his mother drove her car off a cliff.

I put down the stack of stories in shock. My pulse was racing. Wayne's stories were as articulate as his speech was brusque. But these were not entertaining stories. They were desperate.

Still, a sense of recognition compelled me to pick up the stack again. As I read on, I noticed that the writing was touched with humor and a fondness for even the worst of the stories' characters. By the time I read the eleventh story, I was struck by the bravery of some of these people, and the humanity of all of them. By the fourteenth I saw the faint strand of hope that lay beneath the despair, tying the stories together. I drifted off to sleep, now haunted by both fact and fiction.

The sound of rain drumming on the skylights woke me in the morning. I pulled my pillow over my head, longing for the sweetness of slumber, but it was too late. My mind was up and racing. The storm-darkened Saturday invited me to do all the work I had put off for the last three days. I showered to Vivaldi, the hot water and music infusing me with energy and good intentions.

By eight o'clock I was seated at my desk, with all the lights in the room turned on to ward off the gloom of foul weather. I tore through orders, accounts and government forms, listening to the rain on the roof and the wind rattling my doors and windows, secure in the inevitability of my paperwork. When the telephone rang, I answered reluctantly.

"I assume you are awake, alive and well," said a familiar voice on the other end of the line. "No poison in your dinner, no convenient accident on the way from your warehouse?"

"Felix?" I guessed.

"Speaking," he confirmed. "I got your letter."

"Oh, no," I said, remembering the note I had sent him in my spasm of paranoia before going out with Wayne. C.C. chose this moment to burst through her cat-door, a wet and angry black-and-white ball of fur, who denounced me loudly for allowing the downpour.

"Oh, yes! How was the date? Somehow, dinner and the warehouse sounds less than romantic to me." His sarcasm was as strident as C.C.'s howls.

"Forget the letter," I said.

"Like you forgot to tell me about your date with the cop's best bet for murderer?"

"What do you mean, their best bet?" I asked, suddenly alert. C.C. leapt for my lap, muddy paws outstretched.

"Not so fast. Why didn't you tell me?" The tone of his voice brought his hurt face into my imagination. "Here I am, busting my hump for a good story, and you go out with the mysterious man behind the scenes and don't bother to tell me. Me, who has brewed you all those cups of tea, and made your best friend a happy woman.''

It wasn't the time to mention that Barbara was perfectly capable of finding happiness without his presence. She was, after all, soaking up sunshine on a beach somewhere in Maui at this very moment, probably with very little thought of Felix shivering in rainy California. Or of me, for that matter.

"All right, Felix, I'm sorry. But we didn't talk about the murder. Wayne didn't tell me anything important.''

There was silence on the other end of the line. C.C. rolled in my lap to dry herself off. It was time to catch some flies with honey.

"All of us who were there the day of the murder went to a meeting yesterday at Maggie's,'' I said. "Would you like to hear about it?''

"When? What did you meet for?'' he said, his voice quickening, all hurt erased from its tone.

"In a minute. First, tell me what you meant by Wayne being the cop's best bet?'' My heart beat a little faster waiting for his answer.

"My source says they've narrowed the field of their investigation to Wayne Caruso.''

"Why?'' The word came out in a yelp.

"Don't get uptight, Kate. I'm just answering your question, okay. *A*, he inherits. *B*, he was the only one who really knew Younger well. Apparently Younger wasn't even that tight with Renee Mickle. And *C*, it turns out Caruso managed all of Younger's affairs and investments. Bet you didn't know that. Younger hadn't touched anything for years. So they're looking real hard at Caruso for embezzlement, or at least mismanagement.

"Look at all the possible motives for God's sake! Shit, this guy could have had any number of reasons for killing the man. And no one else has a trace of a motive.''

"All right, even granting that he had motive,'' I said, injecting unfelt reasonableness into my voice, "why would he have killed Younger at Maggie's?''

"Answer that yourself. Look at all the suspects. If Younger had been killed at home, there would have only been one suspect: Wayne Caruso. This way, there are nine.''

"Felix, if you talked with him, you'd know he didn't do it. I know he didn't.'' My words compensated for the five percent doubt that still lingered in my mind as I remembered Wayne's angry stance the day before.

"Fine, I'd love to talk to him," Felix replied. "Get me an interview."

"What?"

"You heard me. You said I'd know if I talked to him. So get me an interview. I'll make him a hero in the local paper. 'Quiet man swept into nightmare of suspicion,' that kind of thing. It might help sway public opinion."

"I'll talk to him," I promised.

"And now," he said, his voice thick like a vampire's lusting for new blood, "tell me about your meeting."

Twenty minutes later I hung up the telephone. C.C.'s fur was dry and fluffy again, and Felix had sucked all the relevant information from my brain. I was left with a sodden, furred lap and innumerable questions.

I stared through the window into the branches swaying in the dark storm and asked myself what the motive was for Scott Younger's murder. I hadn't really asked myself that question before. I had only considered who was capable of such an act of violence, and foolishly concluded that no one was. Money was a good motive. The police were right about that. But how about revenge, or jealousy, or lunacy? Or motives I couldn't even conceive of?

Valerie had certainly seemed angry that day. And what about Renee? Was she actually a woman scorned, with the fury to match? Then there was Devi. Devi had known Scott Younger. Maybe he had done her some irreparable harm. Made her pregnant? That was an interesting thought. What if Tanya was Scott's illegitimate child? But that still didn't add up to a murder motive. I shook my head in frustration. Valerie was an unmarried mother. Scott could just as well have fathered her kid. Or Renee's for that matter.

My pulse speeded up. What if one of Renee's kids was Scott's? That would certainly explain why he was so interested in her. Maybe her ready-made family was more than just convenient. Unfortunately, that still didn't make a murder motive. I told myself how angry Renee's husband would have been if he had found out. But Renee was already divorced. I slumped back in my chair, considering the possibility of other guilty secrets. That brought Maggie to mind. I didn't think lesbianism was a secret to kill over, not in mellow Marin. But maybe it was. A conspiracy between Maggie and Eileen? My imagination took flight.

The ringing of the phone interrupted my lurid vision of Maggie's confession under hot lights. It was Valerie.

"I need to speak to you," she said. "I've got some explaining to do."

"You don't have to explain anything to me," I answered, twirling the phone cord nervously. Did "explaining" mean confessing to murder? If it did, I wished she'd go to the police.

"But I do," she said, her voice full of calm certainty. "I feel guided to you. Next Monday evening our ashram has a visitors' night. Would you join me for dinner?"

"Monday," I temporized, as if looking at my calendar. Actually I couldn't even see my calendar under the spread of current paperwork. But I knew Monday was free.

"The dinner is a vegetarian feast," she said. I licked my lips. "And afterwards, a video of Guru Illumananda's last visit." I groaned to myself. She should have closed the deal with the feast.

I was afraid to meet her on her turf, and not for the obvious rational reasons. I had not been raised religiously. When I had occasionally been dragged to other people's churches, mostly by guilty grandparents, the grandeur and power of all that unified spiritual belief had only frightened me, made me feel all the more a despised outcast. Now I imagined crazed disciples of the Guru brainwashing me, their eyes fixed, their grasping hands long and sinewy. Or even murdering me, the fragrance of incense masking the smell of death. Long periods of solitary paperwork had obviously bolstered my imagination's powers.

I asked if I could bring Wayne along. She graciously agreed, and we set the time and place. As I replaced the telephone receiver I realized I was planning to investigate. And I couldn't blame Maggie. I could only blame my need to know that the murderer was someone other than Wayne Caruso.

The rain and wind continued their assault on the house as I did paperwork. Water seeped in under the sliding glass doors. Broken branches danced across the yard. C.C. paced back and forth, occasionally jumping in place, her black ears flattened back against her skull. Suddenly, the minutiae of Jest Gifts held no more allure. I wanted to tackle Maggie.

I wasted no more time. I zipped up my down jacket, pulled up the hood and raced through the cold rain, ready to do battle with the storm from the heated womb of my Toyota. Great gusts of wind tugged at my car as I drove toward Maggie's house. I blasted rock 'n' roll from the radio speakers in defense. Rain slapped the windshield to blind me. I turned up the heat and the speed of the wipers. I was high on the battle by the time I reached Maggie's.

Her brick walkway was drowned in a whirlpool of murky water, dead leaves and bougainvillea blossoms. I splashed through and knocked on her door. The sound of dachshunds yipping and skittering could be heard over the noise of the storm, and then heavier, human footsteps approached.

"Who's there?" came Maggie's muffled voice from behind the door.

"It's Kate."

"Hold on." She opened the door the two inches allowed by the chain lock. The slice I could see of her face was set in an uncharacteristic frown. Doc and Hound clamored for a chance at my ankles.

"Are you alone?" she asked in a lowered voice. Her eyes moved behind me and to my sides.

"Yes, I'm alone. What the hell is wrong with you?"

"Is Wayne with you?"

"No!" I was getting wetter by the minute. I could feel the rain pouring into my Reeboks. "Will you let me in, already?"

She removed the chain and opened the door. Doc and Hound flew out, whirling and leaping at my corduroy-clad legs in an ecstatic frenzy. I walked carefully through the minefield of moving dachshunds into Maggie's brightly colored living room and took off my muddy shoes.

"Jeez, Kate you're soaked," said Maggie. "I'll get you some dry socks!" She rushed out of the room. I sat down on an orange pillow and submitted to an attack of wet tongues, cold noses and hard toenails.

The socks Maggie brought me were bright yellow. They provided an interesting contrast to my black corduroys and Reeboks. While I put them on she hovered over me, twisting a clump of her frizzy red hair around her finger.

"Are you sleeping with Wayne?" she burst out mid-twist.

"No," I answered. "Are you sleeping with Eileen?"

"Of course," she said, her eyebrows rising. "I thought you knew. Didn't you say Renee had told you?"

"Oh, yeah," I answered inanely. Of course; that was Renee's

secret about Maggie and Eileen, the one that I had pretended to know. I blushed, remembering my bluff. Maggie sat down on the green sofa.

"Does it bother you?" she asked, her expression serious and concerned.

"I don't think so," I answered. "I hadn't really thought about it much, except in terms of motive."

"Motive?" she said. She straightened up, her eyes widening with disbelief. "You mean a murder motive?"

"It is a secret," I said defensively. "People kill to protect secrets. And you never told me in all this time."

"Sheesh, it never came up. Should I announce my sexual preference while I'm giving treatments? Or put it on a bulletin board? That's what Eileen would like to do. She's committed to pride, claiming our power, openness, all of that stuff. Personally, I don't think it's anyone's beeswax but ours. How the heck can you get a murder motive out of me and Eileen?" She looked at me with hurt in her eyes.

"I'm not sure," I mumbled. "Blackmail? I mean, wouldn't it hurt your business?"

"Oh boy, Kate. Some motive! Eileen says it wouldn't hurt the business anyway. She says we'd get a whole raft of neat new lesbian/feminist clients. She's probably right."

"I'm sorry, Maggie. It was just an idea."

"At least you're trying," she said, brightening. "I guess I asked for it. But you can stop investigating me. I've got it figured out." She bent forward and whispered. "Wayne is the murderer."

"Not you too. Welcome to the lynch mob," I said bitterly.

"But listen, Kate, it all works." She jumped up from the sofa and began to pace, twirling her hair as she moved. "I didn't think it could be him because he was so gentle, but when I saw him with you yesterday, it came to me. He killed Scott to be free to marry you!" She turned and pointed at me in triumph. Her smile faded as she saw my stunned face.

"Oh boy, I'm sorry, Kate. Are you in love with him?"

"How on earth did you come to the conclusion that he killed Scott to marry me?" I asked.

"Remember Wednesday morning, when you told me Craig had left you?" I nodded. How could I forget the morning of the murder? Maggie began pacing and twirling again. "Wayne was there, listening. He had loved you from afar, watching you in my office, but he knew you were married and held back. Kinda like Eileen and me, before I left my husband. Then he heard you were free and he knew he had a chance.'' She paused dramatically and looked at me. ''But Scott stood in his way, so Scott had to die.''

''How the hell did Scott stand in his way?'' I exploded.

''Blackmail,'' Maggie whispered. ''Why else would Wayne have stayed with him all those years?''

''How about friendships?'' I suggested. ''How come no one is able to accept that Wayne really cared about Scott?''

''Jeez, I'll bet they weren't even lovers. Eileen doesn't think so either.''

''People can love each other without being lovers.''

''Love, maybe. But live with him, and go everywhere with him for all those years. It's too bizarre, Kate.'' I shifted uncomfortably on my pillow. It was bizarre. Maggie sat back down on the couch, her case almost finished.

''I saw the way he looked at you. He'd loved you all that time. It's kinda romantic when you think about it.'' She smiled dreamily at me, inviting my agreement. I bet myself she had a whole slew of romance novels tucked away somewhere in her vividly colored house. So much for my stereotypes about lesbians.

''It is not romantic, Maggie. It's fiction,'' I said with all the force and reasonableness I could muster. I looked her straight in the eye and began the defense. ''In the first place Wayne is incapable of murder. You've said so yourself. . . .''

''But that was before I saw him having a fit yesterday. Jeez, did you see the way he jumped on me? He wanted to kill me, I'm sure of it.'' She squirmed on the couch, remembering.

''Maggie, no offense, but there are times that I'd like to kill you, too. I just don't look as scary as Wayne when I have murder on my mind.''

''You don't mean that,'' she said, blinking. I ignored her and continued.

''In the second place, I doubt that Scott had any nefarious hold over Wayne. If Wayne had wanted to see me he would have. And, in the third place, if Wayne had wanted to kill Scott I'm sure he could have found a way to do it without being suspected.''

''Like what?'' asked Maggie, her tone turned sullen.

''Like an accident, or a drug overdose. Considering Scott's history, a drug overdose would have worked. Wayne could have killed him any number of ways, at his leisure. No, someone else had to kill him, that day in your office. Someone with no other choices." I was convincing myself, as well as Maggie, as I talked.

"But Kate," Maggie said. "If Wayne didn't do it, who did?"

Believe me, I thought about the question on my drive home through the storm. Then I began to think of food. I had missed breakfast and it was nearly lunch time. The image of a large bowl of brown rice, shredded cabbage and green onions, topped with tofu sauce, floated on the rain before my windshield. I was salivating as I turned the key in my front door.

My hunger dissolved instantly when I pushed the door open. I knew an intruder had been in my house. It wasn't intuition; it was the rain and mud-soaked carpet in the entry hall. Not even C.C. could have produced that. And then I asked myself if the intruder was still there. I stood very still, listening for movement, my heart beating loudly against the drumming of the rain.

- Eleven -

I DON'T KNOW how long I stood there, straining to pick up the sound of a human presence. Five minutes? An hour? I was unaware of time, locked into the focus of listening. I could hear, as if from a distance, the beating heart, ringing ears and shallow breathing of my own body competing with the sound of the storm outdoors, and no more.

C.C.'s sleepy mewing broke into my concentration. She came from the kitchen and dropped into her china-cat pose at my feet, her paws curled delicately underneath her, her eyes opening and closing. Would she be napping if the trespasser were still here?

I turned toward the living room to find a weapon. I was still in an altered state of consciousness, my hearing and sight acute, my body vibrating with adrenalin. I saw signs of intrusion all through the room. The piles of junk I had left on the pinball machines were now neatly ordered. My books were rearranged (alphabetically, I discovered later). Magazines and pillows were straightened. The room had not been so much ransacked as tidied. Had my mother been here? I laughed aloud at the thought and then immediately stilled my body again. If there were intruders present, they were now alerted by that foolish laugh.

After listening quietly for any reaction to my laugh, and hearing none, I crept to the fireplace and picked a poker off the rack. I hefted it and practiced a blow, suddenly wishing I had found time in my schedule for the tai chi sword class. I told myself that there was no one in the house anyway. I was right.

As I moved warily from room to room, I noted signs of trespass everywhere. Nothing was gone, only displaced. The papers on my desk had been unscrambled and stacked with military precision. My bed looked as if it had been picked up and then remade. Wayne's stories had been moved from the floor by the bed to the bedroom bookshelf, the manila envelopes disposed of. Even the books in the bathroom were positioned differently on the top of the toilet tank.

The final insult awaited me in the kitchen. There, I found C.C.'s bowl heaped with an amount of cat food it would have taken at least one of her nine lives to consume. No wonder the little glutton had greeted me so sweetly.

Only when I had completed my tour of inspection down to the last reorganized closet, did I believe that the trespasser was really gone. No one skulked in a corner or jumped at me from behind furniture. I was alone in the house.

My fear and quiet focus turned to anger. My home had been invaded! I clenched my fists uselessly in an effort to stem the violent trembling of my body. Quick tears burned my eyes as I dropped into the naugahyde embrace of my comfy chair.

My limbs were weak now. I told myself this was a reasonable reaction to adrenalin aftermath, as well as simple hunger. I didn't admit to fear. My mind wandered in speculation. Who had searched my house? What did they want? I couldn't seem to focus. I told myself I just needed some food.

I considered calling the police as I walked into the kitchen. A menacing thought stopped me in my tracks. What if it was the police themselves who had searched my house? Of course, Felix had said they were only considering Wayne. But maybe that wasn't true. What if they were searching for a clue to a relationship between me and Scott Younger? I tried to dismiss the idea as unduly paranoid, but it lingered.

At least the trespasser hadn't rearranged the refrigerator. Moving on automatic pilot, I pulled out leftover brown rice, vegetables and onions. What was the object of the search? Something that might be under a bed? on a bookshelf? in among my papers or under a pillow? As I poured tofu sauce on my veggies an unnerving possibility slammed into my mind. Craig. But what would he have been looking for? Hidden assets, in preparation for divorce proceedings? No. It didn't make sense. I didn't even take the time to heat my concoction, and took a bite without tasting it. A random prowler? I chewed and swallowed with difficulty. My throat was constricted. *The murderer.* The words came unbidden into my mind. My hands resumed trembling. I couldn't take a second bite. I pushed the dish away violently.

My house had been locked. The intruder had managed to get in without a sign of forced entry. If "intruder" equaled "murderer . . ." My mind refused to finish the thought. Calling the police was clearly the next move, but something in me balked. What were they going to do for me? First, I would have to convince them my house had been invaded. Then I would have to convince them the invasion was related to the murder. And how could it be? What could the murderer have been looking for? And what could the police do for me, at that? Warn me to be careful? I doubted that the intruder had left any telltale fingerprints or other calling cards.

I put my uneaten meal into the refrigerator and cleaned up slowly. I found myself unable to make a decision about calling the police. My adrenalin had burned me up. My fear had immobilized my brain. I wanted a drink, but I didn't drink anymore. I decided to further numb my brain with bookkeeping. For two hours I scribbled and calculated in a trance, allowing nothing to come into my mind but numbers.

Even that refuge was limited. The doorbell broke into my paper retreat at two o'clock. I assumed it was not the intruder. He or she wouldn't find it necessary to ring a bell for admittance. However, I still pushed my face to the cold glass sliding door in my office to see who was on my doorstep.

Wayne stood there in the rain, his green goose-down parka zipped up to his chin, his hair curling out from under a water-beaded knit cap. At that distance he looked frightening, the classic nightmare prowler. I went to the hallway and opened the door.

"For you," he said, thrusting a dripping bouquet of white gladioli, blue irises and yellow daffodils toward me.

"Any more of these and this place will look like a funeral parlor," I replied. The words were out of my mouth before I could engage my brain. "Sorry," I mumbled and hastily took the flowers from him, sprinkling myself with water in the process.

"That's okay," he replied, his eyes crinkling in a smile. "Interesting, how repressed material pops up."

I stood there looking at him. He wasn't frightening up close, especially when he smiled. In the five days in which I'd known him his face had become familiar to me, no longer ugly. Like the features of a battered but treasured teddy bear. The low-hanging eyebrows seemed necessary to guard the warm and expressive eyes from rude attention. The outsize mashed nose and scarred cheeks appeared comfortably worn.

"Don't let me bother you," he said, breaking into my silence and turning to leave. I had lost track of the minutes as I stared at him soaking in the downpour.

"No, come back," I called, as he headed down the stairs.

I got him into the house, took his cap and parka, and offered him a seat at my kitchen table for a cup of tea. I put the flowers into a water pitcher, having used my only real vase on the last bunch, and fired up the teakettle on the stove. As I fussed with the teacups, I considered telling him about the invasion of my house. His kind face invited confidence. Perversely, I limited myself to naming the seven kinds of herbal tea I had available. He chose Red Zinger. Then we fell into a silence filled inadequately by the sound of rain.

"I read your stories last night," I said finally.

"Didn't have to," he replied. His response made me want to take him by the shoulders and shake some self-worth into him. But I didn't know how effective that would be against a black belt in karate.

"I didn't read them because I had to. I read them because they're good." My irritation sounded in my voice. I poured the tea into the pot to steep and brought it to the table.

"Oh." His eyes were lowered and his cheeks were pink. I sat across from him.

"Have you tried to get them published?" I asked, and warned quickly, "and don't tell me they're not good enough."

"No, not yet. And thanks for keeping me in line." He raised his head. He was smiling tentatively.

"That reminds me, Felix wants to interview you," I said.

"Who's Felix?"

"He's a newspaper reporter, a friend. Actually, he's my best friend's sweetie. Anyway, I said I'd mention it to you."

"Consider it mentioned," he said. Was this a polite refusal? I poured the tea, and we sipped quietly for a while.

"How'd you like to visit Valerie's ashram with me Monday night, for dinner and a video of Guru Illumananda?" I asked, as if this were an everyday event.

A groan slipped from his lips, but he added quickly, "With you, a delight. The occasion?"

"She invited me—us, actually. She said she needs to explain something to me. All very mysterious."

Wayne's face and posture stiffened. "Scott?" he asked in a low growl.

"I don't know."

"Damn it, I should be taking the risk, not you," he said, his voice filled with the tension of yet more unexpressed feelings. "It's my responsibility. You could be hurt."

"I understand the danger," I answered curtly, thinking of the invasion of my house. "That's one reason I invited you. But it's up to *me* to decide what risks I'm going to take or not take."

In that moment of assertion, I realized why I hadn't told him about the trespasser. My own fear and confusion were enough. Someone else's panic and warnings could become unbearable on top of it. Wayne's eyes had disappeared under his low brows. I sat glaring in his direction. A gust of wind rattled the kitchen door.

"Lay off the paternalism?" he essayed in a lighter tone.

"Right," I answered softly.

Gradually we both softened into renewed smiles. I poured another cup of tea for each of us.

"Any thoughts on who killed Scott?" I asked. Might as well get down to cases.

"Police think I did. They can't understand why a grown man would take care of another one for so long. Sometimes, I can't either."

"But you didn't kill him?" I needed to hear him say it.

"I didn't kill Scott," he said firmly. At that moment, looking into his liquid brown eyes, I believed him absolutely. But then what was my judgment worth? The judgment of a woman who had failed to notice her own husband's infidelity. I was still stinging from that one.

"Can't see who else would want to, myself," he continued. "In the past, maybe. Scott had lots of enemies. Other dealers whose profits he cut into. But he was already getting out of that business when he hired me in seventy-six. I wouldn't have worked for him otherwise." He paused and stared out the door into the rain. "This murder came out of nowhere, or maybe the past."

A Halloween ghost fluttered up from a tombstone in my mind. The cartoon quality of this mental image made it no less frightening. I shivered and sipped my tea to warm myself.

Wayne shifted in his chair as if the ghost had visited him as well. "Really came to ask you to dinner tonight. Been attempting a dairyless lasagna. Never used soy cheese before, but it seems to work. I'd like you to try it," he said.

It took me a moment to shift gears. I gave my head a little shake, looked into his battered face and accepted. He asked if he could come by and take me to his house at six o'clock.

"I'll leave you to your work," he said once I had agreed, and left without another word.

I went back to the refuge of my bookkeeping, working mindlessly until I needed an accounts payable file.

I walked to my file cabinet, opened a drawer, and saw the hidden work of the trespasser. My files had been completely reorganized. I always arranged my color-coded file folders by subject matter. My own personal system. The invader's method had been less sophisticated. All the folders had been rearranged in strict alphabetical order. I quickly opened the remaining three drawers in that file cabinet and then the drawers in my other two cabinets. All had been similarly violated. Anger and fear welled up in me. My legs and hands began to shake once more and my mind floated into free-style panic. Herbs, I need herbs, I told myself, and headed out into the storm.

Once I reached the health food store, I grabbed a basket and swept through the wet Saturday crowd, ignoring the gustatory lure of barbecue-flavored brown rice crackers and teriyaki tofu balls. I went straight to the herbal remedy section, all the while refusing to consider the invasion of my home. A bit of valerian to relax the muscles? I felt the tightness in my shoulders and filled a small bag with the acrid-smelling herb. Some NatuRest so I could sleep that night? I got a bottle of ninety capsules. A little chamomile tea? I added it to my basket. And a bottle of Calms. Passion Flower, oat, hops . . . Ought to do the trick. I got in line and avoided thought.

Lines were always long on a Saturday. Customers holding bottles of freshly squeezed carrot juice, tiny plastic cups of wheat grass, tofu chocolate bars, blue corn chips and vitamins, awaited their turn patiently as Paul Simon's "Graceland" played on the sound system. The couple in front of me were talking about how they had adopted a turkey for Thanksgiving instead of killing one. I wondered what they'd do with it when it arrived. Keep it in their backyard? their living room? Send it to a turkey kennel?

Finally it was my turn. The cashier was an unnaturally tan and muscular young man who added up my purchases with a look of disdain.

"That'll be thirty-three forty-five, lady," he said. "Why don't you just forget all this crap and buy yourself a bottle of whiskey? It'd sure be cheaper."

- Twelve -

I CAME HOME, cold and wet, and washed down two Calms with some chamomile tea. Then I sat down on the floor next to the blast of the heater vent, waiting to calm down as advertised. After fifteen minutes I had come to the conclusion that there was at least one great difference between whiskey and herbal relaxants. Whiskey worked.

I watched the rain in my yard for a while, then decided to run the risk of disturbing my friend Barbara's vacation in Maui with a telephone call. I rationalized that if she was in her room, she wouldn't be actively vacationing anyway. And if she wasn't in, I wouldn't be able to reach her. Amazingly, she answered the telephone on the first ring. Not so amazing actually, when you consider that she is a practicing psychic.

"Hiya, kiddo, I've been waiting for you to call," she said cheerfully.

I sighed audibly. I should have known she'd be waiting. I had never been able to figure out whether Barbara was really psychic or not, but her ability to foresee my actions always irked as well as fascinated me.

"I suppose you know why I called, too," I said.

"Not exactly. But I get vibes that you've been touched by death again, and perhaps, love?"

My face got hot. "Did Felix call you?" I asked in an accusatory tone.

Her laughter floated over the line. "Okay, I talked to my sweetie." Then her tone deepened. "But seriously, I've been concerned. I've consulted my spirit guides and I don't get any mortal danger for you. But I see confusion and fear everywhere. Tell me about it.''

I did, at great length and long-distance cost. I described the day of Scott Younger's death. I reviewed the suspects. Valerie's record and her dinner invitation. Maggie and Eileen. Renee's relationship to Scott, and her hostility. Devi and Tanya and Ted. And, finally, Wayne.

''But what about Scott Younger?'' she asked when I had finished. ''You've told me he was a former drug dealer and a patron of the arts. He was cold, rich and reclusive, but what else? You haven't really told me who he was.''

''I guess I don't know who he was,'' I said slowly.

''Ah, my dear Watson,'' she said. ''That is exactly the point. Find out.''

I considered her words silently as the charges for my phone call mounted up. I could ask Wayne. He probably knew.

''That's right,'' Barbara responded to my unspoken thought.

''Stop that!'' I said. Apparently, long distance didn't crimp her intuitive powers any.

''Wayne is your best source,'' she prodded. ''For lots of things,'' she added with a lascivious chuckle.

''Is this channeled advice?''

Her laughter came over the line again. ''No, it's culled from all of the mysteries I've been reading while I lie on the beach sunning myself.''

I sighed again, this time with envy.

After hanging up, I found myself centered enough to report the break-in to the Sheriff's Department. I don't know if it was Barbara, or the combination of chamomile and Calms, that had relaxed me. I was thankful that due to my residence in one of the many unincorporated sections of Mill Valley, my troubles came under the jurisdiction of the County Sheriff's Department instead of the Mill Valley police. I certainly didn't want to talk to Detective Sergeant Udel again unless I had to.

The switchboard operator told me someone would visit me in the next two hours. I did forty-five minutes of distracted bill-paying before they showed up.

The two uniformed sheriff's deputies who came through my door were young, white, wet, mustachioed, and interchangeable. They refused to sit down, but nodded with simultaneous sympathy while I told my story. The effect was therapeutic, bordering on hypnotic. Once I had finished, the two men cleared their throats in concert.

"Anything stolen, ma'am?" asked the one on the left.

"Taken from the house," clarified the one on the right.

"I don't think so," I answered. "But I know someone was here."

"We'll file a report," offered the one on the left.

"Talk to the neighbors," said the other.

"Take a look around," continued the first.

"Anything else you'd like to tell us?" asked the second.

I shook my head.

"Call us if you find anything missing," said the first.

They chorused their thank you's and clattered back down the stairs into the rain. They were certainly efficient. The visit had taken less than ten minutes. No plaster casts of footprints. No fiber samples. No fingerprints. At least I wouldn't have to clean up fingerprint powder.

I spent the next hour in a flurry of manic energy, putting my file folders back into color-coded order. I yanked the files from the cabinets and shoved them back in roughly. I slammed drawers and cursed. I trashed outdated files mercilessly. By the time I finished, I felt back in control. By God, I could shove files around!

My illusion of control wavered when I realized I had only fifteen minutes to prepare for Wayne's arrival. I stripped off my clothing and gazed critically at my A-line form in the mirror. My mother's voice told me to wear clean underwear—in case of accident. I chose my newest, brightest, flowered bikinis, a lavender bra with lace cutouts, and lavender socks. In case of love? Then I buried all that frivolity under a purple turtleneck sweater, black corduroys and rain boots.

Breathing deeply, I went to the cedar chest by the bed and drew out a condom. The doorbell rang. I sprinted to the front hall, after throwing the condom into my purse. It seemed to glow through the black leather as I opened the door.

At the sight of Wayne dripping on my doorstep, I began to babble. "What can I bring? Some fruit juice? Sparkling water? Bread?" My heart thumped erratically. A combination of lust and fear.

"Just yourself," he answered. He lowered his eyes as he spoke. His deep voice seemed filled with sexual promise, but I told myself it was probably my imagination, fueled by the radioactive condom in my purse. Maybe that explained my dizziness and the heat spreading through my body.

Once inside the luxury of the Jaguar's belly, I calmed myself down by deep breathing. Wayne and I spoke sparingly, and only of food, while he guided the purring beast through rainy streets, and finally up a twisting road that ended at a set of black wrought-iron gates in the hills of Tiburon.

It was cold, dark, and isolated there. The only light came from a small sentry box by the gates. Wayne excused himself and stepped from the car into the sentry box, letting the chill of the evening into the Jaguar. The black gates opened magically as he got back in the car. We drove up a graveled driveway and parked in a three-car garage near the top of the hill.

A dimly lit, covered walkway led us to the house. It was made of curved slats of wood which ambled mysteriously around soft corners until we reached a door. Wayne unlocked a small box on the door and tapped in a series of numbers. The front door opened and bright lights came on to guide us into the house.

The room we entered was immense and blindingly white after the darkness outdoors. When my eyes had adjusted, I saw that it was contained by chalk-white brick and plaster walls, large windows dark against the night sky, hardwood floors, and redwood beams that peaked at twenty-five feet. It was furnished in minimalist style. Three white sofas, two ice-blue glass-topped tables, and a few silvery grey rugs didn't come near to filling the void. There were six randomly spaced lighted recesses in the walls, for paintings and ceramics. A grey-toned painting depicting a lone fetal figure on the floor in an empty house seemed at home in the room. The brighter works did not.

"I never liked this room," said Wayne. "Reminds me of an empty ice-skating rink. Impossible to keep warm." I jumped at the sound of his voice. Lost in the large room, I had almost forgotten that he was standing by me.

"Take you to the kitchen, my territory," he said, and gestured across the hall.

The kitchen greeted us with warmth and tantalizing whiffs of garlic, tomatoes, yeast and herbs. The walls of white plaster were saved from sterility by wooden cabinets, and cinnamon- and biscuit-colored tiling on the floor and work areas. Plants, baskets and cookbooks sat on top of the cabinets and filled the shelves. A small wooden table sat in the center of the kitchen, topped by a vase of gladioli. The pinks, salmons and whites of the flowers matched the colors in the place mats and cloth seats of the two matching wooden chairs. The contents of the recessed niches here (terra-cotta animals, copper cooking utensils, living herbs and a painting of an avocado with one slice removed) filled the room with life.

"Have a seat while I turn on the oven, then I'll show you the rest of the house," he suggested. "If you're interested," he added uncertainly.

"Absolutely," I replied, too loudly for my own ears. The living room had had the effect of a cathedral on me, compelling quiet and hushed whispers only. I let out the breath I had been holding and breathed in the warm kitchen smells. "Did you cook for Scott as well as yourself?" I asked in a softer voice. I looked up into his eyes, just visible under his brows.

"Yes. I've done the cooking for years. Last few months, developing tastier recipes for Scott. Try and get him interested in food again. But he'd hardly eat, anyway." Wayne's voice had become barely audible. He opened the oven, peered in, and continued in a lighter tone. "But I could always get him with sweets. He couldn't resist my apple crisp." He smiled momentarily, then the light left his eyes as he returned to the present.

"You should move away from this house," I said emphatically. At least it was my mouth that said it. I certainly hadn't consciously planned on butting in.

"Probably right," he replied, pausing with his hand on the oven door. He thought for a moment, then turned on the oven, set a timer and pulled a salad out of the refrigerator. "Scott's house really. Not mine."

"You have your own room, don't you?" I asked. For a moment when he had spoken of Scott I had wondered if they had been lovers after all.

"My own suite. Show you if you'd like. But first, this floor." He smiled and waved me out of the kitchen.

He escorted me first to a stark, formal dining room furnished with nothing but a long, icy, glass-topped table and six grey modern highback chairs. I was relieved when he told me we could eat in the kitchen.

He pointed out the doors to the guest bathrooms, then led the way to a library, where built-in bookshelves occupied two of the white plaster walls. One wall, Scott's, held a tastefully arranged selection of volumes on art and music. Wayne's wall was stuffed with fiction, and a smattering of metaphysics, law and psychology. A piano sat in the center of the room.

"Do you play?" I asked Wayne.

He shook his head sadly. "Scott used to."

A room filled with video games, exercise equipment and one lone pinball machine (Four Square, one of my favorite Gottlieb machines) was next. I was impressed, but not half so impressed as I was by the indoor spa. I'd never seen anything like it, outside of Hearst castle.

In the spa, a good-sized swimming pool shimmered, a hot tub steamed and doors lead offstage to a sauna and dressing rooms. The echoing sound of the pool water lapping inside harmonized with the drumming of the rain outside. The walls of the room were also white plaster, but with scattered, odd geometrically shaped windows that looked as if they had been tossed into the walls. This, along with a series of blue lights and the blue of the water, gave the room a whimsical, fairy-tale feeling. I knelt down and put my hand in the water of the pool. It was heated.

"Go for a swim if you'd like," offered Wayne, his eyes lowered.

I hesitated. I hadn't brought a suit.

"Couple of suits in the dressing room, and a robe," he said. "It's up to you. Dinner will be another forty-five minutes at least. You can see the rest of the house later." God, I thought, we hadn't even seen the whole house.

"A heated pool in November?" I said in awe. "How can I refuse?"

I found two swimming suits as promised in the dressing room. Both were modest one-pieces, the first black with trailing lilac flowers, the other simply lilac. I chose the black. Doesn't black slim the hips? I removed my own clothing and pulled on the suit, feeling something scratch as I did. There was still an inspection sticker on it, although the price tag had been removed. I sat down on the plaster bench with a sudden slap of bare thighs. This suit was new. Wayne had probably bought it especially for me, as well as the lilac one and the robe.

I couldn't remember anyone ever doing something quite like that for me. Certainly not Craig. And the dinner. How much time had Wayne put into preparation? The flowers, the dinner at his restaurant. My legs felt weak. I was touched, but frightened at the same time. How badly could I hurt him? How badly could he hurt me?

Then I switched to the "I wouldn't want to join a club that would have me" mode. Why was he trying so hard? What was wrong with him? Was he trying to use me to replace Scott in his life? Or was Maggie right? Had he fallen irrevocably in love with me? I couldn't believe that. But still . . . I pulled the suit all the way up, threw the robe over my shoulders and came out of the dressing room, feeling like an attractive woman.

Wayne was already in the pool, doing laps. He stood up in the water when he heard me. His upper torso was beautiful. My stomach did a little lust lurch at the sight. I jumped into the pool beside him and we did laps together until I was tired. Then we got out of the pool and into the hot tub. The move revealed his green swimming trunks and well-made legs. We sat silently, staring through the steam into each other's eyes.

"Who was Scott Younger?" I asked. The question bounced off the walls of the room. Wayne flinched. I asked myself why I had broken the mood, the bond. Because you're chicken, came a voice in my head.

"He was a lonely and depressed man," Wayne answered, his voice low. "Always been reserved, quiet. But the last year or so, he was seriously depressed. Did nothing but sit in his study and watch TV. Then it was constant VCR movies. Didn't talk. Hardly ate. Hadn't dealt with the business in years. Even stopped going to his art committee meetings. Wouldn't have gone anywhere if his back hadn't started bothering him." He laughed bitterly. "I thought the chiropractor's would save him from being a total hermit."

"But why?" I asked. He looked up at me blankly as if he had forgotten my presence.

"You mean why was he depressed?" he asked. I nodded. "Who knows?" he replied with a massive shrug of his shoulders. The water in the tub splashed over the sides. Then, with obvious effort, he began to speak again in his low growl.

"I think he backed himself into a corner. Nothing mattered to him. Dealt dope to defy his father. Then he made a success of it. But it wasn't something he could feel really proud of. And women. There were women, but . . . but he couldn't connect emotionally. Then he thought he wanted kids. But he couldn't connect there either. Kids didn't like him much. He really went downhill after Renee dropped him. That was his last try to give some meaning to his life.''

"Why did you take care of him?" I asked. I had to know.

Wayne looked startled by the question for a moment. "Scott was good to me when I first worked for him. We were friends. Well, almost friends, anyway. Met shooting baskets at Crocker. Both frustrated basketball players.'' He paused, his eyes staring out unfocused into the past. "Over the years . . . I don't know. Guess I just got used to taking care of him."

He refocused his eyes. "I've read a lot of pop psychology books lately,'' he continued hesitantly. So *that's* where he got his theories about Scott. "According to them, some of us end up taking care of emotionally disturbed people because we're playing out our own childhood struggles. Maybe I was. Scott was certainly playing out his. His mother died in childbirth. His father never forgave him. I could tell that, the one time I met the judge. No love there. Servants took care of Scott. Servants he wasn't allowed to fraternize with. So he played out his life taken care of by a servant, never emotionally connecting with anyone.''

"And your parents?" I asked softly. He lowered his head even further at the question.

"No father. Mother's a severe manic-depressive. Been in an institution the last twenty years. She couldn't cope after I left home.''

I shivered, cold in the steaming hot tub, remembering his story about the boy and the magically mad mother.

"You don't blame yourself, do you?" I asked. A stupid question. Of course he blamed himself.

"Can't help it. I kept thinking that once Scott was okay, then I'd leave. Couldn't leave him while he was depressed. What if he ended up like my mother? But it just got deeper.''

We sat in the tub for a while. I reached out and took his hand. But he shook me off.

"Need to tell you the worst. He asked me to put him out of his misery. Told me I inherited it all. He acted like he was joking.'' I held my breath for a moment, afraid Wayne was confessing. "I knew it was a cry for help. But I couldn't get him to a therapist. Didn't try hard enough. I keep wondering, did he ask someone else?''

No murder confession. I let out my breath. Then the faces of the people who had been at the chiropractor's that day flickered through my mind.

"I can't imagine anyone who was there as a hired killer," I said.

He shook his head wildly. The water in the tub splashed. "Nor can I. I've checked the accounts. No money missing. He didn't pay anyone to do it, that I can tell. But I still can't stop wondering. Did he feel so bad that he would rather have died?" The last sentence exploded from him, loud and clear. His face was a map of pain.

There was no obvious answer to that question. I moved across the tub to put my arms around him awkwardly from a crouched position. It is difficult to gracefully hug someone who is sitting in a hot tub. His body jerked at my touch. Then he stood, pulling me up with him and holding me in return.

"Kind, as well as witty and beautiful," he said softly after we had held each other for some time. It was a shock to realize he meant me. I held him tighter, squeezing the guilt and despair from him by brute force. Somewhere a buzzer went off, as if we had won a game-show prize.

He jumped. "My lasagna!" he yelped in a voice two octaves too high.

Never had the words "my lasagna" held such comic import. Laughter spilled from me uncontrollably, echoing against the plaster walls, drowning out the buzzer. Wayne's laughter began as a low rumble and flowered into neighing gasps that filled the room.

"God," he said suddenly. "I can breathe. That band around my chest, squeezing my lungs, it's gone." He lifted his arms triumphantly, then hugged me again briefly as the buzzer continued its song.

We put on our robes and walked into the kitchen, our bare feet joyfully slapping the warm ceramic tiles. Then I sat and watched as he produced dairyless lasagna and fresh baked bread from the oven, his battered face glowing. An insolent voice in my head asked me how long this could last, but I dismissed it. I would enjoy it while it did.

It was the best lasagna I ever tasted.

- Thirteen -

WE DIDN'T MAKE love that night. But we lay together for a long time on the bed in his room, surrounded by his books and plants and quilts. As a child on Halloween, I had always set aside the richest, sweetest candies, saving them for later when I would be less glutted and more appreciative. I felt like that hopeful child again at midnight when Wayne left me at my house. I fell asleep savoring the intimacy to come.

Sunday morning, I awoke to romantic fantasies and watery sunshine drifting through the skylights above my bed. But thoughts of business soon intruded. It was time to visit my warehouse and pick up paperwork.

An hour later, wrapped in two layers of sweaters and a down jacket, I was driving across the Richmond Bridge. The weather had returned to an oppressive drizzle. There were very few cars on the bridge that morning. I noticed a black Cadillac behind me and wondered idly if Cadillacs were again going to replace Mercedes and B.M.W.'s as symbols of wealth. Back to basics?

Once across the bridge I drove down the highway to Oakland automatically, snug and warm in my Toyota and daydreams. The warehouse district was deserted. That was one reason I liked to visit on a Sunday morning. No traffic snarls or employees to distract me.

I drove into the warehouse parking lot, lost in an internal dialogue on the relative merits of solitude and love. As I stepped out of my car I heard the sound of another car pulling up behind me. Odd for Sunday morning, I thought, locking the door and dropping the keys in my purse. Then I turned from my car door and saw a black Cadillac not two yards away.

In the time it took for me to consider unlocking the door and climbing back in the Toyota, the doors of the Cadillac opened and two figures emerged into the grey morning. Both were dressed in navy blue suits. The first was tall, thin and neat in his suit. The other was short, stocky, and moving rapidly toward me. But what arrested my attention, as I frantically fished through my purse for my keys, was the similarity of their grotesque heads. Both had rubbery, distorted faces that seemed oddly familiar.

My heart was beating so loud it seemed to shake my entire body. I dug deeper into my purse, jabbing my shaking hand on a pencil. I grasped the car keys just as I realized what I was looking at. These men weren't deformed; they were wearing identical, smiling masks of Ronald Reagan. I felt an instant of relief before I asked myself why they were wearing masks. With renewed desperation, I turned to my car and fumbled my key into the lock. As I turned the key I felt a hand on my arm, a heavy hand that gripped me tightly.

"Lady, you've got something of ours," said a deep voice.

I turned toward the voice slowly and saw the stocky one, his receding hairline evident above Reagan's rubber features. I considered but dismissed the use of tai chi to loosen his hold on my arm. I looked around the parking lot for help, but it was deserted. The only other car in sight was a beat-up old Chevy in the next lot.

"It'd be easier if you'd just give us what we want," the stocky Reagan continued. The great communicator was not communicating to me. I couldn't translate the meaning of his words. The pounding of my heart didn't help any. "The boss says to get them . . . and we'll get them." He paused in silent menace, his rubber face impenetrable except for the slits where his eyes were. "The easy way or the hard way."

My response was a blank look. I could feel my mouth gaping open. I shut it with a snap and tasted bile.

"Give her a chance to answer," said the tall Reagan in an annoyed voice.

"Well?" asked the short one after he had allowed me a full thirty seconds to respond. His mask may have been smiling, but the eyes I glimpsed beneath the mask were small and angry. A shiver ran through my already trembling body.

"Can you tell me what you're talking about?" I asked in a shaky voice. I hoped it was a suitably meek request.

"The fuckin' pictures, lady, the fuckin' pictures!" he shouted, tightening his grip on my arm.

"What pictures?" I asked.

The two Reagans exchanged glances.

"Lady, just get them for us, okay?"

"Honestly, I would if I could. But I don't know what you're talking about." I searched my brain frantically for a way to convince them.

It went around like this for the next ten minutes, with the stocky man demanding, me protesting my ignorance, and the thin man acting as an exasperated referee. After the thirtieth time I was asked where the pictures were, my fear had turned to, not quite anger, but irritation. My arm was sore from being squeezed, my neck hurt, and I still didn't understand what was going on. With this irritation came a spurt of bravery.

"Did you guys kill Scott Younger?" I asked.

"Listen, lady. Scott Younger was the last person the boss wanted wasted," answered the stocky one. The tall one nodded his Reagan-face in agreement.

"Do you know who killed him?" I persisted.

"No, do you?" returned the stocky one.

I shook my head.

"Bunch of fuckin' amateurs these days, punks. Running around with their fuckin' Uzis . . ."

"That's enough, Hugo," the tall one said. "Younger was not killed with an Uzi." He turned his rubbery gaze on me. He wasn't close enough for me to see his eyes. "We'd like to know who killed Mr. Younger, ourselves. If you find out, you'll let us know." It was an order.

"Me?" I squeaked.

"Our boss would consider it a favor," he said. I had a feeling there was a second, social smile underneath his rubber one, but neither of them warmed my heart.

"Just who is your boss?" I asked.

"None of your business," Hugo answered, tightening his grip on my arm once more. "Lady, you'd better not fuck with us on this. If we find out you are . . ." He let the threat trail off into the cold air. It was an effective technique. I began trembling again. But I still had some of my own questions.

"You searched my house, didn't you?"

"How could you tell?" responded Hugo.

"Everything was so neat. The files were in alphabetical order and the cat . . ."

"I told you," Hugo broke in, his rubber face turned toward the tall Reagan. "But you had to straighten up after me. Alphabetical order! I told you I put everything back the way I found it!"

"Shut up, Hugo," the tall man responded. "You're the one that fed the cat." There was a short silence while Hugo regrouped.

"The cat was hungry," he said, turning toward me again. "You shoulda heard her crying. Leaving her like that, without feeding her." He shook his head in sadness while his mask smiled on.

I considered telling him he'd been suckered by C.C., but recognized in time that he was not a person to take teasing well. I was in enough trouble as it was. Spurred by his righteous indignation over the near-starvation of my cat, Hugo threw himself into another round of questioning and arm squeezing. He ended with a magnanimous proposal.

"Lady, we'll give you twenty-four hours to come up with the pictures," he said.

"Forty-eight hours," amended the tall one.

Then the two Reagans climbed back into their black Cadillac and drove away. I tried to catch the license number, but the plates had been liberally smeared with mud.

I collapsed against my car. The cold wind chilled me through sweat-soaked clothing. I opened the door and crawled into the front seat. Should I call the police? All I wanted to do was lie on my car seat and recover. How was I going to convince the Reagans that I didn't have anything to do with "the pictures"? What in hell were these pictures, anyway? And what did they have to do with Younger?

A sharp rap on my side window startled me out of my thoughts and into sitting position. I looked out the window. Two heavily bearded men, with bird nests for hair stared back at me. They shared a crazed ferocity of expression and unspeakably filthy clothing. Rapists, I was sure. As if I hadn't been through enough.

I jammed my key into the ignition, but turned toward the window again when I heard another tap. Something was pushed up flat against the glass. It was a badge.

"Narcotics officers, ma'am," came a voice cutting into my panic. "What are you doing here?"

I babbled. About my business in the warehouse, my fear, the two men in the Cadillac, everything.

"Mind if we search your car?" was the only response.

"My car?"

"No problem, if you don't have anything to hide."

I got out of my car and let them go to it. They pawed through files, gas receipts, Softisculp dolls, maps and Christmas ornaments, to no avail. My glove compartment had a set of emergency tools, a flashlight and an owner's manual I hadn't looked at in years, as well as my current registration and insurance documentation. But no drugs. They checked my license against the registration, looked beneath the body of the car and then gave up. One of the officers turned to me.

"You ought to be more careful, ma'am," he said. "This can be a dangerous place when it's deserted. And you have some mighty strange friends."

Then they turned and headed for their car, the beat-up Chevy I had spotted an eternity of an hour before. They had probably been there the whole time.

My anger at the two narcotics officers fueled me with enough courage to get my paperwork from the warehouse and drive home. I told myself I should have never allowed them to search my car. I didn't have any drugs, but it was the principle of the thing. And they sat there the whole time the Reagans were interrogating me!

I shivered, remembering the threats. My arm ached from being squeezed. I returned my focus to the narcotics officers. It frightened me too much to think of the masked men who had interrogated me. The men who had entered my house without a problem. The men who could do it again just as easily.

When I drove up my driveway all I wanted was to cuddle up somewhere in the womb of my house and make my mind a blank. I wanted to forget the day's events, the weeks's events for that matter, even if that meant forgetting Wayne. I longed to own a TV, if only for the day, to bury my mind in. I told myself a book and a hot bath would do. But even that was not to be.

Maggie was waiting for me on my porch. She sat on the stairs wrapped in an olive-green slicker, her red hair escaping from underneath the hood. It was all I could do to hold back tears of self-pity when I saw her huddled there.

"Jeez, Kate, I'm glad you're here. I was going to wait five minutes longer and then go home," she said, standing up to meet me as I approached the stairs.

"What are you doing here?" I asked wearily.

"I'm here to apologize," she said with a sheepish smile. Then her wide eyes filled with concern. "You look just terrible. What's wrong?"

I toyed briefly with the idea of telling her what had happened to me in four-part harmony, but satisfied myself with grunting, "tired, work." Who knew what Maggie's fevered imagination might make of the real story?

"Wow, you do look bushed," she said. "Want me to make you some tea?" I nodded and immediately regretted it. Now I had invited her in.

She put her arm around me for support and led me up the stairs. I let myself lean on her. It felt good. For all her childish excesses, Maggie was at bottom a kind woman who would always help a friend in need, if she could stop whirling around long enough to notice you were in need. Once inside, she sat me down in my comfy chair.

"Just tell me where you keep the blankets and the tea," she admonished when I tried to play hostess. I sank into my chair and gave her directions. The idea of being treated as an invalid was suddenly appealing. She bounded off in the direction of my kitchen. I could hear cabinets slamming as she searched for tea, and then C.C.'s meows begging for food. I thought of the stocky Reagan and began shivering all over again.

"Are you okay?" she asked as she returned to the room with a blanket.

I attempted a smile. "Fine, just a little tired."

"You're probably coming down with something," she said, her intent gaze on my face. She felt my forehead. "No fever," she pronounced. "Red Zinger, Mellow Mint or Dr. Chang's?"

"Dr. Chang's," I answered. "Maggie, why are you here?"

"Eileen ordered me to come," she admitted, a pale pink blush spreading underneath her freckles. "She really chewed me out about my insensitivity. And I realized she was right. I'm really sorry, Kate." Her wide-open eyes looked into mine. "I've been way out of line. I should never have asked you to find the murderer."

"That's all right," I said. I was too drained to judge her harshly. It was easier to forgive her.

"No, it's not. And I shouldn't have accused Wayne either."

I let that one go by without absolution.

"Eileen said it couldn't be Wayne," she continued. "Even if it was, I should have kept my mouth shut." She sat down across from me and twirled a strand of her hair, her eyes focused on her lap. "I get real excited. I read a lot of fiction. . . ."

"Romance novels?" I couldn't resist asking. The deepening of her blush was answer enough. She kept her eyes averted and continued. "Eileen says that judging without knowing the facts is the same kind of thing that leads to racism and homophobia, and she's right. I want to make amends. . . ."

But before she could finish her sentence the whine of the tea-kettle turned into a scream, and Maggie jumped up and galloped into the kitchen like one of Pavlov's dogs. After a minute she returned with a cup of tea and set it down on the table.

"I want to make it up to you."

"You don't have anything to make up to me," I said.

"But I do, Kate," she answered, tapping my arm for emphasis. I winced and drew away.

"Is your arm hurt?" she asked, concern in her eyes once more, and a pinch of suspicion.

"I knocked it getting out of the car," I lied.

"Shall I take a look at it?"

I shook my head. She shrugged her shoulders and went on. "Eileen and I would like to take you out to dinner tomorrow night."

I remembered my evening appointment with Valerie. "I've got a date," I said. I could tell by the way Maggie was wriggling in her chair that she wanted to ask if my date was with Wayne, but she practiced uncharacteristic restraint. I softened toward her. "How about lunch?"

"You've got it," she answered, her face brightening. "Twelve o'clock. Meet us at the office. There's a great little place down the street that serves tofu burgers and vegetarian tostadas.

"And," she continued, "I want to give you free chiropractic treatments for a while."

"How are you planning to get Renee to go for it?" I asked.

Maggie's eyes narrowed. She pulled her shoulders back before speaking. "Renee does a real good job. But I am the boss."

I burst into laughter before I could stop myself. Maggie added a good-natured chuckle to my squeals.

"Well, some of the time I'm the boss," she said with a lopsided grin. Then her face grew serious again. "There's another thing I need to tell you about. Eileen and I decided you should know."

"What?" I prompted impatiently.

"Renee says she knows something about Wayne that will convict him."

I felt the blood drain from my face. Maggie jumped to her feet and began pulling on a clump of her hair.

"Jeez, I'm sorry. I was afraid to tell you, but Eileen thought I should. That's one of the reasons I suspected Wayne in the first place."

"But what is it that Renee knows?" I asked, managing to keep my voice below a shout only by digging my nails into the arms of my chair.

"I don't know. She won't tell me." Maggie was tugging at her hair with one hand and gesturing wildly with the other. Her voice grew more shrill with each sentence. "Sheesh, I've bugged her for days now. She won't tell Eileen either. And it's no use you asking. She says she won't say anything to you, or Wayne. And, whatever it is, she's told the police!"

– Fourteen –

MAGGIE STARED DOWN at me, her eyes like a deer's caught in oncoming headlights. Looking at her, I could understand why the messengers of bad news were slain. Especially when they brought the news with the best of intentions. I gripped the arms of my chair tighter, gulping deep breaths in an effort to calm myself.

"What's Renee's home phone number?" I asked Maggie through clenched teeth.

"Renee won't talk to you. . . ." she began.

"Just give me the phone number," I snapped.

"Sheesh, Kate," she said.

I threw off my blanket and stomped to my telephone. I yanked the telephone directory from underneath it. The receiver clattered off the hook. I replaced it with a bang, and began thumbing through the directory pages with a great show of purpose. I couldn't remember Renee's last name. But Maggie didn't know that.

"It would be easier if you gave me her phone number," I said, my tone a half-conscious imitation of the stocky Reagan.

Maggie fumbled in her coat pocket and brought out a crumpled list of names and numbers. She handed it to me without further comment.

My conversation with Renee was short and shrill. When I asked her what it was she knew about Wayne, she told me it was none of my business. When I persisted, she told me that she would call the police if I tried to talk to her again. Then she hung up on me.

Maggie remained watchful but blessedly silent when I slammed the receiver down. Her freckles stood out in bold relief against her unnaturally pale skin, and her hair had been tugged into a frizzy horizontal clump on the side of her head. I found a glimmer of pity for her in my heart. She must have seen that glimmer.

"I blew it again," she said. I withheld comment. "I shouldn't have told you." Her shoulders slumped. "Can I say I'm sorry one more time?"

"It's all right." I sighed. It was my mother's sigh of the martyr.

"I'll go now," she muttered. She pulled her hood back up over her hair and walked to the door, dejection evident in each heavy step.

"Thanks, Maggie," I said. "I'll see you tomorrow for lunch."

"Really?" she asked, and turned toward me, her face brightening.

"Yes, really. Now get out of here while you can," I said, infusing my tone with a lightness that I didn't feel.

Once she was gone I fell back into my naugahyde chair and tried to figure out what Renee might know about Wayne that could convict him. The old fear about Wayne came back. Just a whiff, but it was enough. Was he a murderer? I shook my head, rejecting the idea. I refused to believe it. But, what if he was? Did I still want him? What a thought! Where were the days when dandruff was enough to nix a relationship? I got out of my chair and began to pace. C.C. sashayed in and dropped herself onto her back in my path.

All right, let's assume Wayne is innocent, I told myself as I stepped over C.C.'s supine form. She took a swipe at my foot. Did Renee have a piece of evidence that she was misinterpreting? Something she saw or heard that wasn't what it seemed? That was certainly possible. I considered what Maggie had made of Wayne's attraction to me. But Renee didn't seem to have Maggie's imagination. On the other hand, she probably had enough imagination to turn some innocuous act into a murder threat, like the psychology students who were convinced their professor had been threatened with a gun, when, in fact, only a banana had been pointed at him. The power of suggestion. I was beginning to feel better.

And what if she was lying? I could imagine one very good

reason for her to lie. Pinning the murder on Wayne was certainly a way to divert suspicion from herself, the only other suspect who had had any established personal relationship with Scott. The police would certainly weigh that in before accepting her testimony at face value. I was calm enough now to flop back down in my chair. Was Renee the one who had broken Scott Younger's neck? She looked very good to me. Who knew what had really gone wrong between her and Scott? C.C. yowled her agreement and jumped into my lap.

"Should I tell Wayne?" I asked her. Her ears barely twitched at the question. She clawed my thighs happily without answering.

I picked her up and held her in the air so I could see her face. "Will it only drive him crazy?" I asked. *Or get Renee killed*, a dissenting inner voice suggested. C.C. squirmed out of my arms and onto the floor.

Then she was back in my lap, clawing again. I held one of her paws and smiled, thinking how Wayne had subdued her clawing the night he had taken me to dinner. I remembered his halting invitation, the ride to the restaurant, and the black Cadillac which had followed us.

I jumped out of my seat, dumping C.C. on the floor. The black Cadillac had been following Wayne!

I moved quickly to the phone and dialed Wayne's number. As it rang I watched C.C.'s indignant backside disappear through the cat-door. Wayne answered on the second ring.

"Hoped you'd call today," he said. The warmth in his voice seemed to caress me over the line. But I wasn't in the mood for a warm caress.

"Two men in a black Cadillac questioned me today," I said.

A short silence followed, then a soft "Oh God."

"They wanted some 'pictures.' Do you know these guys?"

"Be right over," he said. His voice had hardened. The phone went dead.

I folded my blanket and fought back tears and doubt. It was too much. First, Renee's vague accusation and then the connection between Wayne and the black Cadillac. Angrily, I shook away all thought and gathered up my forgotten paperwork.

I didn't get very far on order forms. Wayne arrived on my doorstep within fifteen minutes. His curly hair was ruffled, as if he had pulled on his sweater in a hurry. His shoulders were stiff, his expression unreadable.

"Okay?" he asked. I looked up at him looming in the door-way.

" 'Okay' what?" I snapped, irritated by his one-word sentence and my own fear.

"Are you okay? Did they hurt you?" His voice was tight, his eyes intense under his heavy brows. Concern or anger? Or both?

I rubbed my arm.

"What did they do to your arm?"

"Nothing. Dammit, I'm alright!" I exploded.

The rigidity of his posture melted. He dropped his head down until his chin touched his chest. Then he sighed.

When he brought his face back up it held a softer expression. "Can we start over?" he asked.

I nodded, ashamed of my outburst. "Let's sit down," I said. "I'll tell you the whole thing."

We took our positions in the swinging chairs. I described the break-in at my house, my interrogation at the hands of the two Reagans, and my realization that the black Cadillac was the same one that had followed Wayne on Thursday night. My neck tightened up just talking about it. He listened intently without interrupting me.

"They visited me too," he said, once I had finished. His voice was steady and clear now. "Friday morning while I was out. They weren't as tidy putting things back at my place. Books, files, magazines, all over the floor. Whole place was ransacked. Took me most of the day to clean up.

"They pulled me off the road as well," he continued. "Wore the Reagan masks. Wondered if they knew I was a Democrat for a second."

I choked down a laugh.

"So what happened?" I asked. "Did they tell you what they wanted?"

"Uh, no," Wayne answered. He was blushing now, his eyes lowered.

"Why not?"

"I took their guns away. They ran off before I could ask." His words were delivered in a low voice, the words barely audible.

"How the hell did you get their guns from them?" I asked.

"Karate," he answered. "Sorry."

"Sorry? You beat the bad guys and you're sorry!" I began to

laugh. My muscles relaxed a little. A mental picture of Wayne routing the Reagans was delicious.

Wayne looked up and smiled hesitantly. I walked over and put my arms around his neck. His now familiar scent drifted up toward me, and with it a wave of tenderness. But there were still too many uncertainties. No time for tender feelings. I returned to my chair.

"So, what do you know about these guys?" I asked. My tone was nonchalant, but fear was tightening the muscles of my neck again.

Wayne closed his eyes for a moment, sighed and then looked at me intently. "Like to go for a walk?" he asked.

I looked out the window into the unappealing grey drizzle. "Why a walk?"

"Might know what the goons were looking for. I think I do. But it's a long story. A walk would help."

I put on my coat and boots quickly, impatient to hear the story. We headed out into the drizzle. The cold damp air burned into my sinuses. Wayne began to speak as we crushed across the gravel of the driveway.

"It goes back a long time," he began. "All hearsay. Scott told me bits and pieces. He was through with this stuff before I met him."

I nodded my encouragement. We headed up the road, past tall fences, overgrown lawns, and gaunt fruit trees to which a few scattered leaves still clung. There were no sidewalks. We squished along the muddy roadside path in rhythm, our eyes on our feet.

"Scott was dealing drugs to students, just starting to make big money. Didn't sell hard drugs. Another organization did that. One night, two goons visited him with a proposition. Join their organization or get out of the business. Scott refused to join. Always a loner. He hired two bodyguards.

"It wasn't enough protection. Couple of months went by. He got an explosive device in the mail. Wasn't set to go off. The letter said it was just to show him what they could do."

"Who were 'they'?" I asked. "The Mafia?"

"Scott never said. I got the feeling they were local boys. Not actual members of The Family. Mob methods, though.

"Letter that came with the bomb arranged a meeting between Scott and the boss of the local organization. The boss came and visited Scott at his house. All very friendly. 'Join us. You'll like it. Be part of the family.' Scott said he'd consider it. The boss made a mistake, though. Told Scott he had two kids going to Crocker himself. Part of the 'one big family' routine. Scott took his picture too, with an automatic camera over the doorway.''

Wayne stopped walking and turned to me. ''You're not going to like this part. Wasn't right. But it happened.'' He resumed walking and I walked with him, watching my boots tromp in the mud as I listened to the story.

''Scott got the boss identified from the picture. Hired a couple of detectives who tracked the kids down. Boy and a girl. Then threw a party. Scott's parties were events. Live music, light shows, catered food, drugs. Later, he added art work, subtracted the drugs and charged people to come. But in those days, no one would refuse an invitation.

''The kids didn't refuse. They couldn't figure out why they were so lucky. Once they got to the party they were separated. Got stoned. Real stoned. Didn't know how to handle drugs. Scott thought that was funny, their father a drug dealer and they couldn't handle drugs.'' Wayne's tone was hard and bitter. I shivered in the cold, at the memory of the man who had thought that funny.

''Girl found herself naked with a gang of men who introduced her to group sex. Boy got two gay men. Won't tell you the details. You can imagine. They weren't forced. Scott said he merely fulfilled their fantasies. Maybe he did. But there were photographs, lots of photographs. He took them himself.

''He sent copies of the photos to the boss, with a letter telling him that Scott had endowed a trust to give maximum publicity to the pictures in case he died, went missing or became disabled. School, porn magazines, friends, relatives, whatever.''

''What happened?''

''The boss backed down immediately. Said 'fine, live and let live.' Scott kept the student trade. The boss kept the hard stuff. Scott didn't let go of his bodyguards, though.''

''But what happened to the kids?''

''Sent to the East Coast with chaperons. The girl eventually got married. The boy became a diplomat. Some African country. Scott kept in touch with the boss. They actually seemed to respect each other as time went on. Once Scott got out of the drug game he told the boss there was never any trust set up to publish the pictures. But that he still had the pictures.''

"God, Scott was an evil man," I burst out. "Didn't he ever stop to consider the hell that he put them through?"

"No. Never could understand him on this one. He really was a good man most of the time. But he saw this whole incident as a personal triumph and nothing more. His biggest triumph, beating the boss at his own game. Insisted the kids weren't harmed."

We reached the main road and stopped walking. I looked into Wayne's face. It was closed to me.

"How can you still defend Scott?" I asked angrily.

He shrugged his shoulders.

I turned away from him.

"Any of the slime rubbed off on me?" he asked softly.

I didn't answer, but it had. I began walking up the path by the main road. Wayne followed behind me.

"So those are 'the pictures,'" I said after we had walked two blocks in silence.

"Think so."

"So it's simple. Give them the pictures," I said, stopping in my tracks.

"Couple of problems with that. First, I burned the pictures the day Scott died." I turned to look at him. The slime seemed to be slipping away. He saw the look.

"Forgave the sinner, not the sin," he said and turned his eyes from me once more. "Second, I don't know who the boss is. Scott never mentioned his name. I burned his picture with the others."

"What are we going to do?" I asked.

"Thanks for the 'we.' Don't know why you're even involved, though. Why do they think you would have anything to do with this?"

I thought. And I remembered the black Cadillac across the street when Wayne had dropped me at my house Thursday night.

"The envelopes!" I said. I grabbed his arm. "You handed me your stories in manila envelopes. They thought you gave me the photos."

A smile crept across his face. "Of course," he muttered. But the smile disappeared as he said, "How do I tell them they've made a mistake?"

"First, a tofu burger to celebrate," I said. Now that I knew what they were seeking, I was no longer terrified of the Reagans. Afraid, but not terrified. It was two o'clock and I hadn't eaten since breakfast. I was starving.

I led Wayne down the side of the main road, past fenced-off houses and gardens, to the neighborhood 7-Eleven. We walked single file to avoid the stream of cars cruising closely by, their tires spraying muddy water as they passed. When the path turned to sidewalk, I slipped my hand into the crook of Wayne's arm to continue by his side. A sudden memory of a similar walk with Craig startled me with its pain. I walked faster.

Wayne and I shared tofu burgers and carrot juice, sitting on a cement block in the cold damp air at the end of the 7-Eleven parking lot. We discussed the problem of the Reagans, the photos and the boss. The only solution we could come up with was to wait until the next approach and explain the situation clearly to them. And then hope to be believed.

We walked back home in companionable silence, listening to the sound of our matched footsteps and the cars whooshing by. We were crunching back up my gravel driveway when Wayne broke the silence.

"Wish this solved Scott's murder. But it doesn't, does it?"

The gloom of the day came pouring down on my head. In unraveling the minor mystery, I had managed to forget the major one. And I had forgotten Renee's claim. I stole a quick glance at Wayne's face.

"What's wrong?" he asked.

"I don't know whether to tell you," I said.

"Tell me." His eyes were on mine, steady.

"Renee claims to have told the police something that will convict you."

"What?" he asked, unblinking. His voice was pitched low.

"She won't say. Do you know what she means?" I asked, the last words wrung out of me in a painful yelp.

"No," he answered sadly. "All I know is that you're afraid again."

– Fifteen –

HE WAS RIGHT. I was afraid again. But I went ahead and re-counted what Maggie had told me about Renee's claim. And then I described my fruitless telephone call to Renee herself.

When I had finished speaking I waited for Wayne to answer me, to reassure me. But he just stood silently, staring in my direction without focus, his scarred face expressionless once more. My insides became as cold and dead as the grey day.

"It's okay," he said finally, and left without another word. I watched his Jaguar crawl away.

I spent the rest of the day and evening in concentrated paper-work. No hurt. No doubts. No fears. Only paper, pencil and ink. I moved my hands carefully as I worked, so as not to disturb my frozen body. I mouthed the numbers and words on my papers as if they formed a mantra which could block all thought. I had buried all feeling.

At ten o'clock that night I knocked myself out with a large dose of NatuRest. But I awoke at midnight, my face wet with tears. The details of my nightmare dissolved into undefined fragments of fear and loneliness as consciousness returned.

Consciousness brought a barrage of unresolved questions that banged against my drowsy mind. I squirmed under the covers, kicking and dodging, until one question engaged my attention. What if one of the people in the waiting room that day had been the boss's kid, grown up, or the boss himself, for that matter? The faces of the suspects moved before me, mounted on a spinning carousel. The carousel turned slowly at first and then faster and faster until the faces blurred again into sleep.

* * *

Monday morning was bright blue through the skylights. I blinked and then rolled out of bed, giving myself a pep talk. Time to move. Time to feel again. I jumped into a hot shower, enduring the return of sensation to my body. If Wayne was a murderer, so be it. My body tensed, not seeming to agree, but I continued the talk. If Wayne didn't want to see me anymore, I would live. A sigh sneaked out of my mouth. I'd call him. If only to share my midnight inspiration. I toweled myself down and looked in the mirror.

Multihued blotches of bruising decorated my arm where the stocky Reagan had squeezed it. Maybe I had the key to Scott's murder, I reminded myself, and pulled my eyes away from the reflection.

Ten minutes later, my bruises aptly covered by a black turtle-neck and blue sweat shirt, I sat down at my desk and dialed the phone. My hands were ice cold. I watched C.C. enviously as she basked in the cat-sized patch of sunlight that came through her clear plastic cat-door. After two rings Wayne answered.

"So what if the murderer is one of those kids, all grown-up?" I asked, without further introduction.

"Kate?" he said softly. The relief in his tone was unmistak-able even in that one soft word. Somewhere in my chest ice began to thaw.

"That's me. Kate Jasper, office chair detective, reporting. The boss's kids. What do you think?" I was attempting the bantering tone of Nora Charles.

"Guess they'd be somewhere in their late thirties now," Wayne answered slowly. I could picture his brows lowering over his eyes as he considered. "That would let out Ted or Tanya."

"Unless Ted was the boss," I said.

"He doesn't look anything like the boss," Wayne answered.

"You mean you know what they look like!" The blood pump-ing through my body speeded up. We had a chance of identifi-cation.

"Know what they *looked* like, past tense," he corrected. "I saw Scott's old pictures of him and the kids before I burned them. Mediterranean features, maybe Italian or Greek. Long strong faces, large noses, olive skin, black hair, big dark eyes."

"Hold on a minute," I said. I shoved my stack of paperwork to the side and grabbed a pen and yellow legal pad. "I'm going to list every one that was there that day. For starters, I was there.'' I wrote "Kate Jasper" on the pad. Wayne didn't know I wasn't one of the boss's kids. Anyway, I like complete lists.

Wayne was silent on the other end of the line. Was he thinking of my rather large nose?

"Wayne?" I prompted.

"No, your face isn't quite right. Your eyes are too small, too close together." I winced at his choice of words, but went on.

"Then there's you," I said. As I wrote his name down I said "Caruso," aloud. Damn. Caruso was an Italian name.

"Birth certificate lists Enrico Caruso as my father," he said, his voice so low I had to press my ear against the receiver to hear. "A joke on my mother's part. She loved opera. Never would say who my father really was. She may not have known."

"I'm sorry," I said simply, my face burning for his pain and my own blundering.

"Just put a question mark beside my name," he suggested. His voice had returned to normal, soft and low, but blessedly audible and cheerful once more.

"All right," I said, matching his cheerful nonchalance, while my mind tried to encompass the experience of growing up the illegitimate son of a crazy mother.

"Check off Ted and Tanya," he continued. I dutifully wrote down their names on my list, with an "X" next to each. "And Valerie. They weren't black." My pen scratched.

"How about Devi?" I asked.

"No, features are too delicate," he said. I felt a tingle of jealousy. Devi's features were "delicate." My eyes were "too small, too close together." I added her to my list and X'd her off reluctantly.

"So who's left?" I asked. Between my worries about Wayne's childhood and my jealousy of his description of Devi I had lost track.

"How can you forget Maggie?" he asked dryly. I smiled. How could I forget her? "But she's all wrong, anyway. Big bones, red hair and freckles. Renee's not even close, features too pinched. Eileen is the closest physically." He paused. "No, don't wash," he answered himself finally. "Face isn't long enough. Eyes the wrong shape. Lips too full. Can't be the same person." But I still heard a hint of doubt in his voice. I wrote down Eileen's name and put a question mark beside it.

I looked down at my list, "But that's everyone," I said. My perfect theory was crumbling.

"I appreciate the idea," Wayne said gently. "But it won't work. Too much risk in murdering Scott, for the boss or the kids. That was the purpose of the pictures in the first place. The threat of publication is still effective, witness the hoods the boss sent. And why wait to kill Scott? Has to be fifteen years ago at least, maybe twenty."

"How about the heat of the moment?" I insisted. "Say the daughter in the pictures suddenly recognizes Scott after all this time. Couldn't she get angry enough to strike out at him without regard to the risk?" I wanted the theory to work.

"Not the girl, none of them." He said gently and firmly. But I remembered his hesitation about Eileen. I'd ask her about her parents at lunch, just to make sure.

"Wait a minute," I said. "What if it's not the boss or the kids, but someone who loves them—a wife, a husband, a friend?"

I could hear his soft sigh. "I want it to work, too, Kate. But it won't. If they knew about the pictures, they'd know about the risk of publication."

I crumpled up my list and threw it forcefully on top of the overflowing wastebasket. It rolled on to the floor, where C.C. leapt on it with murderous intent. But I wasn't finished yet.

"Did Scott ever blackmail anyone else?" I asked.

"Never told me so," Wayne answered, his voice slowing as he considered. "Probably would have told me if he had."

"Damn!" I said. I jabbed my pen into the pad of paper in front of me. "Shouldn't we tell the police about all this?"

"Do you think they'd believe us?" he responded.

I could see his thoughtful look in my mind's eye. And I knew what he meant. Sergeant Udel would be just as likely to believe the whole story was an elaborate red herring conceived, directed and produced by Wayne Caruso and Kate Jasper in an attempt to divert suspicion from Wayne. There were no witnesses, except possibly the unnamed narcs. And I never even got their badge numbers. Stupid, I told myself. And the pictures were gone, except from Wayne's memory.

"They probably wouldn't," I finally said reluctantly. Dead end. I slumped in my desk chair.

"Got an idea," said Wayne.

"To catch the murderer?" I asked, my ears perking up.

"No, to get the boss's hoods off your back. Personal ads. 'To the boss: The pictures have been burned. Your secrets are safe. Call off the Reagans.' All the local papers. What do you think?''

"Pretty good," I said. "But your short stories are better."

Low, appreciative laughter floated over the line. "Thanks," he said. "You're a funny and beautiful woman."

"Even if my eyes are too close together?" I asked in a saccharin-flavored voice.

"Should have said your eyes are perfect, theirs were too widely spaced," he said quickly. Once he heard my answering chuckle he went on, but in a suddenly serious tone.

"Kate, back out now if you need to. I tried to give you the chance yesterday. Didn't think I'd hear from you again, but . . ." He sighed. "The police may arrest me."

I sat there holding the telephone to my ear and looking at the blank pad of paper on my cluttered desk. Telephones are such strange devices, separating the words from the physical beings who utter them. If only I could have seen his face or touched him, maybe I could have answered him with one hundred percent assurance. As it was, I had to settle for almost sure.

"You told me you didn't kill Scott. That's enough," I said firmly. I was grateful that he couldn't see the tremor in my hands over the telephone. "Now, do you want to drive to guru-ville to see Valerie tonight or shall I?" I asked.

He duplicated my no-nonsense tone. "I'll pick you up at six o'clock. And I'll call in the ads for tomorrow." After a pause he added, "See you soon." His last words were as soft as C.C.'s fur, and just as sensual.

"Soon," I answered and hung up.

The moment the receiver went down, all of the air I had been holding in my lungs came whooshing out. I hadn't realized until that moment just how tight I had been holding it in.

I had twenty minutes left before I needed to leave for my monthly appointment to have my hair cut. Plenty of time to do paperwork, I told myself. But for once my body rebelled. I found myself opening the curtains of my dark office wide enough to allow in a large person-sized patch of sun. Then I lay down on the floor to bask in it.

Half an hour later I entered the gilded doorway of the Golden Rose Beauty Salon. Although located in Marin County, the Golden Rose did not specialize in hair design consultations. It was an old-style salon, untouched by yuppie values, decorated in shades of pink and gold, and staffed by an all female troupe of gossips. You could get a good haircut there for twelve dollars, as opposed to the thirty dollars plus, charged by the more up-wardly mobile establishments of Marin. The Golden Rose had not raised its prices in the three years I had been a customer. I appreciated the time warp.

The receptionist directed a friendly pop of her gum my way and pointed me to the plush pink love seat to await my hair-dresser. I nodded to the two elderly women sitting across from me and thought about Wayne's mother. A single mother with a strange sense of humor. Only people didn't talk about "single mothers" in those days, they talked about the shame of illegit-imacy. Was that what had driven her mad?

My thoughts were interrupted by the arrival of my hairdresser, Carol. Carol of the snapping scissors and perpetual motion mouth. She was a nervously thin woman who survived on cig-arettes, Coca-Cola, and being right about everything. Politics, psychoanalysis, music theory, economics. You name it, she was an expert. And the more she opined during any given appoint-ment, the shorter she cut my hair. That day, her own constantly changing hair was swept up in a mass of cascading blond curls that gave her bony face the look of a country-music singer.

"Hiya, honey," she greeted me, brushing her glossed lips lightly across my cheek. "Hear you're acting crazy again, trying to find out who killed that drug dealer. Jesus Christ, you must be nuts! Though, if you ask me, drug dealers deserve everything they get. Let them kill each other off, do the world some good." The two older women across from me looked up curiously. The receptionist stopped popping her gum to listen.

"He wasn't really a drug dealer. He just used to be," I whis-pered as I stood up to follow her to my chair.

"Crack, it's more addictive than heroin, you know, a terrible business." She shook her finger. "My kids had better just say no, if they know what's good for them."

I climbed up into the pink vinyl barber chair as she lowered her voice to a conspiratorial whisper. "Everyone's jealous I get to do you. Finding the body like that, you're a celebrity. Look at old radar-ears over there."

Carol waved her scissors in the direction of a young woman who had stopped buffing the nails of her silver-haired customer long enough to stare our way, open-eyed and slack-jawed. I rec-ognized her pink and blond head. She was Tiffany, the manicurist. She had been trying without success to take charge of my stubby, unkempt nails for the last three years.

Carol draped a gold, rubbery sheet around my neck and turned me to the mirror, now reflecting a scenic panorama of interested faces. "Smile, you're on Candid Camera," she said, her voice once again loud enough to carry to all present, except those whose heads were encased in the sound-muffling hoods of their dryers.

"How'd you find out about Younger's murder?" I whispered.

"Renee Mickle recommended you to me, remember?" I nodded. Renee had had a great haircut before her permanent. "That woman always wants too tight a perm. I keep telling her, tight perms are out, soft curls are in." Carol caressed her own curls briefly before grabbing her scissors. "Renee ought to go back to her husband," she continued. "She still loves him. She just won't admit it." I wondered if she was right. That might explain Renee's ultimate abandonment of Scott Younger. Carol trimmed some hair from the top of my head.

"So, Renee told you about the murder," I hazarded.

"No, no. Bonnie told me. Renee wouldn't tell me if my ass was on fire." She cut a path down to my ear.

"Who is Bonnie?" I asked, turning my head toward Carol's face.

"Don't move," she said. "Ted Reisner's wife, Bonnie."

"You mean Ted, who was there the day . . ."

"The day the drug dealer got it. Yeah." Her scissors snipped at the back of my head.

"He wasn't really a drug dealer," I said once more. Creep that Scott Younger was, he was a man, an individual, not just a "drug dealer."

"Bonnie's too young for Ted. But who am I to judge? They seem happy, even if she is young enough to be his daughter . . . or granddaughter. You know old men." She rolled her eyes without missing a beat with her scissors. "Bonnie knew the drug dealer, you know."

"He wasn't . . ." I began. "Oh, never mind. How did Bonnie know Younger?"

"Some art committee together. She's a good artist. I've seen her work. Good sense of style. Had a graphic-design business before she married Ted. They both work at the hardware store now, and she paints on the side, New Wave naturalism."

I remembered Ted saying something about an art committee.

I felt a tingle in my chest. Was this a motive? Insecure older man. Young wife.

"I'm a better judge of art than you'd think," Carol was saying. "Never painted myself, though. Never had the time. But I know quality." Younger was probably richer than Ted. Did that pose a threat? Did Bonnie marry an older man for money? Would she prefer a younger one with even more money?

"Excuse me," came a voice from behind me. I looked up. It was Tiffany, the manicurist, her blue eyes roundly staring.

"Don't move," Carol snapped at the back of my head. She accelerated her pruning operation.

"I couldn't help overhearing," Tiffany began.

"I'll bet," said Carol.

"You're investigating that terrible murder. I'm so impressed." Tiffany smiled encouragingly at me. I could just see her pink-cheeked face in the mirror without moving my head.

"Thank you," I said. "But I'm not really investigating." Except for a little trip to see Ted and Bonnie at the hardware store, perhaps. I was fairly certain I still had Ted's business card.

"Of course she's not investigating," said Carol. "The man's a drug dealer. Whoever killed him should get a medal."

"But you'd just have to know, wouldn't you?" Tiffany said breathlessly to my reflection in the mirror. "You can't just let something like that go by."

"The police are on the job," I said. Busily trying to build a case against Wayne, I added silently. I shifted uncomfortably in my seat.

"Don't move," said Carol. "The police are so corrupt. I was reading this book about how the cops—and the FBI, mind you—phony up evidence all the time to put criminals away." God, that was an awful thought. My stomach kinked. Don't panic, I told myself. I would see Maggie and Eileen for lunch, and Valerie for dinner. I could always call Devi. I had her phone number.

"The police wouldn't do that," Tiffany argued. "Not here." Not in Mill Valley or not in America? Either way, I hoped she was right.

"You wanna bet?" asked Carol and she was off and running. For the next ten minutes she clipped hair furiously and voiced her opinions on everything from corrupt police officials to the failure of the Vietnam war (actually a damned clear analysis), to what we ought to do about Libya's Qaddafi. I closed my eyes and let her voice roll over me. Tiffany's disagreement was reduced to a series of indignant peeps by the time Carol had finished.

"Well," Carol said, putting her hand on my shoulder. "What do you think?"

I opened my eyes and looked in the mirror. My hair was shorter than my ex-husband's.

"I could always become a skinhead," I said softly.

"Now, skinheads," she said, picking up her scissors once more. "They're real scum. Do you know about the neo-Nazi link to the Fundamentalists . . . ?"

I fumbled in my purse for her tip, placed the dollar bills in her hand and leapt down from the pink chair.

- Sixteen -

I WAS LOST in the consideration of Ted and his younger wife, Bonnie, as I paid my bill and made my escape from the Golden Rose Beauty Salon. The receptionist mumbled something at me through her gum, which I was too distracted to decipher. I just smiled as if I understood, and left. I was halfway to my car, reaching to scratch the itchy hairs that had worked their way under my sweat shirt, when I realized I was still wearing the rubbery gold sheet that Carol had draped around my neck.

As I returned the sheet, I felt that kind of mental tickle that tells me I've forgotten something. It couldn't be the sheet around my neck. I was handing that over. But something. Damn. I couldn't quite coax it into consciousness. As I drove home I did a mental inventory of those items I might have overlooked. I'd set the answering machine, fed the cat, locked the doors. I hadn't left anything on the stove or forgotten any appointments. The inventory was useless. By the time I returned home I knew I had lost it, whatever it was.

There was one message on my answering machine. I pushed the button to listen, hoping to hear Wayne's soft growl. Instead I heard my husband Craig's smooth tones, as disappointing as the taste of stale white bread after a loaf of fresh baked whole-wheat. I indulged in a shoulder-heaving sigh that I instantly regretted. I would become my mother yet if I kept those sighs up.

"Let's get together soon," Craig's voice said. "We need to talk settlement."

Settlement? Three days and he wants settlement.

"Call me when you get in," the voice continued. "Talk to you then."

I turned off the machine and began to dial his number. But mid-dial a revolutionary idea waltzed into my mind. I didn't have to return his call! I sat in my comfy chair and submitted this idea to rigorous testing. Did I have a moral obligation to call him as he had requested? Not really. A legal one? No. How about common courtesy? No way, I assured myself. But the sudden shriek of the doorbell obliterated that self-assurance. I jumped up guiltily to answer the door.

When I saw Sergeant Feiffer standing in the doorway I froze. The fear that Wayne had been arrested grabbed my chest and squeezed. I couldn't breathe. Feiffer's look of concern seemed to confirm my fear.

"What happened to your hair?" he asked.

My hand shot up to touch the ends of my cropped hair, and I remembered. "An overzealous hairdresser," I answered briefly. "It's not a criminal matter, no matter how it looks."

He gave a faint smile in reply.

"Why are you here?" I asked, my voice tight. I couldn't even pretend nonchalance.

"Just to ask a few more questions about Scott Younger's death," he answered. "Sergeant Udel wanted to interview you, but I thought it would be easier for you to talk to me." He was smiling again, his Santa Claus blue eyes twinkling in friendliness. Was he playing the old good cop/bad cop game with Udel? Or was he really trying to make it easy for me?

"They haven't arrested anyone yet, have they?" I had to ask. At least I didn't mention Wayne.

"No, they're still in the process of gathering information," he answered. I let my breath out slowly and silently, trying to hide the relief that was flooding my body. Feiffer's eyes never left my face.

"Like to play a little pinball?" I challenged. Let him think I was calm enough to play. Actually, it would have helped to have something to do with my hands.

"No," he said, wistfully glancing over my shoulder at Hayburners. "I really can't." I knew then that this was to be a serious interrogation.

I invited him in and directed him to sit in a swinging chair, hoping that the absurdity of that seat would interfere with his interrogatory mind-set. It didn't. He led me back to the day of the murder with some general questions. Then he narrowed the focus to Wayne.

"When Mr. Caruso came back from the treatment room, did he display any signs of agitation?"

"Not that I noticed," I answered honestly. "Mr. Caruso" sounded so strange to my ears; all it conjured up for me was the operatic tenor that Wayne's mother had admired.

"Was he holding anything in his hands?" asked Feiffer. *Like a metal bar,* I silently finished his sentence.

"No," I said.

"Was there anything different about his clothing? His face? Was he sweating? Trembling?"

"No," I answered to these and the other questions that followed. The repetition of the word lulled me into a state of drowsiness. I swung in my chair, my eyes half-closed.

"How long have you known Mr. Caruso?" Feiffer asked quietly. My eyes popped open. I saw his eyes observing me closely. This question required more than "no" for an answer.

"I saw him at Maggie's a few times but I really never *knew* him until after . . . after Younger was killed," I said. I could feel the blood rising in my face. I wondered if Feiffer would interpret the word "knew" in the biblical sense. My face burned hotter. I looked down at my hands. C.C. chose that moment to announce her arrival with a plaintive meow.

"Did you ever see him, outside of your chiropractor's, before the day of the murder?" he asked, ignoring the cat.

"No," I answered, relieved to be able to use that simple word once more. C.C. rubbed up against his legs. The little traitor.

"Just exactly what is your relationship to Mr. Caruso?" Feiffer asked.

I swallowed a series of possible replies. "None of your business" or "that's a good question," among them. It was difficult to articulate a coherent answer. I found a little smile forming on my face as I remembered Wayne's fumbling approach and my equally fumbling response. How to explain? I looked up and saw that Feiffer was not smiling. His look was the look of an angry father who discovers his daughter has done something very foolish. I wondered if he was really angry, or if that look was just one in his repertoire of looks to unnerve reluctant witnesses.

"We've gone out a couple of times," I mumbled. C.C. tentatively clawed one of Feiffer's pants legs. I looked at her with new fondness.

"In less than a week?" he asked. His tone was incredulous. He continued to ignore C.C., who clawed more and more enthusiastically.

"Yes," I answered sullenly. How easily I had slipped into the role of teenage daughter.

Having established the fact that I was foolish enough to have communicated with Wayne, Feiffer asked me a series of questions. Had Mr. Caruso and I discussed the murder? Was I aware of any financial problems on his part? Did I know if he had been angry with his employer, Scott Younger? Or if he and his employer had been lovers? Just what was their relationship, anyway?

A quick summary of my various mumbled answers might have been "no comment" or "Jeez, I don't know." And I wasn't just feigning ignorance. I still couldn't understand, much less explain, Wayne's connection with Scott. I was toying with the idea of telling Sergeant Feiffer about the boss. But how could I put him in a more receptive state of mind?

"Ms. Jasper," Feiffer said in a softer voice, "I know you, and I know it might be useless, but I've got to warn you." He paused and looked at me, concern in his eyes. "Ouch, goddammit!" he bellowed, and exploded out of his chair.

I jumped in my seat, on the alert. Was this a new interrogation technique? Then I followed Feiffer's angry gaze down his body to C.C., who sat nonchalantly licking her paw. Feiffer's grey pants leg was newly frayed. He reached down and gingerly touched his leg.

"The little bugger drew blood," he said, licking his finger in awe.

C.C. turned to me, her eyes squinting smugly, drew herself to her feet majestically and strode out of the room, tail high. I resisted applauding, but was not quick enough to erase the grin that appeared on my face.

"Can I get you a Band-Aid?" I asked meekly. "Some alcohol?"

"No," he snapped. But his subsequent recovery of composure was admirable. He relaxed his posture and his tone. "No thank you," he corrected himself and flashed a sickly grin. "It's not going to do any good to tell you to be careful, is it?"

I shook my head in confirmation, relieved at his return to reason.

He walked toward the door. "Tell your cat I won't arrest her this time . . .'' he began. I laughed. "And I hope you enjoy talking to Sergeant Udel,'' he finished. My laughter died in the air.

For some time after Sergeant Feiffer left I sat paralyzed with dread. But not for too long. The dread eventually turned to anger. Anger toward a predisposed police force focusing on only one suspect. This anger slowly burned my doubts about Wayne down to a thin layer of ash. And with the anger came the adrenalin-fueled determination to find out who *had* killed Scott Younger. But I needed information. Felix, I thought. A reporter would know everyone's background. I reset my answering machine, said goodbye to C.C., and was out the door.

Felix lived and worked out of an apartment in downtown Mill Valley. He paid for the address. That same small apartment would have gone for six hundred a month in Novato. It was nine hundred in Mill Valley. But he could walk to the local bookstore/café in the morning for a cup of literary espresso and pastry, and to the health food store in the afternoon for his penance of wheatgrass juice. I parked my car down the hill from his apartment and wondered if I had come too early to find him back from breakfast. It was a few minutes past ten o'clock. Downtown Mill Valley was just awakening.

I was relieved to hear the whine of the Rolling Stones coming from his door as I hurried up the stairs. Felix was in. I rang his doorbell.

"Howdy, hi,'' he greeted my hurtling backside as I shot through his doorway into the living room. I wasn't giving him a chance to challenge my arrival.

He shrugged his shoulders, took my coat and threw it over the six-foot inflated Godzilla that guarded the entryway. Then he followed me into his living room. It was decorated in neon. A hot-pink neon flamingo dominated one wall, a lime-green neon palm tree another, and over the mantelpiece the five letters of Felix's name glowed in electric blue. I flopped down on the turquoise futon that served as his couch, ignoring both the blinking word processor that signaled his work in progress and the overflowing laundry basket that sat in the middle of the floor.

"What happened to your hair?'' he yelled over the Stones.

"Is it that bad?'' I yelled back, my hand involuntarily reaching up to my shorn skull.

"No, not really," he shouted. He fiddled with a knob, mercifully reducing Mick Jagger's shrieks to whispers. "Actually, it's pretty punk," he continued at normal volume. "If Barbara was here she'd show you how to spike it." I saw a twitch of a smile underneath his shaggy mustache. I took my hand away from my hair. If he was teasing, I didn't have time to play. I had a mission.

"Sit down," I ordered.

"Yes, ma'am." He saluted and dropped his wiry body to the floor by the laundry basket. "Mind if I sort my laundry?" he asked and simultaneously upended the basket. A small brightly colored mountain of cloth appeared.

"The police are harassing me about Wayne," I ventured. The twinkle went out of Felix's brown eyes. He looked serious and uncomfortable. "He didn't do it," I said. My anger kept my belief strong.

"Kate, he probably did. . . ." he began softly.

"No, you're wrong! There are things going on the police don't even know about." I told him the story of Scott's blackmailing the boss and about my encounter with the men in the Reagan masks. When I had finished, Felix sat without moving, an unfolded purple washcloth in his hand.

"Has it occurred to you that Wayne might have made up that story?"

My head jerked back as I sucked in my breath. How could Felix ask that question? But, unbidden, my mind sought to answer. Because it hadn't ever occurred to me.

"But the Reagans," I objected. "They were real. I have the bruises to prove it."

"And what did they say exactly? A lot of vague threats about some pictures. Wayne is the one who told you a story to fit the facts."

I ran back in my mind to Sunday morning. "They knew who Scott Younger was," I said triumphantly. "They even wanted me to find out who killed him."

"How do you know these guys weren't actors? Maybe Wayne hired them." Felix was still holding the washcloth and watching me sadly.

My mind came back to center after this last scenario. Wayne wouldn't hire actors to frighten me, and then advise me to keep it from the police. I took a deep breath. Felix was just wrong. But if Felix reacted this way to the story, I was just as glad I hadn't told Sergeant Feiffer. Wayne was right. The police wouldn't have believed us.

"All right," I said. "You think Wayne is guilty. I don't. Someone else did it and I want to find out who that someone was. Will you just pretend for a while that you have an open mind, and tell me what you know about the other suspects?"

He hesitated.

"I'll help you fold laundry," I said.

"How about an interview with Wayne?" he asked.

"I can't promise that. I told him you were interested. Maybe, if you and I break the case . . ." I let my sentence trail off in a tantalizing whisper.

"I give," he answered finally. He stood, scooped up half the pile of laundry and dumped it in my lap. "What do you want to know?"

"I realize it's not likely," I began, in order to forestall objection, "but I'd like to rule out any of these people as being the boss or one of his kids. And for that I need background." I picked out a Betty Boop towel and folded it carefully. "Parents especially. Do you have that kind of background on these folks?"

"Hang on a second," he said. He went over to a black file cabinet next to his computer and rummaged through it. I folded some washcloths and admired Felix's shorts. No plain white Jockey for him. I made a pile of skimpy red and white stripes, turquoise polka dots and black silk bikinis. I wondered if Barbara had picked them out. Felix came back with a thick manila file. He blushed and turned his head when he saw his neatly piled underwear.

"I've got a little background on everyone. Just in case," he said. He sat back down on the floor.

"Just in case what?" I asked.

"Well, let's say the police arrest one of these guys today. I've already got his background story ready to go. Or, say one of them is a second victim. The same goes."

A second victim? I shuddered.

"What do you have on Eileen?" I asked. I still hoped she might turn out to be the boss's daughter.

"Eileen," he repeated, rifling through the papers. "Here it is. Eileen Garza, thirty-four years old, parents: Felipe and Delores Garza. She was crowned Football Queen at Cal State Hayward in seventy-five. Her parents own a nursery in San Rafael."

"A nursery!" I threw down a sock in disappointment.

"Yeah, plants. Felipe did gardening for twenty years, his wife did the bookkeeping. Saved enough to buy a nursery six years ago. An American success story."

"How do you find these things out?"

"From the publicity blurb when they opened the nursery. Hey, here's something interesting. She has the same address as Maggie Lambrecht."

"I knew that already," I said. "They're . . ." I trailed off. Should I offer the private facts of Eileen and Maggie's relationship to a reporter?

"Lovers," Felix completed my sentence for me. His voice was filled with annoyance. "Thanks for the information. Anything else you're holding out on me?"

"Well, Ted has a much younger wife, Bonnie," I offered.

"Ted," he mumbled, back to his file. "Ted Reisner. Sixty-nine years old. Married to Bonnie Harris, never changed her maiden name, twenty-nine," he rattled off. "That is pretty young for the old boy."

"How about kids?" I asked.

"None for her. He has three grown boys from a former marriage." No girl. That let him out as the boss. I began sorting socks. "Ted was an electrical engineer before he opened his hardware store. Runs the Bay to Breakers every year. Bonnie Harris is a pretty successful artist, according to her notices," Felix continued.

"And she was on an art committee with Scott Younger," I added.

"Really?" said Felix. His eyes were lighting up. I was glad to see he'd consider someone else besides Wayne as a suspect.

"How about Maggie?" I asked.

"Maggie Lambrecht, forty-two years old. Parents: Doris and Henry McCurdy." The Scottish Mafia? "They live in New Jersey." Wrong coast for the boss. "Maggie moved out here with her husband, Donald Lambrecht. Married for seventeen years, divorced two years ago. One boy, sixteen years old, lives with his father. She's been a chiropractor for a little over ten years."

I looked down at the socks I was sorting. Bright blues, purples, lime-greens. Maggie would love the colors. I wondered idly if her husband had insisted on drab socks. Grounds for divorce?

"Julie Moore, a.k.a. Devi Moore. Thirty-eight. Parents: James and Carolyn. Father was a pharmaceutical magnate."

"Drugs?" I interrupted, now on alert.

"Legal drugs. Guy made a fortune in aspirin and such. Didn't need to sell illegal drugs. Anyway, he died seven years ago." I went back to sorting socks. "Mother died some years before. Devi and her brother split a bundle when Daddy died. Devi is one rich woman. One daughter, Tanya, fifteen, illegitimate. Who needs a father when you have those bucks, huh?" Felix asked in awe.

"Valerie Davis, forty years old. Parents: John and Celeste Davis. Father is a dentist in Oregon. First black man admitted to the local chamber of commerce. One younger brother. One daughter, Hope, eighteen. You already know about her, and about Valerie's prison record. Also, Valerie made the papers some years back as a founding member of Community Drug Watch, an organization which has since died out," Felix said.

"What did the organization do?" I asked. Felix looked through some notes.

"Looks like they kept an eye on whoever was dealing drugs and made it public. Even picketed outside drug dealers' homes. A few slander and libel suits were brought against Drug Watch, but then dropped."

Maybe this was how Valerie had known about Scott Younger's past life as a drug dealer. And she certainly had been angry. An obsession about drug-dealers . . .

"Renee Mickle, thirty-two. Parents: Carl and Rosa Polvino. Carl was a machinist. He passed away in eighty-two. Rosa is a saleswoman at Penny's." I shook my head. The boss's wife wouldn't work at Penny's. "Two kids, twelve and fourteen. Renee divorced husband, Tom, two years ago."

"Who's left?" I asked.

"Kate Jasper," he said with an evil smile.

"Forget it," I answered.

"Wayne Caruso, age thirty-eight." he read. "Parents—this is weird—father listed on the birth certificate as Enrico Caruso."

He looked up from his papers at me. I was angrily twisting a pair of blue jeans in my hands, outraged at his intrusion into the intimate details of Wayne's genealogy. Never mind my own prying into the lives of others.

"Enrico Caruso," Felix repeated. "Wasn't he a third-baseman, with the Giants?"

- Seventeen -

"A BASEBALL PLAYER? He was an opera singer!" I shouted. Then I noticed Felix was laughing.

"I know that, you dimbulb," he said. "I just wanted to lighten you up. You looked ready to strangle me with my own jeans."

I dropped the jeans, took a few deep breaths and forced a smile. After all, Felix was helping me. He smiled back, like a shark.

"So answer me this," he commanded, "Was this another guy named Enrico Caruso, or did Mrs. Caruso just steal the name?"

"Mrs. Caruso?"

"Yeah, maiden name Martha Atcheson. She began calling herself Mrs. Caruso after Wayne was born." He looked up at me. "She's in a loony bin you know," he added softly.

"I know," I said, and then groaned. What chance was there that the police would interpret this piece of information as further evidence of Wayne's mental instability, by reason of bad blood?

"Wayne's got a pretty impressive scholastic record. Third in his graduating class at U.S.F. law school. Why didn't he ever practice?" Felix's look indicated he hoped for a sinister reason.

"Too many lawyers in the Bay Area," I answered.

"Yeah, so I hear," he acknowledged. His face bore an expression of disappointment at the simple explanation.

That expression grew more pronounced as I answered the rest of his questions about Wayne. I didn't think there was anything in what I said to give him a handle on Wayne as the murderer. And there was nothing left in his files to give me a handle on anyone else. School records, job histories, residences. Nothing screeched out "clue."

I returned home, tired and frustrated, to the sound of my own recorded voice cheerfully announcing my absence to a telephone caller. I clicked off the answering machine with a stab of my finger, stilling the cheery voice mid-sentence, and snarled "hello" into the receiver.

My friend Ann Rivera was on the other end. She needed to talk, she said, about the death of Scott Younger. She was feeling an unwarranted surge of guilt and responsibility over his death, although she hadn't seen the man in over fifteen years. Maybe if she had been more sensitive?

I reassured her impatiently that it wouldn't have made any difference. When she heard the impatience in my voice she concluded that *I* needed to talk. By the time I got off the phone she had lovingly bludgeoned me into a visit for a "real talk" the next day. I didn't know whether to be touched or annoyed.

There were no more messages on the machine. I had over an hour to kill before my lunch with Maggie and Eileen. I pulled my chair up to my desk with every intention of working, but the towering mounds of paper on my desk seemed alien to me, forming a small, coldly distant Stonehenge. I pushed them aside, put my elbows on the desk and rested my face in my hands. Would I ever know for certain that Wayne was not a murderer? The police believed that he killed Scott Younger. Would they arrest him whether he had killed Scott or not? I remember what my hairdresser had said about the police phonying up evidence.

I pulled my face out of my hands and reached for my purse. Fishing around in it, I found Guru Illumananda's pamphlet, the scrap of lavender stationery with Devi's phone number and address, and Ted Reisner's business card. Reisner's Hardware was local. I could always use a box of nails.

But I wanted to talk to Devi as well. I just didn't trust anyone so damn ethereal. And she had known Scott Younger. I dialed her number, wondering if she would agree to meet with me or somehow float her way out of it like a wispy cloud. The question was moot. No one answered her phone, not even a machine.

I picked up Ted's card and left my ruined paper Stonehenge behind without a backward glance.

Ted's store was only a few blocks from Maggie's office, between a Chinese take-out and a lingerie shop. "Reisner's Hardware'' was painted on the window in the silvery shapes of tools against a blue background, just as it was on his business card. And below this a small sign announced ''art gallery upstairs'' in tasteful black calligraphy.

I pushed open the door, my eyes seeking Ted's wife, Bonnie, among the light fixtures, wheelbarrows and paint cans displayed at the entrance. I saw a young woman, wearing makeup more appropriate to a Las Vegas showgirl, standing at the checkout counter. Had she been Scott Younger's type? Forcing the muscles of my face into a ''let's chat'' smile, I advanced upon her.

''Are you Ted's wife, Bonnie?'' I asked. ''I've heard so much about you. . . .''

''Bonnie,'' the young woman hollered, cutting me off mid-socialization. ''Someone for you.''

It took my tired mind a few seconds to realize the young woman in front of me was not Bonnie at all. The real Bonnie ambled down the polished wooden stairs that led to the gallery. She was pinkly plump with fluffy blond hair and round blue eyes. Once she stood in front of me, she smiled pleasantly, no doubt trying to remember if she knew me.

''Can I help you?'' she asked.

''Nails,'' I said. ''Tell me about your nails.''

She looked down at her short fingernails for a second before answering. ''Oh, nails. They're three aisles down, against the wall.''

Damn, I thought, I should have asked about something complicated, like bathroom sink drain assemblies. I knew from experience those were worth at least a ten-minute lesson from which I might have segued into a friendly question like, ''Was you husband jealous enough of Scott Younger to kill him?'' As I was trying to formulate a credible question about nails a voice spoke into my ear, startling me into a little jump.

''Kate, heh, good to see you,'' Ted said. ''What happened to your hair?'' He moved to Bonnie's side. He was in top form, his eyes twinkling and his mustache twitching merrily.

''New hairstyle,'' I said shortly.

''Have you met my Bonnie?'' he asked, putting his arm around her. She moved herself close up against the enclosure of his arm like a cat. I expected her to purr any minute. They did not look like an unhappy couple. In fact they looked nauseatingly in love.

''Glad to meet you, Bonnie,'' I answered. ''Ted's told me you're an artist.''

Bonnie looked up at him with glowing eyes. "He tells everyone about me, like I was famous."

"Well you are to me, sweetie, and you're a heck of a good artist," he said, giving her a glowing look in return. I began to feel like a voyeur. Their pheromones were turning my own skin warm and pink.

"Weren't you on an art committee with Scott Younger?" I asked abruptly. They both turned their eyes back to me. Bonnie looked somewhat confused by the question.

"Kate was with me at the murder," he explained to her. An interesting choice of words.

"Oh, that poor man," Bonnie said, her voice and face both filled with compassion. "He seemed so unhappy. he hardly came to meetings anymore. I felt so sorry for him."

"Bonnie feels sorry for all of us sinners," Ted said, squeezing her affectionately. "Especially us old ones."

Was Ted just a little too eager to explain his wife's concern for Younger? She didn't look concerned about Younger for long, though. She was laughing and staring into Ted's face with adoration again after his last comment.

"How about a look at Bonnie's paintings?" Ted suggested.

I agreed and the three of us climbed the polished wooden stairs to the gallery above the store, leaving the Las Vegas showgirl to mind the hardware. Bonnie's paintings were landscapes, but landscapes as an alien might paint them, stark with an eerie luminescence. There was tension in each painting, as if something was about to explode, a rainstorm or even a nuclear holocaust. How could a fluffy woman like Bonnie produce such spooky images? They made me shiver. Bonnie and Ted didn't shiver. They were cuddling again.

I found myself resenting their romance, and immediately felt guilty. In penance, I bought four kinds of nails and a new hammer. But at least I didn't leave Reisner's Hardware with one of Bonnie's paintings.

It was twelve on the dot when I parked my Toyota in front of Maggie's office. For once the waiting room was empty, filled only by space music and the ever present sterile smell. Renee was at her desk, but she wasn't speaking, at least not to me. Apparently she had not forgotten, or forgiven, my last phone call to her. She pursed her lips and compressed her eyes to barely visible slits in greeting. Was this the face of a murderer?

"She's here," she shouted over her shoulder, all the while watching me through those slits, as if daring me to steal the furniture.

Maggie and Eileen walked down the hall together, suddenly looking very much like lovers to me. True, they were not as obvious as Ted and Bonnie about their relationship. But there was some sort of invisible link between them, which integrated the rhythms of Maggie's lope and Eileen's glide into a solid couple's walk.

They both glanced at my hair but didn't comment. Women usually are more subtle about these things. Though I was surprised at Maggie's show of sensitivity. Maybe Eileen was a good influence on her.

"Don't take too long," Renee commanded. "I want to get out of here on time today. My kids are tired of waiting all afternoon for me in an empty house."

"We'll be back in a flash," Maggie assured her.

"Make it an hour or less flash," Renee muttered.

Maggie chattered all the way down the street about how much I was going to love the Starship Café. It was a really "neat" new restaurant, not to mention "far-out." I noticed she avoided any mention of Wayne, murder—or my hairdo, for that matter.

When we got to the Starship I saw that "far-out" was an understatement. The restaurant's entrance was designed to look like the transporter room in *Star Trek*. And once through the transporter we were met by a space hostess wearing silver tights and a navy blue tunic, who seated us at our table. The table was topped by a silver metallic cloth, and sat under a lamp resembling the planet Saturn, complete with rings.

"Neat, huh?" asked Maggie.

"Neat," I acknowledged.

"Look at the ceiling," she suggested.

I looked up to see a panorama of the night sky painted in shades of midnight-blue and purple, and littered with silvery stars. I was still staring upward when our waiter arrived, also attired in silver tights and a navy blue tunic. I nodded in sudden approval of the uniform. He had great legs.

"Rocket fuel anyone?" he asked, lifting a pot of coffee in our direction. Maggie held out her cup. He filled it, and recited the rest of the available beverages. I chose a Quantum Carrot Juice. Eileen asked for Martian Mint Tea. He told us the soups of the day were Rocket Booster Bean and Split Atom Pea, and then left us with our menus.

The menu was printed on what appeared to be laminated computer printout paper. I ran my eyes over it, searching for dishes without animal products. I reluctantly bypassed the Nova Nachos and the Warp Drive Wiener, narrowing my choices down to the Venusian Veggie Burger or the vegetarian version of the Twenty-First Century Tostada. As I had suspected from the decor, the prices were astronomical. Eileen's gentle voice interrupted my consideration.

"Wayne's a good man," she said softly. "Not a murderer. I just wanted to let you know I believe that."

I looked at her lovely face through suddenly moist eyes, and realized just how much I had longed to hear that assessment of Wayne from someone else. She gave my hand a quick squeeze as our waiter returned to the table, bearing carrot juice and tea.

"So, are we ready to order?" he asked. He looked in my direction, white teeth and blue eyes sparkling. I would have bet he got damn good tips from his female customers.

"Vegetarian tostada, no cheese or sour cream," I answered brusquely, embarrassed by my own libidinous thoughts.

"Veggie burger for me," Eileen said.

"Melt Down Patty," ordered Maggie diffidently.

"That's got a hamburger patty in it, you know," he told her.

"I know, I know!" she said. A little blush was creeping in under her freckles.

Once the waiter had left, Maggie defended her selection to Eileen. "Jeez, one little hamburger isn't going to hurt!"

Eileen lifted sorrowful eyes to Maggie's and said, "It's up to you what you put in your body. You know that." Maggie squirmed in her chair like a bad puppy.

"Are you a vegetarian?" I asked Eileen conversationally. I felt a misguided urge to get Maggie off the hot seat.

"Almost. I still eat fish sometimes."

"Then you're a fish-etarian," I told her and took a sip of my carrot juice.

She smiled gently at the description. Maggie giggled.

"Once I stopped smoking dope, I gradually started cleaning up my body," Eileen said. I noticed she had the same fanatical gleam in her eye that my almost ex-husband Craig had exhibited. Now, that man knew how to make meat eaters miserable. By the time he would finish his description of slaughterhouse conditions, people would either go pale and order something vegetarian, or never speak to him again.

"First no dope, then no alcohol, and then I started looking at my diet," Eileen continued, her lovely smile in place under the gleam of her eyes. "Caffeine, sugar, meat. It really comes down to how much you're willing to pollute your body."

I nodded. But, much as I agreed, I still felt sympathy for Maggie's rebellion. I've often wondered if I would have become an abstemious vegetarian if it hadn't been for Craig's not so gentle nudging.

"Jeez, drugs are one thing. Caffeine and alcohol are another," objected Maggie. Was I in the middle of their current disagreement? "I mean, look at all these people addicted to crack and stuff," she said, her freckled face thrust forward earnestly.

"Look at all the people addicted to alcohol," Eileen responded.

"I know, I know. But lots of people are just fine with a little alcohol," Maggie insisted. I suspected she was talking about herself. "And drugs. Why look at . . ." She braked her tongue for a moment of self-censorship. Was she about to say a client's name? "Look at you-know-who's brother," she said finally, with a significant glance at Eileen. "Their parents escape the black ghetto and heroin and all that, and then the kid goes to college and burns out his brains on psychedelics. Now that's a real bummer, a real tragedy."

Could she be talking about Valerie's brother? I hadn't seen that many black clients at Maggie's. Mill Valley is not known for its ethnic diversity. If it was Valerie, that might explain her antipathy toward drug dealers. My heart jumped. What if Younger had personally sold Valerie's brother drugs? But my thoughts were interrupted by the arrival of our waiter, bearing space food.

I looked down at my Twenty-First Century Tostada. It looked disappointingly ordinary to me. Tortilla and beans with salad, guacamole and salsa on top.

Once the waiter left, I opened my mouth to find out just who Maggie had been talking about. But Eileen's mouth was quicker than mine.

"I agree that's a tragedy," she said. "But how about another unnamed person? You know the one. Her father owned a prescription drug company and was a belligerent alcoholic." That had to be Devi, I thought with excitement. "Then her mother

O.D.'s—not on heroin or anything illegal, mind you—but on prescribed sleeping pills. So her teenage daughter is left at the mercy of a physically and emotionally abusive drunk. Not that he would be called a 'drunk' of course, because he was rich and had a socially approved habit. I know what she went through until she was old enough to leave home. And all because of alcohol.''

I was convinced, if only by the bitterness in Eileen's usually sweet voice. I took a bite of guacamole-garnished lettuce without enjoyment, imagining Devi's ruined adolescence. It had to be Devi they were talking about. No wonder the poor woman was such a space cadet.

''I've tried to get her to an A.C.A. meeting, but I guess she has enough on her plate right now,'' Eileen continued sadly, picking at the veggie burger on her own plate. At least she had spoiled her own appetite as well as mine. Maggie seemed unaffected however, biting into her cheesy hamburger with an appetite bordering on ecstasy. She wiped the grease from her chin and spoke.

''That's alcohol abuse, hon,'' she said in a surprisingly soft tone. ''A little glass of wine at night is not abuse.''

''I really know that,'' Eileen conceded, her voice gentle once more. ''I guess growing up with alcoholic parents has given me a skewed outlook. Not that they were as cruel as her father. And my parents kicked it, both of them. They've been in recovery for seventeen years now. But you're right.'' She turned her South Sea Islands smile on Maggie. ''I'm sorry if I got on your case about the wine.''

Somehow even my tostada tasted better when she smiled at Maggie. I dove into it hungrily. But my mind was churning as fast as I was shoveling beans and lettuce into my mouth.

''Maggie,'' I asked nonchalantly, mid-tostada. ''Was that Valerie you were talking about earlier?''

Maggie looked up from the remains of her hamburger with a guilty start. She obviously hadn't thought I might guess. And she refused to confirm that guess.

''Confidentiality,'' she said. Eileen nodded solemnly.

''But we're talking a murder motive here,'' I insisted. ''I don't see how Devi's experience could be a motive.'' Now Eileen looked startled. She had been indiscreet as well. ''But Valerie— if it was Valerie—can't you see it? Scott Younger was a drug dealer for God's sake.''

Maggie and Eileen looked at each other with identical expressions of concern on their very different faces.

- Eighteen -

I NEVER DID get either of them to confirm Valerie's identity. Or Devi's for that matter.

Eileen became quietly professional. She apologized for the ethical breach and asked me to keep confidential anything that either might have let slip. Maggie exploded in a flurry of self-deprecation. She repeated "Jeez, I have a big mouth," ten or fifteen times in between Eileen's calm sentences. I had to agree with her on that. Though, unfortunately, her mouth was not big enough to positively identify Valerie Davis. She wouldn't even unburden herself when Eileen left her at my mercy to go to the restroom. However, I concluded from all the uproar that I must have guessed correctly.

I did get the name and location of Eileen's parents' nursery from Maggie with no resistance. She was so relieved by my change of subject that she never questioned my interest, and burbled about their sweetness, their roses and their superior potting soil until Eileen returned from the restroom and the three of us left the Starship.

On the way back to my car I saw a familiar wispy figure puffing up the sidewalk toward Maggie's office. It was Devi, swathed in layers of fuchsia, with a jade and fuchsia scarf knotted around her neck. As far as I was concerned, Devi had some questions to answer. Why had she been so hostile to Scott the day of his death? His "bad reputation" wasn't adequate explanation in my book. Just how well had she really known Scott?

I called her name. She looked up at me with a start.

"Oh, Kate," she greeted me, breathless as ever. "I was just going . . ."

"To Maggie's," I finished her sentence for her. "Devi, can I ask you some questions about Scott?" I arranged my face into what I hoped was a disarming smile.

"Well, yes," she replied. "I mean, I guess so. I didn't really know him. Not very well, I mean. But go ahead, if you'd like." She peered in my direction, blinking expectantly and breathing hoarsely.

"How did you know Scott exactly?" I asked.

"Oh, around, at school. At least I thought I knew him, but I didn't really. I mean, how well do we ever really know anyone? I guess God's in all of us, but the way we manifest . . ."

"About Scott," I interrupted. "Why did you dislike him so much?"

"Scott?" she asked, her eyes open and blank.

"Yes, Scott," I said, holding my smile in place with difficulty. She closed her eyes to think and then opened them again, along with her mouth.

"Oh, I don't know. It's hard to explain. I mean, he wasn't a very nice person, was he? His aura was yucky, you know, kind of dark and awful. And then there was the drug thing. . . ." Mid-dithering she glanced down at her wristwatch and back at me in alarm. "Oh, I'm late again! I tried so hard to be on time, and now I'm late again."

On that note, she hurried back down the street to Maggie's without so much as a wave goodbye in my direction. I watched her fuchsia backside disappear through Maggie's door and breathed a sigh of frustration. It was lucky that woman had money, I told myself, because I couldn't imagine her earning her own way in the world. Then I felt a pang of guilt-laced sympathy, remembering what Eileen had said about Devi's abusive father—if it was Devi's father Eileen had been talking about. I didn't even know that for sure. I shook my head, sighed again, and got in my car to go home.

By the time I opened my front door I had done a lot of thinking. About Valerie's brother, Devi's father and Ted's wife, Bonnie, among other things. I walked over to my answering machine absently. It had one message on it.

I thought of Wayne and smiled. I was eager to share the fruits of my investigation with him. In the seconds it took me to rewind the tape I imagined the answering smile on his battered face, and his soft growling praise.

But it was a woman's voice that spoke when I pushed the playback button.

"This is Inez from the law offices of Lee and Davies," the bland voice said. "We have a message for you from Wayne Caruso. Mr. Caruso wanted us to let you know that he may be unable to keep his date with you tonight, since he has been detained by the police for questioning." I stopped breathing. "And he also wanted you to know that he did have time to place the ad that you had discussed." She recited the phone number of Lee and Davies. Then I was listening to the recorded dial tone.

I replayed the tape, hoping I had misheard, but the message remained the same. Afterwards, I stood with my hand frozen on the answering machine, a confusion of thoughts bursting like little bombs in my mind. How long could they detain him? It was only one-thirty in the afternoon and he was expecting to miss his evening with me. Would they really hold him that long? My body had gone entirely numb. Only my mind was frantically functioning to the sound of my shallow breathing. Were they really arresting him? Was that it? It couldn't be. It wasn't fair, my mind whined.

I collapsed into the comforting embrace of my favorite chair and dialed Lee and Davies. Inez answered the phone. She told me she had merely relayed the message given to her by Mr. Lee. She didn't really have any more information. But perhaps Mr. Davies could help me, she suggested.

Mr. Davies was more forthcoming, but no less distressing. He said that his partner, Gary Lee, was representing Wayne. Gary and Wayne had been law-school friends. When I pressed him for details about Wayne's detention, he was initially silent.

"They're leaning on him," he finally replied, his tone apologetically gruff.

"Are they going to arrest him?" I asked, my own vocal cords squeaky with fear.

"We can't tell for sure at this point," he said. But the sigh in his voice told me his estimate of Wayne's predicament was not optimistic.

I thanked him for the information, and hung up the phone gently. Then I cried. I cried for the injustice of Wayne's detention, for the possibility of losing whatever our relationship might have become, and for my own inability to absolutely believe in his innocence. I paused to snatch a Kleenex, blew my nose and burst into renewed tears. Wayne's suffering, my husband's treachery, even memories of the family dog who had died when I was fourteen, all conspired to flood me with misery. I wetly lamented what seemed to me, at that moment, to have been a lifetime of loss and loneliness.

There came a time, finally, when I could cry no more. I picked up the telephone and called Wayne's number. When and if he came home, I wanted him to hear my welcoming voice on his answering machine. I told the machine that I believed in him and wanted to hear from him as soon as he was released, no matter what time. But only after I had hung up did I whisper "I love you," and wonder if it might be true.

I walked over to my desk. It was a time for reason. The solution to the problem was simple. I would find out who Younger's real murderer was and deliver him or her to the police. "Right," my internal critic commented in a voice marinated in sarcasm. But I ignored the critic and cleared my desk of Jest Gifts paperwork as a start. I hadn't seen the bare top of my desk in years. I hurried to cover its nakedness with two pads of lined paper, one for a list of murder suspects and their motives, the other for action items. I have found that list-making has an almost spiritual power to comfort me and focus my thoughts in times of crisis. Probably a result of far too many years of bookkeeping.

Eileen, possible motives: daughter of the boss, other unknown, I wrote. *Action item: visit her parents at the nursery.* It seemed very unlikely that she was the boss's debauched daughter, but I owed it to Wayne to find out for sure, and maybe I would uncover another motive by speaking to her parents.

Maggie was a little more difficult. But there was always her lesbian secret or some unknown threat Younger might have posed to her business. No action item on Maggie, though. I didn't think I could handle another conversation with her right away.

Valerie looked promising. There was her general antipathy to drugs, her daughter, and the possibility that her brother was one of Younger's customers. *Action item: grill her about her brother tonight at dinner.* I was beginning to feel the faint pulse of hope as my action list grew.

Ted, motive: jealousy of Younger's attentions to his wife, Bonnie. Bonnie and Ted deserved another visit. Perhaps their display of mutual affection was just good acting, or maybe Bonnie's current affection for Ted was the engineered result of his murdering Scott Younger.

Devi, motive: some deeply remembered wrong from her college days with Younger. He had been a pretty sleazy guy. Who knew what he might have done to her? From getting her pregnant to . . . To what? I needed to get some real answers out of that woman.

Tanya? What could a fifteen-year-old have against a man she had never met before? I left the space next to Tanya's name blank.

Then I got to Renee. My pulse speeded up. *Motive: a woman scorned.* I had only her word that she wasn't irreparably wounded by her relationship with Younger. And who was there that could contradict her? Her kids, I thought in answer, that's who. Her kids who waited for her alone after school. They would know how she really felt about Scott Younger. *Action item: visit Renee's children for a talk.* And to see if either of them resembled Scott Younger, I reminded myself.

Wayne, I wrote reluctantly. I had to complete my list. *Motive,* take your pick: *money, freedom, mercy-killing.* But I listed no action items. The Mill Valley Police Department were taking care of Wayne.

That was it for suspects, I thought, looking at my lists. No one else had been there, excepting myself. We would have seen anyone else come in the front door. But how about the back door? The thought surprised me. There must be a back door! I even had a vague memory of having seen it.

I called Maggie's office, my hands tingling with excitement. Renee answered the phone. I asked to speak to Maggie.

"Do you want to make an appointment?" asked Renee.

"No, just to talk to her," I responded.

"She's spent enough time talking to you," Renee said. "Call back if you want to make an appointment." Then she hung up.

I could feel the hot flush of anger creeping into my face. I redialed Maggie's number.

"Now, listen," I said as soon as I heard the receiver picked up. "I want to talk to Maggie now."

"Maggie is with a client now," Eileen's benign voice floated over the line. "Can I help you?"

"Uh, yes," I mumbled. "I wanted to know about your back door."

"My back door?" she asked, her voice gently confused.

I decided to start over. "Hi, Eileen. This is Kate," I said. "I was wondering if anyone could have slipped in and out of your office through the back door, the day of Younger's murder."

"We do have a back door," she answered slowly. "But it only opens onto an outside stairway to the offices above us. Because of the way the building is set on the side of the hill," she explained. "And I think it was locked. It usually is. But I'll check on it."

"Who's upstairs?" I asked.

"A dentist is on the top floor. A Rolfer and an acupuncturist are on the middle floor. Do you want me to speak to them?" she asked.

"No, I'll come down and talk to them myself," I answered. I noted this intention in bold letters on the top of my action-items list. "But thanks for offering. And thank you for believing in Wayne," I added softly as an afterthought.

I could almost feel Eileen's answering smile over the phone line. I was glad she was on our side. Once I had hung up, I gathered up my purse and my lists, abandoning my naked desk to drive to Maggie's office for the second time that day.

Renee was not pleased to see me. But she grudgingly announced my arrival to Eileen. This degree of cooperation was probably due to the presence of two new paying patients in the familiar waiting room.

"Why is Renee so angry with me?" I asked Eileen as we walked down the hall toward the back door.

"I've wondered too," she said. "I think it's because she's afraid she might be wrong about Wayne. She thinks he killed a man, and she's helping the police to prove it, but she's not absolutely sure. She knows you care for him and believe he's innocent." Eileen turned her concerned brown eyes on me. "So, whenever she sees you she feels a surge of guilt, and she covers it over with anger."

A kind interpretation from a compassionate human being. Personally, I wondered if Renee's guilt, if that was what her malevolence really masked, might have a cause a little closer to home. Her guilt over murdering Scott. I reminded myself to arrange a talk with her kids as soon as I checked out the upstairs.

The back door was located conveniently between the bathroom and the last treatment room, the one in which Scott

Younger had been bludgeoned to death. I caught Eileen's startled look of realization.

"But it *is* locked," she said.

It certainly was. The door was secured by a push-button lock on the doorknob *and* a slide chain.

"Did the police check this door?" I asked, hoping I was the first to consider its use.

"I know they saw it," she answered. "They asked me if it was kept locked. I had forgotten until now. There were so many questions that day." I remembered the day and the questions, and then, with a sinking sensation, Sergeant Udel. What was he doing to Wayne right now?

"I still want to try the stairs," I said. The door might have been unlocked and then locked later in the confusion. I wanted to know where it led.

She nodded and pulled back the chain to let me out. The door opened outside onto a chilly narrow platform overlooking a steep muddy-looking hill. Glancing up, I saw a wooden staircase that zigzagged up the back of the building with a platform at each level. The whole structure was peeling for want of a paint job, and the stairs were warped with age. I placed my foot on the first step carefully, assuring myself that chiropractic assistance was available if I should fall and break my neck. I grasped the handrail firmly and got a handful of splinters. I jerked my hand back.

"Are you okay?" asked Eileen from the still-open door.

"Fine," I lied. "Do you have any gloves?"

"I'll get you some," she said and disappeared.

I looked out onto the day as I waited. Its grey luminescence reminded me of one of Bonnie's landscapes, filled with the threat of rain, or worse. Eileen returned with a pair of disposable clear plastic gloves. She didn't even ask why I needed them. I liked her better all the time. I put the gloves on, hoping they were thick enough to protect my hands from any more splinters. Then I began my ascent.

The warped steps creaked under my feet as I climbed, and the handrail wobbled in my plastic-coated grasp. But I continued upward, turning and rattling the doorknobs at the second and third platforms with no luck. They were locked securely. Then I mounted the final flight of stairs that led to the roof of the office building. I stepped onto its tar surface and turned around. That was a mistake. I was looking out into open space. And that space was suddenly whirling. I closed my eyes and sat down on the tar with a *whumph*.

Keeping my eyes closed, I breathed deeply until my head stopped spinning and the feel of moisture seeping through my corduroy pants from the wet tar roof spurred me to stand back up. Then I shakily searched the roof for other exits. I found none. No murderer had escaped this way without a waiting helicopter or a pair of wings. My trip back down the stairway was made of deep breaths, quivering legs and plastic-covered sweating hands. I kept my eyes glued to the wall.

"Did you find anything?" asked Eileen when I dove gratefully into the open back door of Maggie's office.

"Nothing but splinters," I answered, pulling off the plastic gloves and holding my prickly hand out to her.

After she had plucked the worst of the splinters out of my hand, with Maggie joining in to coo sympathy, I decided it was time to tackle the building from the inside. Just because the upstairs doors were locked now didn't necessarily mean that they had been locked the day of the murder.

I walked out Maggie's door under Renee's baleful gaze, then turned right and right again, into a second doorway which led to the inside staircase of the building. I ascended that staircase appreciatively, savoring the worn maroon carpet, the smooth wooden handrails, and the safely enclosing beige walls. I climbed all the way to the top floor. The gold and black lettering on the glass door there read PETER O'HARA, DENTIST.

When I opened the door I was met by the dread whine of the dentist's drill and the friendly inquiry of the receptionist.

"Do you have an appointment?" she asked. She was young, Asian and pretty. She was also smiling. I couldn't help but compare her style with Renee's. But this receptionist did not have the monumental task of keeping Maggie on track, I reminded myself.

"No appointment," I hastened to assure her. God forbid I should have my mouth invaded any more often than I had to. "I've come from downstairs. I wanted to ask you a few questions about last Wednesday." I gave her my friendliest "just between us gals" smile.

"Oh, you mean when that man was killed?" she asked, her eyes brightening with excitement.

"That's right," I said. "Did you know him?"

"No, I didn't," she answered, disappointment evident in her

eyes. "No one here did. The police interviewed us all, even the patients that were here that day. Are you a private investigator?" Her last question was whispered.

"Something like that," I whispered back. "Is there a rear door to your office?"

"Yes, but it's always locked," she said. "The police asked us about that too."

I felt my smile fading.

"Sorry," she added.

"It's all right," I told her and turned to leave. "Thank you for your time."

"Have a nice day," she called as I walked out the door. Maybe Renee wasn't so bad after all, I thought. At least she had never resorted to that awful phrase.

I descended the stairway to the second floor. There were two glass doors on that landing, one that led to an acupuncturist and the other to a Rolfer. What a choice.

I have experienced acupuncture firsthand, my friend Barbara having recommended her acupuncturist to me when I had a painful ganglionic cyst on my ankle. After an initial consultation, that acupuncturist, a Mr. Lum, had placed me on a table and asked if there was anything else bothering me physically. Glad of a sympathetic ear, I poured out a ten-minute list of complaints. At one needle per problem, I looked like my grandmother's pincushion by the time Mr. Lum had finished skewering me. In all fairness, none of the needles had been deeply painful individually. Except, of course, for the one in my ankle.

Rolfing was something I hadn't tried personally. I've heard it described as a painful deep-tissue manipulation that restructures your posture and the accompanying mind-set. Not something I was eager to experience.

A known evil being more acceptable, I opened the door to the acupuncturist's office. A large blond woman sat behind a teak desk, which was covered in cacti. One glance at all those nasty little spines was enough to spur me to efficiency. Within three minutes I had ascertained that she was the acupuncturist and that, according to her, she worked alone in her office, did not know Scott Younger, and had no access to the back stairs. The back stairs were reached through the Rolfer's office. I thanked her for the information and hurried out her doorway. Then I turned to the only office left, that belonging to Nancy Thomas, Certified Rolfer.

- Nineteen -

A BLOWUP OF a newspaper advertisement for Rolfing was posted on Ms. Thomas' glass door, beneath her name and title.

"Is your body chronically tense?" it asked. I wiggled my stiff shoulders and neck impatiently. "Do you move with ease, grace and balance?" it continued. I thought defensively of my clumsy ascent to the office rooftop. "How's your posture?" it probed. I straightened my spine with a painful jerk. The advertisement then offered a ten-session series of "connective tissue manipulation." That sounds harmless, I thought. Then I reminded myself that I was not here to "restructure" my body but to ask questions. I opened the door.

Upon entering, I found myself alone in a small Spartan room, its only furnishings a desk and a chair. But I could hear sounds coming from behind the wooden door to the left. Sounds of moans and whimpers. Generally, I try to respect privacy, or to at least be subtle when invading it. But these sounds were too much to ignore in a building where murder had already been committed once.

I crept to the door and opened it slowly. A muscular man wearing nothing but underpants lay on his back on a massage table, his knees drawn up to his stomach in a fetal position. A small dark-haired denim-clad woman was grinding her elbow slowly down the back of his left thigh with the intense concentration of a sculptor working in irreplaceable marble. I had found the source of the moans and whimpers. Was this Rolfing?

My involuntary groan of sympathy alerted the woman to my presence. I slapped on a smile as she turned toward me. She was a middle-aged woman with intense dark eyes. Those eyes were regarding me in a most unfriendly fashion. I did have to admit she had great posture.

"I'm sorry," I said lamely. "There was no one at the desk."

"Take a break, Jason" she said in a surprisingly compassionate tone to the man on the table. "I'll be right back to you." He didn't look delighted by the promise. He stretched his body out on the table and heaved a long, quivering sigh.

She led me back to the reception area and asked in a much less compassionate tone what I wanted.

"I'm from downstairs," I answered, as if this explained everything. "I wanted to ask a few questions about your back door."

"Why?" she asked, her eyes focused unblinkingly on mine.

"Maggie asked me to," I said. The lie sprang out of my mouth much too easily. I shifted my weight guiltily and thought about a career in politics.

She sighed. I took that for assent.

"Do you have a back door?" I asked, knowing full well she did.

"I have a back door and it's always locked. I told the police that."

I opened my mouth for another question.

"I also told the police I didn't know the dead man and did not see clients that Wednesday," she added, without a change in expression.

"Well, thank you," I said and turned to go.

"Wait," she commanded. I turned back hopefully. "Did you know that your left shoulder is higher than your right? Have you ever considered Rolfing?" she asked.

"No," I answered. She looked ready to tell me more about it. "But I read your ad. I'll certainly consider it."

I turned and took my graceless, stiff, malformed body through her door, down the stairs and out onto the street with a sense of relief marred only briefly by the visions of drills, needles and elbows that lingered as I emerged into the cold bright day. Looking back at the building with new perspective, I suddenly recognized it for what it was, a New Age torture chamber.

My relief at having escaped its upper floors gave way to a grinding sense of failure as I stood there. What had I learned? Only that it was highly unlikely that the murderer had used the back staircase. Or so the tenants would have had me think. But what if one of them had lied? Damn. There was really no way I could be sure they had told me the truth. And none of this was helping Wayne any. I returned my thoughts to my original set of suspects, focusing on Renee.

I looked through the window of Maggie's office. Renee was working quietly at her desk. There were two patients in their chairs, reading magazines. I wanted to talk to Renee's children. All I needed was an address and some luck. I opened the door and stepped in.

"What do you want now?" she hissed when I reached her desk. I could just see the top of the sheet of paper she was working on.

"To talk to Eileen or Maggie again," I answered. I didn't need to tell Renee what I wanted from them was her address. My eyes focused on the paper beneath her hand. It was her bank statement.

"No way; they've spent enough time with you today," she said, readying herself for further argument.

But I didn't have to argue with Renee. I could see her name and address at the top of her bank statement. I transposed the upside-down letters to right-side-up as fast as I could. *Mickle*, that's right, *675 Willard Avenue, San Rafael*. Renee noticed my focus and turned the paper over with a slap. But she was too late. I didn't need her zip code.

"Well, thank you anyway," I said sweetly and left.

I glanced over my shoulder as I went through the door. Renee's mouth was gaping. She saw my glance and snapped it tightly shut. I hurried to my car, only pausing briefly to jot the address down as soon as I was out of Renee's line of sight.

I decided to drive to San Rafael as I thought up a plan. It was three o'clock. I hoped that Renee's latchkey kids would be home, and that Renee would be held up at the office for at least another hour or two. It was time to strike.

But how was I going to get them to talk to me? I considered what Renee had told me about her children as I pulled onto the highway. Her boy, John, liked punk rock, I remembered. So what could I do with punk music? And her daughter. What was her name? Something very young California. Kimberly, that was it. She liked malls, I thought, as I saw the sprawl of the Marin Shopping Center approaching on the right-hand side of the highway. And stuffed animals! I pulled my steering wheel sharply to the right and screeched toward the exit ramp. I was going shopping.

Zoe's Ark was aptly named. Her store sold a stuffed version of almost every beast, clean or unclean, that Noah could have had for company during the flood. Plus a few he might not have ever met, like tribbles, dinosaurs, soft robots, unicorns and wookies.

I walked into the store and was immediately swept away by the magic of the animals. I fondled a small plush otter and patted the head of a life-sized pony. I was playing with a comically bobble-eyed cat puppet when I remembered what I was there for. Think twelve-year-old, I reminded myself. Then I turned and saw him. A six-foot-tall white Snoopy dog with black floppy ears, a black ball of a nose and black yarn eyes creased into a smile. *I* certainly couldn't resist. And I was sure Kimberly wouldn't be able to either. Of course, I made my living with joke gifts. I was predisposed toward cute.

The cuteness began to wear off when I wrote the check. Anything over two figures always makes me a little shaky. And I was giving this away. The cuteness completely evaporated while I was lugging the dog out the door to my car. I hadn't realize how heavy six feet of fluff could be.

I laid him across the back seat of my Toyota, but his feet hung out the doorway. Was this how it must be to dispose of a dead body? At least rigor mortis hadn't set in. I folded his legs up, but before I could shut the door they flopped back out. Damn. Maybe I could pull his head up. I climbed in the back seat, trying to straddle the dog without putting my weight on him, but I just sank into his considerable girth. I had a sudden flash of how sexual, not to mention bestial, this position must look and glanced back out the open door. Sure enough, a small crowd had gathered to watch me ravish the innocent dog. A tall redheaded man winked at me.

"Let him sit up," his little girl suggested.

It was good advice. I pulled Snoopy up into sitting position, seat-belted him in and drove off, with all the dignity that could be expected of a woman chauffeuring a stuffed dog.

This is the way I pictured my interview with Kimberly and John, on my way up the highway: I would bring the stuffed dog to the door and introduce myself as a friend of Renee's, with a gift for Kimberly. The children would be so overwhelmed by the magnificence of the gift that they would invite me in for a friendly conversation. (When I was that age I would have told a stranger anything about my parents in exchange for a stuffed animal taller than myself. I just hoped Renee's kids weren't too hip for such an approach.) Once I got them talking I would lead them into a discussion of their mother's feelings toward the late Scott Younger.

A wave of ethical queasiness overtook me. What if I was successful? What if the innocence of Renee's children led them to tell me something that might help to convict their mother? I shook the queasiness off and thought of Wayne being held by the police, perhaps because of whatever Renee had told them about him. And I was only going to question the kids. I could decide later what to do with anything of importance that they told me.

The address on Renee's bank statement was a modest three-storied redwood apartment building, dotted with balconies. I parked my car on the street and walked up to the front entrance. I was in luck. Nobody was in the lobby. And I found a listing of 2D for Mickle on the mail slots. I went back to my car and retrieved the stuffed dog. I dragged him up a carpeted stairway to the second floor.

Apartment 2D was at the end of the hall. Something like music was coming from that direction, something made up of voices angrily shouting to the accompaniment of screeching amplified guitars. I hesitated, then knocked loudly. The sound of the music stopped abruptly, and I heard footsteps.

The boy who answered the door had a shaved head that was tattooed with a red circle and a cross near his temple. He wore khaki fatigues and black lace-up boots, but he looked too young for the army. The blue eyes that stared out of his head were a match for Renee's. He narrowed those eyes as he looked at me and then at the stuffed dog.

"Yeah," he said. The word was infused with enough hostility to make me step backward. There was no sign of the girl.

"You must be John," I answered with false cheeriness. "I have a present for Kimberly."

"Yeah," he said again. "Who are you?"

"Suzanne," I answered, remembering Craig's new girlfriend's name. I only wished I had known her last name so I could really get her in trouble.

"Yeah, so?" he snarled.

"Is Kimberly in?" I tried.

"No," he answered. Damn. I looked into his glowering eyes and tried to think of an appropriate conversational gambit. Heavy metal? Neo-Nazism? Tattooing? No, I decided, I just couldn't carry it off, not even with my new haircut. I told myself to act normal.

"Do you think Kimberly will like this one as much as the one Scott Younger gave her?" I asked, adopting a cheerful tone again. I nodded at the dog in my arms.

"What the fuck are you trying to pull here?" he asked, his eyes narrowing even further. Then he advanced on me, arms and shoulders stiff, hands balling into fists.

"Never mind," I said quickly. "Give this to your sister."

I shoved Snoopy into his stiff arms and left without looking back.

As I drove away I hoped that Kimberly would actually enjoy the stuffed dog. Maybe its fluffy smile could compete with her brother's surly scowls. Then I wondered what Scott Younger could have found attractive about John as a surrogate child. Did he identify with the boy's anger? love him for qualities of character that I was unable to perceive upon one meeting? perhaps just view him with aloof amusement? Or was John just a boy only his real father could love? I shrugged. I would have to find a way to talk to Kimberly without John.

Once in my front door, I walked quickly to my answering machine, hoping for a message from Wayne. But the only message was from my warehousewoman, Judy, demanding my usual daily call to Jest Gifts. I dutifully called in, but my heart was not in funny cups and Christmas ornaments that day. Judy berated me about my negligence for a while, but softened when she convinced herself that I must be sick with the latest flu. I didn't challenge her conviction. She advised me to take a hot bath and lots of aspirin, and then hung up.

I went back to my desk to study my action-item list. I could check off one visit to Renee's kids and the exploration of the office building's backside. But the check marks were a poor substitute for any real discovery. I turned the list over and dropped my head into my hands. All the sadness and dread that my frantic activity had kept at bay came rolling back over me. Keep moving, I told myself sharply. I turned the list back over and sought the next action-item.

It was time to talk to Devi again. She had known Scott, no matter how far back that connection was. She was a source of information and I was determined to pin her down. I dialed the number she had given me.

"Hello," answered a young voice. It had to be Tanya.

"Is Devi there?" I asked.

"No." She was succinct as Devi was diffuse.

"May I leave a message? Can you ask her to call Kate Jasper at . . ." She cut me off before I could leave my phone number.

"She doesn't want to talk to you," Tanya said, and slammed down the phone.

Boy, did I have a way with adolescents! I decided it was time to interview some older folks.

I found Garza's Nursery listed in the telephone book. It was located in San Anselmo, just as Maggie had said. My watch read four fifteen. Just enough time to visit them before they closed. I looked at my telephone longingly, willing Wayne to call me and tell me he was released, and the real murderer discovered. But it remained silent.

On the drive to San Anselmo, I surveyed the clear weather resentfully. How could the skies have turned so bright and blue just as Wayne's prospects had become so murky? But it was good weather for a nursery.

Garza's was located in an attractive Spanish-style stucco-and-tile building which opened onto a quarter acre's worth of cement patio filled with flats of plants. A small, attractive brown woman was cheerfully ringing up sales at the register. Eileen's mother? On the patio, a slightly taller and browner man was assisting customers, who were nervously eyeing the sky and frantically gathering annuals, perennials, shrubs and vegetables to plant in their gardens while the weather held.

I wandered in the primrose section as the woman rang up flowering plants, seeds, fertilizer, bulbs and even squares of lawn sod, and the man calmly fielded anxious questions about frost, fuchsia blight and fast-sprouting grass seed. His serenity under the barrage of questions convinced me he was Eileen's father.

Finally there was a lull between customers. The register stopped ringing and the patio was empty except for me and a few hundred thousand green life-forms. The man moved to join the woman behind the counter. I grabbed two six-packs of fairy primroses and followed him.

"Are you the Garzas, Eileen's parents?" I asked conversationally, setting my primroses on top of the counter.

"Why, yes," replied the woman. Her tone was pleased, her

words slightly accented. "Where do you know our Eileen from?"

"I'm a patient of Maggie's."

"Oh, that Maggie," she said, nudging her husband. "Such a character. But we love her." Mr. Garza smiled and nodded. He put an arm around his wife's waist. The boss? Impossible. But I had to try.

"Didn't I know one of your children at Crocker?" I fished.

A pleasant look of inquiry settled onto Mr. Garza's weathered face. "Crocker?" asked Mrs. Garza. She too looked mildly confused.

"The school," I explained. "North of here."

"Oh, I know where you mean," said Mr. Garza, comprehension now evident in his expression. He turned to his wife. "That expensive college. Where Mrs. Peter's son, Jerry, goes."

"Oh, that one," she said. "No, our kids didn't go to expensive schools. Couldn't afford to. But all three of our kids have graduated from college." She told me about her children. A boy who was a CPA, a girl who was a pediatrician, and Eileen, who was soon to be a chiropractor herself. She asked me what I did. I told her about Jest Gifts. They nodded appreciatively.

Finally, after we had run out of small talk, Mrs. Garza rang up my primroses. Her husband picked up an African violet plant from a shelf and handed it to me.

"A gift, for a friend of Eileen's," he said. I accepted the gift from those rough and calloused hands and decided once and for all that he couldn't be the boss.

I could feel myself blushing as I turned to leave. I promised myself that as expiation for my terrible suspicions I would buy all my gardening supplies at Garza's Nursery for the rest of my life.

Arriving home, I dropped the primroses I was carrying in one hand onto the deck and rushed into the house to see if Wayne had called in my absence. My answering machine had a new message. African violet still in the other hand, I hit the playback button. Craig's voice emerged.

"Are you really there?" he demanded. A new, whining tone in his voice had marred its smooth surface. "You are going to be sensible now, aren't you?"

- Twenty -

I ERASED MY soon-to-be ex-husband's message. Sensible? A woman who had given an expensive six-foot ball of fluff-dog to a skinhead? Guess again. Hurriedly, I chose an outfit for my visit to Valerie's ashram, refusing to allow myself time either to return Craig's call or to review the day's futile investigations.

What does one wear to visit a spiritual center? I threw on black corduroys, a black turtleneck and a purple sweater. Purple was a mystical color. And black? The color of death, mourning and depression. I told myself I just happen to look good in black.

I had left my house, pumped gas into my Toyota, and was on the highway headed toward the Marin Ashram, spiritual home of Guru Illumananda, before my fear about visiting a religious institution resurfaced. The fear came back in a sweaty remembrance of a childhood visit to a Catholic church with my grandmother. Suddenly, I was drenched in the long forgotten darkness of that church and the eerie sounds of those disembodied voices raised to God. I felt again the unaccustomed scarf tied tightly under my chin, which served to remind me that I didn't belong and might be unmasked and turned upon at any moment.

I tightened my grip on the steering wheel and brought myself back to the present. Not that the present was any great improvement. But at least Valerie had invited me to visit her ashram. That was a relief after a day of barging in on people uninvited, to ask unwelcome questions.

What was it that Valerie wanted to explain to me? I couldn't believe that she would choose me to hear her confession of murder. That wouldn't make sense. And if she was planning to do away with me, she wouldn't have so graciously agreed to my bringing Wayne along. With a lurch I remembered why Wayne was not coming with me. Damn. I had actually managed to forget for a few minutes.

I concentrated on preparing my questions for Valerie. I had quite a few. Why had she been so angry with Scott Younger the day he was killed? How did she know he had been a drug dealer? And how about her brother? Had Scott sold drugs to him? Is that why she killed Scott? Little old questions like that. I spent the rest of the drive trying to think of a slightly more subtle way to ask those questions.

The directions in the ashram brochure led me past the soft sensual hills of open range land into the northernmost reaches of Marin. I was glad I had gassed up my car, and relieved when I finally saw the well-lit sign that announced simply MARIN ASHRAM. I pulled into the parking lot with a strong sense of having been there before. Briefly, I wondered if I was experiencing some kind of spiritual homecoming. But then I realized that I *had* been there before.

This was the site of the old El Paso Inn. I looked at the wooden buildings in the fading light and remembered the motel, resort cottages, restaurant and bar as they had been. The bar had hosted live country music, uninhibited dancing, and innumerable seductions. The adjacent motel was perfect for a little country cheatin'. A recently divorced girlfriend had taken me there one night when Craig was out of town, assuming I would be up for a bit of adulterous intrigue in his absence. I had taken a taxi home as soon as I recognized the misguided game plan, leaving her happily swaying in the drunken embrace of a weekend cowboy. Sitting there in my car, ten years later, I wondered if I too should have indulged.

Once I got out of my car and went to the "you are here" map I saw that things had changed. The bar was now a meditation sanctuary, the old prime rib restaurant a vegetarian dining hall, and the hotel lobby an information and registration center. Behind the main building were a newly built auditorium, bookstore and art gallery.

Valerie hadn't told me exactly where to meet her, so I walked over to the registration center. The smell of incense wafted on the air as I opened the door, and the sound of many voices buzzed against a background of celestial electronic sitars.

Once inside the old El Paso lobby, I saw something that looked

like an airport ticket counter. Four separate lines of seekers were
bellying up to the peach-colored counter where men and women
in matching white jumpsuits answered their questions and took
their reservations. On the sky-blue wall high above their heads,
television monitors listed the offerings of the Marin Ashram. There
were beginning courses and workshops in meditation, yoga,
chanting and vegetarian cooking, just for starters. Then there
were the more esoteric offerings in Kundalini, goddess energy,
sadhana and fire-walking. Some of these were evening courses,
but most were week-long seminars complete with accommoda-
tions. A metaphysical Disneyland. Boldly radiating letters
proclaimed an upcoming personal appearance by Guru Illumananda.

The buzz of voices was as soft and polite as the pastel decor, but an undercurrent of excitement tingled through the room.
What were they so excited about? I was completely lost in the
question when I felt a light tap on my shoulder. I whirled around
to see Valerie, her six feet imposing and erect as ever, in a
flowing cream-colored caftan.

"God, you scared me," I hissed.

"I'm sorry," she replied in a gentle voice. She smiled down
at me. Now I was embarrassed.

"Are there always so many people here?" I asked, pointing
to the lines.

"Not usually, but Guru Illumananda is going to visit."

"When is she coming?"

"In February." Valerie's eyes began to sparkle.

"But that's three months away," I objected. This was no
Grateful Dead concert we were talking about. Why were these
people lined up three months ahead of time?

"Ah, but Guru Illumananda is the living embodiment of supreme bliss."

What's the comeback to a statement like that? I said, "Oh."

"So where is Wayne?" she asked.

"He's . . . He's being questioned by the police." I was surprised at how hard it was to say the words. I felt the prickle of
impending tears.

Valerie patted my shoulder and changed the subject. A truly
sensitive woman. Maybe there was something to all of this guru
stuff. "Want to go to the dining hall?" she asked.

A peek through the dining-hall door told me that all traces of
the old prime rib restaurant had been erased. Antlers, dark wood
grain and black leather booths had given way to mauve plaster,

long white tables and portraits of Eastern saints. Valerie told the sari-clad doorwoman that I was with her. We swept past a line of people surrendering their dining tickets, into the crowded hall. Valerie sat me down between herself and a plump, blond young woman who began gushing about Guru Illumananda the minute my bottom hit my chair.

"I am so blessed," she kept repeating. Her eyes were as round as silver dollars and just as shiny. "Have you experienced Guru Illumananda's love?" she asked.

The sound of a gong saved me from having to answer. With that sound all the people at the tables and even those still in line at the door began to chant. The "om" began as a low hum and slowly swelled in volume and intensity. I could see the peace on the faces of those surrounding me, but that didn't make the group energy any less disturbing for me. Old fears arose. I kept my own lips stubbornly pressed together, as if to dare the inevitable unmasking and expulsion of the infidel.

The chanting came to an abrupt close. That was the signal for women in saris to begin serving our food. I turned my face to Valerie before the blond on my other side could gush at me any more. Over a first course of *dal* (a soupy dish of spicy lentils) and *chapatis* (a thicker, Indian equivalent of tortillas) Valerie told me how she came to be at the Marin Ashram.

"I first met Guru Illumananda when I was two years out of prison." As she spoke, a muscle began twitching spasmodically in her face, just above her jaw bone. Her dark eyes searched mine for a reaction.

"I heard about your prison record," I told her. She let out a breath, but the muscle twitched on. The waitress began retrieving the first-course dishes.

"Thank you. Sometimes it's difficult to tell people the first time." She forced a smile onto her tense face, and went on. "When I first met my Guru, I knew I had found my path. Now, I've committed my life to . . ."

The waitress spilled some leftover *dal* on the shoulder of Valerie's cream-colored caftan. Valerie turned on her.

"Shit! What you think you doing, girl. You stupid or something!"

My mouth must have dropped open as I stared at her. Catching my look, as well as the looks of the others at the table, Valerie issued a snort of laughter and apologized politely to the waitress. The waitress nodded in confusion, smoothed the folds of her sari and collected the rest of the plates. Once the waitress was gone, Valerie turned back to me, a sheepish expression on her usually proud face.

"Some habits are hard to break. I learned to talk like that in prison. I had to, to survive. I sure didn't learn that kind of talk at home, let me tell you. But, then, I learned yoga in prison, too. Even if I did lose the first years of my daughter's life." Her eyes were soft and out of focus. "Perhaps prison was one of those obstacles meant to liberate." She laughed again and the focus returned to her eyes.

"What was your family like?" I asked. I was eager to follow the lead-in from "home" to her brother. But before she could answer, the waitress returned with our main course. She put a dish in front of Valerie carefully, then jerked her hand back.

"I really am sorry for snapping at you," Valerie said to the woman. She reached out and touched her hand softly. "I won't do it again, I promise you. If I do, just pour some water over my head to cool me down, okay?" A smile blossomed on the waitress's face. "Okay?" asked Valerie again.

"Okay, it's a deal," said the waitress, with a little bow. "We all have these karma attacks once in a while."

The main course included basmati rice, curried garbanzo beans and vegetables with fresh apple/raisin chutney, and some hot vegetable fritters called *pakoras*. I took a bite of a hot *pakora* and let the rich spicy flavor melt in my mouth. Then I tasted the chutney. Yum. Indian food is often three parts grease, sugar and spice to one part vegetable. Not exactly health food. But delicious to those with strong stomachs. I gobbled my way through the food on my plate in silence, almost forgetting Valerie. I decided against licking my plate clean before reintroducing the subject of Valerie's family.

"How does your family feel about your life here?" I asked. She was finishing up the last of the curry. I watched her enviously.

"My folks think I'm nuts," she said with her mouth full. "And after doing their part in raising my daughter, they weren't very happy to see her become part of the community here. But Hope went off to college anyway this year, pre-med, so they're satisfied. And they are gracious enough to be happy for my bliss. I even think they understand it a little, every once in a while."

She wiped her lips with her napkin and continued. "I'm not a success in their eyes. I exchange services here for room and board. And I work part time selling dresses at Larkspur Landing. Not exactly what you call a career. They would have preferred me to be a doctor, or at least to have married one. I'm sorry to have disappointed them."

"You could always go back to school," I suggested.

"I've considered just that. But I'm not really committed to completing my education. And I am committed to a path of grace. I'm not sure I could do both. So, I choose the inner awareness of truth, the greater wisdom." Her serious expression softened once more. "Except that the greater wisdom doesn't exactly account for my parents." She shook her head ruefully.

"Do you have sisters? Brothers?" I asked innocently.

"One brother," she answered.

Our dessert arrived at that moment, an unidentifiable fruit in sugary syrup accompanied by a chocolate chip cookie. I was ready to snap at the waitress myself. I had done so well leading up to Valerie's brother before food intruded. I watched Valerie spoon fruit into her mouth. Would it be too rude to pursue the subject of her brother when her mouth was so occupied? She had talked with her mouth full before. I was formulating a question when the blond gusher on my other side asked if I wanted my dessert.

I said "No" and let her take it. I didn't need any more sugar. The main course had been a hypoglycemic mine field. She thanked me profusely and started up about her many blessings again as she slurped. I turned away as soon as I could, only to encounter Valerie's wink.

"The new ones are always like that," she whispered.

"Eating extra desserts?"

"No." She laughed. "Going on about the blessings of the Guru." She caught the look in my eye. "Okay, Okay. I guess us old ones go on too. But the love I have for Guru Illumananda helps me to transcend. And I have had a lot to transcend, believe me."

"Don't we all," I agreed offhandedly.

"Yes," she answered pointedly. Her steady look into my eyes went straight to my heart and released a painful series of longings in me. Longings for the guidance of a human representative of God, for the love of a community of spirit, and for the Truth with a capital "T" as the Marin Ashram knew it.

But I stubbornly stuffed the longing back where it came from. My solitary meditations had brought me rare glimpses of the infinite, my own truth, with a small "t." I would continue on my unsociable inner path. It was the path I knew, the low road to God, and you'll be in Scotland before me.

Valerie smiled and touched my hand as if she had heard my thoughts. She seemed like pretty good Guru material herself, right then.

The hall was filling with the rumble of people pulling back their chairs and leaving. They had finished their desserts and were eager to go to the auditorium to see Guru Illumananda, even if she was only a flickering image on videotape. I also slid back my chair to get up, but Valerie motioned me to remain seated.

"We have some time before the video," she said. "I'd like to talk to you some more."

All thoughts of God and transcendence left me. The devotees were flocking out of the room like homing pigeons. Soon Valerie and I would be alone in the dining hall. I looked at her serene face and no longer saw Guru material. I saw murderer material.

"I want to tell you why I blew up at Scott," she began. "Is that all right?" She cocked her head in inquiry. She was allowing me a choice. Had she sensed my panic?

I nodded my head. My panic began to recede.

"I have a brother, Gregory," she said. "Two years younger than me. When he was a kid he was a math whiz, always in a book, always doing problems. He loved brainteasers." She was looking up over my head now, remembering. "My parents were so proud of him. They thought he'd be a mathematician or a physicist at least. First black President even." Valerie shook her head and laughed. "He graduated top of his class in high school. Got a scholarship to Crocker." She paused. The muscle in her face was twitching again.

Suddenly, I wanted to tell her that I knew about Crocker, that she didn't have to tell me the sad tale. But maybe I didn't know the whole story. I thought of Wayne and kept quiet.

"At first, Gregory did fine at Crocker," she continued. "But then he started taking drugs, mostly psychedelics. Acid, mescaline, peyote, anything he could get his hands on. Some people can handle that stuff. He couldn't. He got weirder and weirder. He dropped out of school. Lived on the street for a while. Got rousted by the police over and over. He got himself a job at an ice cream store once. He kept it for three weeks. And on, and on." Her voice was exhausted. "You've known people like that, right?" she asked suddenly.

I nodded. I'd known a few. She didn't have to tell me the details.

"By the time I got out of prison, Gregory had come back home to live with my parents. He had stopped taking the heavy psychedelics, but he wouldn't stop smoking dope. My parents pretended they didn't know what he was smoking. And his motivation was gone. No physicist. No mathematician. He couldn't even hold down a janitor's job for more than a month." She paused.

"I saw the waste of a man who had been my shining star of a brother. There was nothing behind his eyes anymore. Just space. I couldn't believe it." Valerie's voice was bitter now, her eyes narrowed in anger. "Not that I hadn't seen what drugs could do to people. In prison, I saw the grief drugs brought people every day. But he was my brother!

"So I came back to the Bay Area and did some community organizing. Became part of an organization called Drug Watch. First, we found out who the drug dealers were. We had connections all over—cons, ex-cons, police, even rival drug dealers. And we didn't bother with the obvious guys on the corners. We found out who the big dealers were. The ones that were getting rich. The ones that the police knew about but couldn't touch.

"Then we went public. We published a newsletter naming names. We put posters up on phone poles, kiosks and bulletin boards, with lists of local citizens who made their money from drugs. We even picketed their houses. So their neighbors would know just who lived on their block. We went on talk shows, talked to newspapers. We did a lot of nasty shit."

Suddenly she grinned. "I have to admit I enjoyed it. I had a lot of rage in those days. But then I met Guru Illumananda. After a while I just didn't have the anger to fuel me anymore. Except when something came up to remind me."

"Like Scott Younger?" I prompted.

She looked at me like she had forgotten where she had started her story. Then she nodded.

"Like Scott Younger. I had never met him personally, but I knew his name from Drug Watch. When I saw the smug yuppie face that went with that name, and remembered my brother's empty eyes, I exploded. I do have a temper." I looked at her strong dark features, now chiseled by remembered anger into frightening severity.

"Uh-huh!" I agreed fervently.

She threw her head back and laughed, long and loud.

- Twenty-One -

HER LAUGHTER ECHOED through the now deserted dining hall. We were the only people left among the remains of the feast.

"You know what I do now for my temper?" Valerie asked. Her eyes were gleaming.

I shook my head. I hoped it wasn't anything violent.

"I laugh," she said with the intonation of a comedian delivering a punch line. As audience, I dutifully produced a nervous chuckle. Even that wasn't easy. I was still caught in the pathos of her brother's life story.

"Guru Illumananda taught me that. I don't think I really laughed once in my entire adult life before I met her. Everything was serious. Everything was a cause. She taught me to laugh." Valerie did look better for the laughter. The tension was gone from her face.

"Whatever happened to your brother?" I asked. I had to know the end of the story. I braced myself for further tragedy.

"He's a computer programmer now. How do you like that? Not what my parents hoped for maybe, but enough. Just like my life is enough." Upon that positive note she rose to leave the hall.

But the heart-to-heart was not over as far as I was concerned. Now I motioned her to sit back down. She stood looking at me for a moment, head cocked quizzically, and then gracefully lowered herself back down into her chair.

"Was Scott Younger the one who sold your brother drugs?" I asked. Valerie's face grew serious again.

"I suspected as much. He was selling drugs at Crocker at the time my brother went there. But I don't know for certain. And I'm not sure it's even important to me anymore."

I looked into her face and believed her. At that moment, it was probably not important to her whether Scott Younger had been the individual who sold her brother psychedelics. But I had seen her personality shift firsthand. The question was not whether this transcendent Valerie cared, but rather whether the angry Valerie would have cared, cared enough to kill over. How could I answer that one? I moved on.

"Why did you want to tell me about your brother?" I asked. Valerie leaned forward in her chair with a little sigh.

"When the police questioned me about Younger's death I panicked. Prison is . . . is unimaginably terrible." The mahogany sheen of her skin greyed as she spoke. "Not even so much prison itself, as the person you must be to survive there. I don't ever want to go back. And I have a record. I was afraid the police would decide that I had killed Scott Younger, and fill in the blanks with evidence that supported that decision. Whether I killed him or not." She looked me in the eye. "And I didn't kill him."

Pinned by her eyeball, I found myself nodding in agreement, although I wasn't really sure I believed her. She went on.

"I meditated on my fears. And my Guru's voice came to me. She told me that total openness would save me. To tell the police everything. So I did. Then Maggie said you were going to find out who killed Younger. So I decided to tell you too. This way there are no terrible secrets to be uncovered, no wrong conclusions to be drawn."

"I see," I said slowly. For all of her openness, I was still uneasy with the interview.

"But primarily," she said with a sudden burst of energy, "I wanted to introduce you to Guru Illumananda." She sprang up and reached for my hand. "So, let's go."

I had to admit that Valerie's guru had presence, even on the video screen. Her lecture on "Siddhas, the Path of Grace," was sensible, intelligent and witty. And she embodied serene enlightenment. But I felt no connection to her, no spark of awakening spirit. So I sat alone and unmoved in a sea of rapt devotees who hung on her every word, and wondered if Valerie had killed Scott Younger.

There was still no call from Wayne when I returned home at nine o'clock. That meant that the police had been questioning Wayne for over eight hours. What kind of questions could take that long? Serious ones, I answered myself. I didn't want to think about it anymore. I turned off the answering machine and turned up the volume of the telephone bell. When Wayne called I wanted to answer the phone personally.

Then I went to bed, where I was visited by hopelessness instead of sleep. I lay stiffly on my back. No murder solution. I turned on my left side, seeking comfort. No Wayne. I turned on my right side. No spiritual enlightenment. I curled my body into fetal position. Not even a cat. C.C. had gone night-prowling. I straightened out and lay on my back again. After repeating this performance a few hundred times I succeeded in twisting both my sheet and my mind into a labyrinthine tangle.

I threw off the sheets angrily. Then I got up and did paperwork in my pajamas until three o'clock. When I returned to bed I managed to untangle the sheets, but I never did quite untangle my mind.

I got almost two hours' sleep before the telephone rang. Drowsily, I waited for the answering machine to kick in. Then I remembered I had turned it off for Wayne's call. I jumped out of bed and ran groggily down the hall, bouncing off the walls like a human pinball a couple of times along the way.

"Wayne?" I shouted eagerly when I picked up the phone.

"Yes," his voice answered. I felt warm relief flooding my body. "Didn't mean to wake you. Thought you'd have the machine on." His voice sounded strange, devoid of feeling. My relief began to ebb.

"You are home, aren't you?" I asked. "They did let you go?"

"For now," he replied. Still no enthusiasm in his voice. It might have been a robot's. Now I felt very cold standing there in the dark in my pajamas.

"Anyway," he continued, his voice tinged with the faintest of feeling, "I got your message. Wanted to let you know I was home." He paused. "Thank you for caring." On the last words his voice cracked.

"Oh God," I said. "I do care. It'll be all right. You'll see." I was babbling.

"Kate, you shouldn't . . ." He stopped.

I waited for him to finish.

"Sorry," he said finally. "I'm just too tired. Need some sleep." I looked at the clock. It was almost five in the morning. Had they questioned him for sixteen hours? No wonder he was tired.

"Go to sleep," I said. "Don't try to explain now. Will you come over when you wake up?"

"If you want. But I shouldn't involve you." His voice had gone dead again.

"We'll talk about it when you come over. Don't worry now," I said, willing my shaky voice into a soothing tone. I wanted to ask him if he thought he was going to be arrested, but it wasn't the right time.

"Will eleven or twelve be okay?" he asked.

"Perfect," I said. "See you then."

After Wayne hung up I went back to bed. I lay hovering in that twilight zone between waking and sleeping for half an hour. Black and white horror images startled me into wakefulness each time I began to drift back to sleep. Wayne in prison, Valerie in prison, Wayne gruesomely executed to the delight of cheering crowds. I gave up on bed.

I went to the bathroom and ran steaming hot water into the tub. While it was filling, I chose a volume of *Far Side* cartoons to read. Judy had suggested a hot bath for my flu. I didn't have the flu, but I was certainly heartsick. I shed my pajamas and stepped into the tub, deriving a good measure of masochistic joy from the searing heat of the water. Then I opened my book of cartoons and began to sweat.

Two hours later I woke up shivering in cool water. C.C. was yowling. How could she claw my lap if she had to go underwater to get there? And my *Far Side* lay soggily at the bottom of the tub. It was the beginning of another day.

I showered and dressed. My new hairdo looked a little better after being washed, but not much. The morning was appropriately overcast. I went to the kitchen, fed the cat, stirred some oatmeal into boiling water, and tried to clear my brain of fuzz. Not an easy task. Four hours of interrupted sleep does not begin to un-fuzz a brain like mine, especially under stress. I had started working on a mental to-do list, my version of brain calisthenics, when the doorbell rang.

Wayne? I rushed to the door and threw it open. My heart was racing. It stopped when I saw who was on my porch. Two rubbery smiling Reagans.

I tried to slam the door, but the stocky one already had his foot and most of his body inside. I executed a swift tai chi backstep before thinking. It took me temporarily out of arm's reach, but now both the Reagans were inside my hallway. I looked out my doorway for a source of rescue, but the weekday morning neighborhood looked deserted as usual. The tall Reagan saw my look and shut the door. So much for rescue.

"Hi," I said. I was aiming for a friendly, casual note. I hit high and squeaky. My body began to tremble. I wasn't sweating yet. I wondered idly if the hot bath had boiled all the sweat out of me.

"Lady, it's been forty-eight hours," the stocky one boomed. Hugo, I remembered, that was his name. I asked myself how I could have forgotten these guys. Because I had. Wayne's detention had wiped them from my mind.

"Wayne burned those pictures as soon as Scott died," I said. I kept my voice as low and steady as possible.

"We saw the fuckin' ad," Hugo replied. There was a trace of uncertainty in his deep voice. He turned and looked at the tall one. The tall one nodded. I had no idea what the signal meant. Their masks hid all facial expression.

"Perhaps we could sit down?" suggested the tall Reagan.

"Oh, I'm sorry," I apologized. Mere terror had not extinguished my social reflexes. I led them to the living room. The tall one sat on the couch. I sat in the swinging chair. Hugo remained standing.

"We were not able to visit Mr. Caruso yesterday," said the tall one. "He was gone all afternoon and evening."

"The police were questioning him," I said.

"Aw, that's too bad," said Hugo. His voice sounded almost friendly. "What about?"

"Scott Younger's murder. They held him for sixteen hours."

"Fuckin' cops," he said, shaking his masked head.

"Enough, Hugo," the tall one said and turned back to me. "I would like to believe you and Mr. Caruso are being straightforward about this matter. Convince me." His voice was quiet and polite.

"If either of us were going to use these pictures for blackmail, don't you think you would have heard by now?"

"Perhaps," he answered.

"I didn't even know what pictures you were talking about until I asked Wayne. And he wants no part of them, no part of your boss's business, no part of your boss's money. That's why he burned them. Anyway, you know who he is. He'd have to be crazy to try any blackmail."

"And he hasn't skipped town?"

"No," I replied bitterly. "He isn't going anywhere. The police wouldn't let him."

"I think we'll believe you for now," he said, rising from the couch. I let my breath out.

"I don't like it!" objected Hugo. He was at my chair in two angry strides. He grabbed my arm and yanked me up out of my seat. Now I began to sweat. I guess I hadn't been boiled dry. "You'd better not be fuckin' with us, lady."

I shook my head furiously, fighting back tears. He gave my arm a vicious squeeze.

"Don't worry," said the tall Reagan, carefully pronouncing each word as if for a deaf person. "We will research this further. And, if she is lying, she will be very, very sorry." The sweat on my body turned cold.

"Yeah," growled Hugo in assent. He squeezed my arm one last time and abruptly dropped it.

Then they left. I looked out of my window at their black Cadillac as it backed out of my driveway, hoping to catch a license plate number, but their plates were still smeared with mud. At least they had gone. I sank into my comfy chair.

They weren't going to kill me! The realization pulled me back out of my chair. I hugged myself and danced a giddy impromptu jig at being alive. It's amazing the kind of chemicals fight-or-flight experiences can release.

A burning smell interrupted my victory dance. My oatmeal had boiled over. But I whistled while I cleaned up the gummy mess, still glowing with the relief of being alive and unharmed. I had started another pot of oatmeal cooking when the phone rang. I turned down the flame and answered the phone with a cheery hello.

"This is Inspector Parker of the Mill Valley Police Department," the gloomy voice informed me. My glow flickered. "Sergeant Udel wants to talk to you." The glow faded to a glimmer.

"When?" I asked. I looked at the clock. It was a quarter to nine.

"Now," he replied.

"Oh." Not a lot of room for scheduling. "I need to be back by eleven," I said.

"That'll be up to the sergeant."

I told him I'd be down in ten minutes and went back to my oatmeal. This pot hadn't boiled over, but the oatmeal had congealed. Yuck. I tossed a couple of pieces of whole wheat bread in the toaster. When they popped up I grabbed them and ran out the door to my car. The faster I got to the interview, the faster

I would get out. I left a note on the door for Wayne in case I was late anyway. But I was going to do my damnedest to be back in time to meet him.

My last glimmer of relief dissolved into fear as I walked through the glass doors of the police station. I told the desk officer I was there to see Sergeant Udel, and sat down anxiously on the familiar plaid couch. I wondered if Wayne had sat there last night. I even sniffed unobtrusively for his scent. But I couldn't smell anything but carpet cleaner.

I didn't have to wait long. Inspector Parker escorted me into the windowless interrogation room before I even had time to work up to a full-fledged anxiety attack. He didn't look too happy himself. His plump shoulders were uncharacteristically slumped, his round red face unsmiling. And Sergeant Udel looked worse than ever. His skin was far too pale, his eyes round and staring. A happy thought brushed my mind. These guys did not look like police who were confidently prepared to arrest a man for murder. They looked more like guys who were ready to give up.

"How well do you know Wayne Caruso, Ms. Jasper?" asked Sergeant Udel, as soon as I sat on the metal folding chair. His voice was as cold as Alaska, his face expressionless.

"About as well as you can know someone in a week's time," I said. Probably not a bright answer. But I decided to compound it. I had convinced the Reagans this morning that the blackmail pictures were burned, maybe I could convince the cops that Wayne was innocent.

"Mr. Caruso is not a murderer. He is a kind and gentle man, a nonviolent man. He is probably the last person who would have killed Scott Younger, because he was the only one who actually liked Scott, even loved him, as a friend." I went on in this vein for another five minutes. I listed Wayne's many saint-like qualities and cited evidence of his compassionate nature. Wayne had cried when Scott was murdered, taken care of Scott unselfishly, and defended Scott to this day. I was moving myself to tears.

But Sergeant Udel's deadpan never changed as I spoke. There was not so much as a flicker of emotion behind his staring eyeballs. I resisted an urge to wave my hand in front of his face to make sure he was at least conscious. The only sign he was still alive was his finger tapping on the table in front of him.

When I had finished speaking, Sergeant Udel said only, "When did you first meet Mr. Caruso?" Had he even heard my five-minute defense? It was hard to tell.

"I saw him at Maggie's a few times, but I've only gotten to really know him since last Wednesday," I answered.

"The day of the murder?" he asked eagerly. There was an "ah-ha" in his voice as if I had just conceded an important point. He thrust his head forward to hear my reply.

"Yes," I confirmed nervously. Was he just trying to rattle me? I looked over at Inspector Parker for a clue. But his head was dutifully bent over his notebook.

"Do you pick up men at murders often, Ms. Jasper?" Udel snapped. My mouth dropped open. What an offensive question! Was he purposely trying to provoke me? I decided to limit my answers to the fewest syllables possible from that point on.

"No," I answered.

Sergeant Udel sat back in his chair and broke into high-pitched laughter. His laughter ended abruptly after a few moments, and he thrust his head forward again.

"How well do you really know Mr. Caruso?" he asked. Now his voice was angry.

It went on like that for another two hours. Udel asked every question about Wayne that Sergeant Feiffer had, plus a few more. Then he repeated them. And all accompanied by rapid mood swings that would have done any manic-depressive proud. I wasn't sure whether his performance was part of an interrogation technique. If it wasn't, I was afraid he was having a nervous breakdown. At the end of the interview he starting pressing me again about my fingerprints being on the murder weapon.

"Are you sure that Mr. Caruso didn't ask you to pick up that bar?" he asked again, for the third time. How long could this go on? At least sixteen hours, I answered myself.

"Yes," I answered. "Quite sure."

"He didn't hand it to you?" Udel snapped. He had asked me this nearly a dozen times.

"No."

"Okay," he said abruptly. "You can go."

I sat in my chair, trying to figure out how to answer this last question. Only after he himself had left the room did I realize that his final words were not a question but a dismissal.

Inspector Parker escorted me out of the interrogation room. At the door he gave me a weak, sad smile and thanked me for my cooperation. I was touched by his kindness. But maybe he just looked good to me after Sergeant Udel.

- Twenty-Two -

WAYNE'S JAGUAR WAS in the driveway when I got home. Wayne himself lay slumped in one of my peeling white porch chairs, his chin on his chest and his hands dangling over the sides. For a breath-stopping moment I thought he was dead, but as I ran up the stairs I could see his chest moving up and down rhythmically. He was only dead asleep.

I bent over him and kissed his pitted forehead. My lips brushed a stray curl of his soft hair. Princess Charming awakening Sleeping Beauty. Or perhaps Sleeping Beast.

His eyes opened and partially focused on my own. A sweet smile spread across his rough features.

"Kate," he murmured. The voice of a trusting child.

I leaned over and kissed his lips. His lips returned my kiss for a few breaths. Then he sat up abruptly.

"No," he said, his voice an adult's once more. "This isn't what I came here for."

"What did you come here for?" I asked sharply. I pulled up a chair and plopped down next to him.

"To slow you down," he said, turning toward me. Then he corrected himself. "To slow us down. The police are sure I did it. They're doing everything they can to prove it. I don't want you to be tainted."

"I'm not going to be 'tainted,' " I said impatiently.

"But they keep asking me if you were part of it, if you helped me to murder Scott." He shook his head in disbelief. "Suspect me, yes. But you?"

"I can take care of myself," I said. It was an effort to keep my tone even. He opened his mouth to argue but I kept talking. "Sergeant Udel interviewed me today. I don't think he's sure of anything, much less ready to arrest you."

"They believe they have enough evidence." He turned his face from me.

"What evidence?" I could feel my heart thumping now.

"Same old stuff and some new. My fingerprints on the table Scott was lying on. I must have touched it when I said goodbye to him." Wayne's voice had gone dead again.

"But of course you did. That's not evidence."

"Payments from our business accounts to the institution where my mother lives," he continued as if I hadn't spoken. "Approved by Scott verbally, but not on paper. Employee benefit, paid directly. Not smart for a man with legal training, but I didn't think."

I reached out and put my hand on top of his. He kept his eyes away from me and went on.

"And finally, Renee's big contribution. Scott once told her he was waiting for me to put him out of his misery. As if they needed another motive."

This was Renee's damaging information! I felt a burden of doubt slide off my chest. "That's all?" I asked. "That can't be enough to convict you. You know the law. Don't you have to be found guilty beyond a reasonable doubt?"

"Technically, yes. Gary Lee keeps saying the same thing." A trace of a smile touched Wayne's mouth. "Lucky to have him as my attorney. You would like him. You're both optimists."

"So, he thinks your chances are good?" I asked. The trace of smile disappeared entirely.

"He thinks it depends on the D.A. Mill Valley cops would arrest me today. The County Sheriffs' Department thinks I did it too. Only the D.A. is undecided. Not that he doesn't think I'm guilty. He's just not sure if he's got a good enough chance of conviction. But there's always my face." He turned to me. I saw the dense low brows hiding his eyes, the huge cauliflower nose, the scarred and pitted skin.

"What do you mean, your face?"

"The face of a murderer. Doesn't even have to be mentioned. Jurors will take one look at me and make up their minds."

"No! That's not true. All you have to do is speak up and people will know your real nature." I realized I had raised my voice. It helped to warm my sudden chill.

"Maybe they will," he accommodated me. His smile was sad and tired. "But that's not what I came here to talk about anyway. Got sidetracked. You shouldn't be involved with me, not until this is resolved. Can't do you any good." He turned his face away from me again.

"Wayne," I said as steadily as possible. "I *am* involved. I can't uninvolve myself."

"But . . ." he began.

" 'But' nothing. I'll decide my own risks. And I choose to be involved with you." I had his attention. He was now facing me, his eyes intense beneath his brows.

"Kate, I'm serious," he tried.

"I know you are. So am I." He opened his mouth again but I wouldn't let him talk. "Come into the house," I said, pulling him up out of his seat. "I'll tell you about *my* investigations."

A new look of concern gripped his face. But I opened the front door and walked inside before he had time to get protective. His sigh as he followed told me that he was giving up on trying to warn me off, at least temporarily.

Once in the house I brewed orange-cinnamon tea and then told him about Ted and Bonnie, Valerie's brother, Eileen's parents, my exploration of the upper floors of the chiropractor's building, and my misguided meeting with Renee's son. When he laughed over the Snoopy incident, even choking on his tea when I described my struggles to get the stuffed dog onto the back seat, I knew I had won him back over. The sound of his laughter was an auditory massage, loosening the tense muscles of my neck and shoulders.

Then I gave him a brief summary of the Reagans' morning visit. Wayne's original spurt of anxiety gave way to relief once I got to the part where the tall Reagan relented. After that, we discussed murder suspects for over an hour but came to no conclusions, except frustration.

"Maybe we need to look at this in a new way," he said after a while. He was thinking, his eyes hidden by his heavy brows. "You've dug up everything you can on motives and backgrounds. Nothing there. How about the day of the murder itself? Can you reconstruct the crime?"

"You mean go down to Maggie's and walk through it?" I asked. It sounded interesting.

"No!" he said, far too loudly. Then he lowered his voice. "Don't need to. We can do it on paper." Was this a trick to keep me safely indoors? Even if it was, I realized it was still worth a shot.

I got a yard-long pad of graph paper that I used for designing and laid it on the living room rug, along with some pencils and erasers. Together, we sketched out the floorplan at Maggie's, complete with desks, chairs and therapeutic tables. I had been in all of the rooms at one time or another. And what I couldn't visualize, Wayne could. It was amazing what we could remember between the two of us. Maybe the shock of Scott's death had engraved the rooms and fixtures on our memories.

Located on one side of the central hallway were the waiting room, the business office, storage area and bathroom. On the other side, three therapy rooms and the X-ray chamber. The treatment room that Scott had been murdered in was across from the bathroom. All the rooms had connecting doors except for that bathroom.

"Now, for the people," I said. I got out some Scrabble tiles and found a letter for each person's first initial. We agreed on a Y for Tanya, since both Ted and Tanya began with T.

I put S, W, V, and T into position in the chairs they had sat in when I had walked through the door that day, and the R for Renee behind the desk. I was just walking my K through the door when I noticed Wayne covertly eyeing his watch. It was past one o'clock.

"Do you need to go?" I asked.

"Work," he said. Guiltily, I remembered he managed several businesses, and that I purported to manage one myself. "Should take care of a few things."

"I'll only let you go if you promise to come back tonight," I said softly.

He hesitated, then chuckled and shook his head as he stood up. "Okay. Seems you can talk me into anything. You've almost convinced me I'll come out of this a free man." There were circles under his eyes, but his mouth held a crooked smile. I smiled back.

He stretched his arms out to me. When I stood, he held me tight for a moment and then picked me up off the floor in a sudden swoop. My feet dangled, bringing back memories of being sleepily carried in my father's arms. I closed my eyes, nuzzled his now accessible warm neck, smelled his herbal scent and thought decidedly un-daughterly thoughts.

He set me back down gently, his hands still on my waist, and looked at me intensely from underneath his brows for a moment. Then he turned and moved quickly out the front door.

The sound of the door closing brought with it a surge of fear. Was this the last time I would see him? I resisted an urge to chase after him, and returned to my floor plan.

I put my *K* on a chair. I thought for a moment. Then I brought in the *D* and *Y*. I was about to put them into position, when I remembered that Valerie had changed her seat while Scott and Devi were talking. And then what? When exactly did Eileen arrive? And Maggie?

I lay down on the rug, my eyes closed, to better conjure up the scene. And fell asleep mid-conjure.

In a dream I was walking down the block, across the street from the chiropractic building, when I saw a large crowd gathered in front of Nellie's "vintage clothing" store. I recognized my favorite uncle in the crowd. Everyone was looking in the direction of Maggie's office. My uncle pointed. I followed the direction of his finger and saw that the whole building was now made of glass. I could see a dentist drilling some teeth in a huge gaping mouth. Blood spurted from the mouth, splattering the glass walls. "No, the bottom floor," my uncle whispered. I lowered my eyes and saw a flurry of movement there. Maggie, Eileen, Renee and all the patients were moving from chair to chair in a circle. In the middle of the circle of chairs lay Scott Younger's bludgeoned body. Musical chairs, I thought. And then the chairs began to ring.

The persistence of the ringing grew until I opened my eyes. Damn. The doorbell. As I got up off the living room rug I wondered what I would have seen if I had stayed in the dream. Did my unconscious know who the murderer was? Or was it telling me that someone from across the street had seen something? I opened the front door.

Ann Rivera was standing on my doorstep. She was wearing a crisp linen suit and a look of curiosity on her friendly brown face. I had forgotten that she was going to visit. There went my time for investigation, or work, for that matter. However, she was a big improvement on the Reagans.

"What time is it?" I asked. I was still groggy.

"Four o'clock. I got off early." She walked into the hallway and gave me a quick squeeze and then a sharp look. "Were you asleep?"

"It's a long story," I said, groaning hopelessly. I had lost more than two hours of worktime to my nap.

"Well, let's go out for an early dinner and you can tell it to me," she suggested.

My stomach growled in assent. I hadn't eaten since the two slices of wheat toast that morning. My mouth opened to second the motion, but then I remembered Wayne.

"I've . . . I've got a date," I said. I felt suddenly embarrassed.

"Craig?" she asked. She cocked her head questioningly.

"No, Wayne," I said. I avoided her inquiring eyes. "Look, I'll make us a snack."

I turned to walk into the kitchen.

"Wayne who?" asked Ann, following me. "What's going on with you? Why are you acting so guilty?"

"Wayne Caruso," I answered. I found some sesame rice crackers in my goodies basket and ripped the package open with my teeth. I dumped them into a bowl and put them on the kitchen table. Then I opened a jar of pickles and set it next to the crackers. When I looked up, Ann's brown eyes were on me, searching for answers.

"Scott's ex-bodyguard," I explained briefly. I pulled a container of tofu "no-egg" salad out of the refrigerator and added it to the food on the table. "The police think he murdered Scott." I went back to the refrigerator for carrots.

"Stop with the food!" shouted Ann. She put her hand on the refrigerator door, blocking my move to open it. "Do *you* believe he murdered Scott?"

"No!" I answered automatically. Then I looked into her concerned eyes and remembered she was a friend. "At least mostly I don't think so," I amended honestly. "But I have this niggle of doubt."

"Tell me about Wayne," she said, and took her hand away from the refrigerator door.

So I did, at length. While I cut up carrots I told her how I had come to know Wayne. I found myself smiling as I described his shy wooing, brusque speech, and self-deprecation. But the smile was short-lived as I sat down at the kitchen table and recounted the details I knew about Wayne's relationship with Scott, the evidence against him and his night of questioning. Ann crunched pickles and nodded sympathetically as I spoke. I spread some "no-egg" on a cracker and related what Wayne had told me about his crazy mother. I stuffed the cracker in my mouth and chewed thoughtfully before I went on.

"He scares me sometimes," I finally admitted.

"How?" Ann asked.

"I guess it's physical. He's a big man, very strong and he is . . . Damn it, he is ugly. If I didn't know him and I saw him, walking alone on a dark night, I would cross the street to avoid him. He's just scary-looking," I finished defensively. I wanted to cry, knowing Wayne was absolutely correct about how he'd look to a jury.

"But you do know him," Ann prompted.

"You're right," I said. "All I have to do is look into his eyes, or hear him speak, and I recognize the gentleness in him. And I know he would be incapable of hurting anyone intentionally, much less murdering someone."

"So?"

"But the police think he killed Scott. What if they're right? How can I love a murderer?"

"Listen," said Ann, tapping a carrot stick on the table for emphasis. "I know you. You have good judgment. If you really think he's dangerous, stay away. But if you don't think Wayne is a murderer, trust that. Trust your own judgment."

I thought about what she had said, while we chomped our way through carrots, pickles and crackers. Then I realized that, at gut level, I didn't believe Wayne was dangerous. I really knew he wasn't a murderer. But I still wasn't comfortable. There was still something wrong, nagging me from my unconscious. Suddenly I had it.

"But even if he's not a murderer, is he a sicko?" I felt a huge sense of relief, putting this underlying fear into words. I breathed out tension.

"What do you mean?" Ann asked.

"All those years taking care of Scott and defending him. Isn't that sick?"

"Listen," Ann answered, with a flash of passion in her brown eyes. "I work in a mental hospital and see truly sick people all day long. Wayne sounds neurotic, but who isn't? He's probably just a caretaker."

"A caretaker?"

"He spent his childhood taking care of a sick mother. Emotionally, it's what he knows how to do. Then this sick man shows up in his life, so he takes care of *him* until he's not needed anymore. But with you he'll be okay. *You* won't abuse his love like his mother did or Scott did. He'll bloom with you." She smiled across the table at me, her teeth white against her tan skin. "Really," she assured me.

I felt a warm glow suffuse my body. Was she right? I returned her smile and thought, This is what friendship is about. I walked around the table and hugged her, crushing her linen suit. She hugged me back for a moment, then let me go.

"You're okay," she said. "Now, let me tell you about *my* problems for a while."

And she did. It was five-thirty by the time she left.

I rushed to the phone to call Jest Gifts. Judy was just leaving. I said I still wasn't feeling well, but I was keeping up with my paperwork. It wasn't entirely a lie, I told myself. She grunted in answer and told me that the temporary help had broken most of the last case of faw-law-law mugs. Somehow, I didn't really care. I assured her that, illness or no illness, I would get the paychecks to everyone on time. That seemed to satisfy her. I hung up while I could. The phone rang immediately after I set it down.

"Kate, finally you answer! Why haven't you returned my calls?" As usual, my estranged husband's timing was less than perfect.

I sighed in response to his question.

"Did you get my messages?" he asked impatiently.

"Yes," I said. "I've been busy."

"Oh." His voice smoothed over. "Let's go to dinner tonight. We can start working on the settlement. Pick you up at seven?" I sure was popular that night.

"I can't, honey," I said, instantly regretting the "honey." Old habits die hard. "Too much work to do."

"And you always said *I* worked too hard. Well, start thinking about it, anyway. You can do that, can't you?"

"Give me a little breathing time," I snapped. "It's been less than a week since you decided to divorce me." This was the man I had loved wholeheartedly for years. My faith in my own judgment began to sink.

"I'm sorry," he said, his voice hurt. I could just imagine the look in his puppy-dog eyes. He probably was sorry.

"It's all right. I'll think about it."

"Suzanne says . . ." he began. But the rest of his sentence

was mercifully drowned out by the sound of my doorbell ringing.

"Got a date," I said. "Talk to you later."

"A date? I thought you said you were working tonight!"

"Sorry, got to go," I said and hung up. I grinned at my own audacity as I walked to the door. I flung it open, ready to see Wayne's smiling face, but he wasn't there. Nobody was there.

– Twenty-Three –

I STARED OUT the doorway into empty space and asked myself who the hell had rung the doorbell. Was it one of those over-zealous UPS delivery men who ring, drop your package on the doormat and disappear before you can say, "I'll sign for that, thank you"? I looked down. There was no package on the doormat.

I walked out onto the porch, but I still couldn't see anyone. I had started down the stairs, when I heard a sudden mechanical coughing noise. I froze, one foot still in mid-step, suddenly alert. As my senses revived, my mind also woke up. If someone had wanted to lure me out into the open they had certainly done an effective job. But then the coughing noise turned to a roar, and a motorbike zoomed off somewhere nearby. I set my foot down and chided myself. What an imagination! I had thought the coughing noise was gunfire. I turned to go back in the house, wondering if I had imagined the sound of my doorbell as well. Anything to get Craig off the phone.

Then I saw it: FUCK OFF OR DIE! Spray-painted in slanting foot-high black letters across the redwood shingles on the front of my house. Next to the letters was a Rorschach-style black blob that I interpreted as a skull and crossbones. I felt the damage to the redwood shingles like a physical blow. My stomach cramped and I doubled over. My beautiful house!

I fought my nausea with concentrated deep-breathing as I walked back inside and dialed the Mill Valley Police Department. My hands were sweating. The cop on the other end was sympathetic, until I gave him my address. I was outside city limits.

"Is Sergeant Udel there?" I asked truculently. My fear and shock were quickly turning to anger. Maybe I wouldn't throw up after all.

"Yes, ma'am," he answered.

"Then please ask him to come to the phone. Tell him it's connected to the Younger murder."

What I got was Inspector Parker. He took down the information without much interest. He didn't buy the connection to the murder. "Sounds like kids to me," he said. Then he suggested I call the County Sheriff's Department, since my house was in their jurisdiction. I asked him whether he would at least tell Sergeant Udel about the incident. He promised he would, and hung up.

I was trying unsuccessfully to remove the spray paint with solvent when Wayne drove up. The black letters were remaining aggressively in place. However, I was fairly certain I was removing all the sealant I had spent the summer applying shingle by shingle.

Wayne was halfway up the stairs when he saw the black message. His body was rigid. Then he looked at me. I felt instantly to blame for the whole mess. But before I could make an unwarranted apology, he marched the rest of the way up the stairs and took me into his arms. I buried my head in his down-jacketed chest, blocking the black letters from my sight and feeling a great affinity with the unjustly maligned ostrich.

"Did you tell the police?" he asked.

I whispered an affirmative from my downy refuge.

"Let's go," he said.

Half an hour later we were eating Chinese take-out in Wayne's warm kitchen. By tacit agreement neither of us had said a word about the spray paint, or discussed the murder for that matter. In fact, neither of us was saying much at all. The only sound was the clicking of our efficient chopsticks across bright pottery plates, to deliver brown rice, garlic broccoli, spiced string beans and Szechuan bean curd to our hungry mouths. I found to my surprise that the most recent shock had sharpened my appetite instead of dulling it.

"Hot tub?" suggested Wayne after the last string bean had been consumed. His eyes were intense as they peered out from beneath his eyebrows.

"Sure," I agreed. More decadence sounded good.

We walked to the spa in silence. Once there, I changed into the black and lilac bathing suit that still hung in the dressing room. I had considered leaving the bathing suit off, but years of misguided monogamy had left me too shy.

I joined Wayne in the tub, where he sat quietly emitting clouds of male pheromones into the steam. I lowered my body into the hot swirling water and closed my eyes. After a lifetime of effortless babbling, I suddenly found myself unable to form words. I leaned my body back and let my mind float. Then I felt the hesitant, soft pressure of his mouth upon mine. I laced my hands into his silky curls and pulled his head closer. The hesitancy vanished and we sank into a kiss which threatened to drown us both, literally.

"Bedroom," I whispered, once our lips had untangled. Good God, woman! objected someone in my brain but I told her to butt out.

We passed a mirror on the way to his bedroom. He stopped me, put his hands on my shoulders and turned me toward the mirror.

"Beauty and the Beast," he whispered.

I started guiltily, remembering how I had used those very words to describe Scott and him as a pair. Then I realized he meant us. I was the beauty. I laughed nervously.

"Are short, dark and A-line beauties in now?" I asked.

But he was serious. He pointed out my beauty, spot by spot. And I began to see myself through his eyes: cellulite-dimpled thighs, sagging breasts and pale yellow skin became, respectively, lush, sensual and creamy. And the Beast: Muscled shoulders gave way to a brown woolly chest, small waist and powerful thighs.

I turned to embrace him. We held each other for a long time. Then he picked me up and carried me the rest of the way to the bedroom.

I had forgotten what it meant to be made love to. I remembered sex, where foreplay consisted of, "You feel like it tonight?" "Yeah, I guess so." But this was true lovemaking. Spells of gentle sweetness punctuated by flurries of passion carried us into the early morning hours. And in those early morning hours came the realization that I had, after all, become too involved. Before, I might have survived Wayne's possible arrest and conviction. But, now, it was inconceivable to me that I could give him up.

Late the next morning, following a breakfast of fresh baked bread and blushing smiles, Wayne drove me back home. After a brief protest, I allowed him to search my house for intruders while I waited in his Jaguar. He didn't find anyone lurking there and drove away with a promise to visit again in the evening, Mill Valley Police Department willing.

I walked up my stairs in the cool air and faced the ugly black lettering on the front of my house. I found that I could look at the message now without overwhelming nausea. Only a fleeting shiver and elevated pulse rate marked the event. So I allowed my mind to consider the words.

FUCK OFF OR DIE! Whose message this was? And what did it mean? It had to be a warning to stop looking into Younger's murder. But I paused to evaluate Inspector Parker's explanation of "kids." There was that little girl down the block whose feelings had been hurt when I had shooed her basset hound out of my yard. She couldn't understand that I didn't hate her dog, only his excretory habits. But she was only seven years old. She probably couldn't even spell the "f" word. I hadn't offended any other kids as far as I knew. A random graffiti gang in Mill Valley? Not likely.

Hugo popped into my mind. He certainly enjoyed the use of the "f" word, but I wasn't entirely certain he could spell it either. No, the Reagans had other methods of terrorism. Tanya? Somehow I couldn't picture her wielding the black spray paint. But Renee's kid, John. His shaved head and hostile blue eyes reared up in my mind. My pulse shot up a notch higher. There was no way of knowing for sure. I shook my head and walked into the house, reminding myself that if I unraveled the murder of Scott Younger I would probably find my graffiti artist tangled in there, too.

But the murder remained obstinately enmeshed in a rat's nest of loops, snarls and knots. I changed my clothes, made a pot of Dr. Chang's Long Life Tea, and knelt back down on the living room rug to move Scrabble pieces on my graph paper floor plan. After half an hour I was no further enlightened. I needed help. I rolled up the graph paper, put the Scrabble pieces in a Baggie and set out for Maggie's office.

When I got there, I opened the front door cautiously. I knew

Maggie would help me with my murder reconstruction if I could just get around Renee. But no such luck. Renee spotted me the minute I stepped over the threshold. Her eyes narrowed.

"You!" she shouted. She aimed a red-nailed finger at me. "Did you give my son a six-foot Snoopy dog?"

The head of every patient in the waiting room swiveled toward me. I allowed an expression of complete mystification to envelop my face.

"Why would I do that?" I asked innocently. Why indeed? my mind echoed sarcastically.

Renee's finger wavered, then dropped. But she continued to stare at me, eyes still narrow with suspicion. I kept my own wide eyes on hers, unflinching, and wondered if her son had spray-painted my house.

"Never mind," she muttered finally and lowered her gaze to her desk. I felt a surge of triumph. I decided to push my luck.

"I need to talk to Maggie for a moment," I said. "Or Eileen, if Maggie's busy."

"They're both busy," she snapped, not moving her eyes from her desk. "This is a chiropractor's office," she added pointedly.

"So when can I talk to them?" I asked.

"Maggie takes her lunch in an hour. If you want to bug her then, that's up to you."

I decided I could wait the extra hour to see Maggie, but not in her office. I went back outside into the cold. At least the sun was shining. A definite improvement on the atmosphere in the waiting room. I knew I would have to straighten Renee out eventually, but right now murder was my top priority. My only question was how to use my spare hour. I glanced across the street and saw Nellie's vintage clothing store. With a start, I remembered my dream of the day before.

I crossed the street eagerly, compelled by the hope that my dream had been prophetic. Had the police bothered to question the people at Nellie's about what they might have observed on the day of the murder? I doubted it. And they could very well have seen something out the glass windows at the front of their store.

I stopped at one of the two-dollar bins on the sidewalk. A purchase would probably make my questions go down easier. And I could always add whatever I bought to my collection of nails and primroses. The bin was filled with a hodgepodge of belts, underwear, hair clips, scarves and knit hats. Nothing I would really want to wear. I dug deeper, not wanting to completely waste two dollars. I pulled out an attractive purple scarf. It looked familiar, especially the black yin-yang symbols embroidered on the ends.

I stared at it. Then I remembered where and when I had last seen it. It had been wrapped around Devi's wispy neck the day of Scott Younger's death. But that wasn't right, was it? I could also remember her wearing a necklace of sparkling crystals that day.

That was what my unconscious had been nagging me about when I removed the hairdresser's rubbery sheet from around my neck! Devi was wearing the purple scarf over the necklace before Scott's death, but not afterwards. At some point in between she had removed the scarf. And presumably hidden it here in this bin. But why?

I took a closer look at the scarf in my hand. There was a small brown stain on one of the neatly stitched corners. I recoiled. Blood? Was this Scott Younger's blood?

I rushed into Nellie's, scarf in hand.

"I found this in your bin!" I shouted.

The woman at the counter looked up at me and smiled tentatively. I laid the scarf in front of her.

"Silk, very nice," she said.

"Did you ever see this scarf before?" I asked.

"No." Her smile looked strained.

"Look, I'm going to leave this with you, but I want you to keep it behind the desk. The police are going to be interested in it."

"The police?" Her smile was gone now.

"It's important that the police know this was found in your bin. Were you here last Wednesday?"

"No, I wasn't," she said, her voice suddenly hostile. "And about this scarf thing. I don't think that's one of our scarves, and I didn't see you get it out of our bins. What are you trying to pull?"

"But . . ." I began. Then I realized she was right. She only had my word for it that the purple scarf came from her bin. And the police? Would they believe me? But it was Devi's scarf, I assured myself. Someone else had to remember her wearing it. And it did have blood on it. At least I thought it had blood on it.

I ended up buying the scarf for two dollars. And even then I couldn't talk the woman behind the counter into giving me a receipt describing it. All I got was a cash register slip showing two dollars plus tax. So much for documentation.

I started back across the street to the chiropractor's office, hoping to find someone who remembered Devi wearing the scarf. But halfway across I stopped. For once, I needed to think before acting. I changed course and walked slowly to my car to drive home.

All the way home my mind buzzed. This proved Devi was a murderer, didn't it? Not necessarily. If Scott's blood was on the scarf it could have gotten there as innocently as my fingerprints on the murder weapon. But then, why hide it? To protect Tanya? Had Tanya killed Scott? No, I couldn't believe that.

But there was something about Tanya. I remembered her dark hair, blue eyes and heart-shaped face. Then a picture of Scott Younger formed in my mind. Again, the contrast of dark hair and blue eyes. And the triangular face. Was Scott Tanya's father after all? Had I been blind to the real motive for murder? Tanya was fifteen years old. How long ago had Scott and Devi known each other? I couldn't remember. But, even if Scott was Tanya's father, how did that add up to a credible murder motive?

I shook my head in frustration. There was only one person who could answer these questions, and that was Devi herself.

- Twenty-Four -

I PHONED WAYNE the moment I barreled through my front door. I didn't even let the black letters on the face of my house slow me down. I was afraid he would never forgive me if I went to talk to Devi on my own. But he didn't answer his phone. His answering machine did. So much for forgiveness.

"Devi might have killed Scott," I blurted onto the tape. "I'm going to see her. I'll call you later."

I found the lavender slip of paper with Devi's address and phone number still on my desk. She was close by, on the outskirts of downtown Mill Valley. On the way out the door I paused for all of a minute to consider the risk in visiting her. But the woman was so frail and indecisive. I remembered her wispy body, faltering requests and continual breathlessness. For a moment I even doubted her actual ability to kill Scott. Could she hit someone in the back of the neck hard enough to kill them? Or even make the decision to do so?

It was up to me to find out. The police hadn't ferreted out the truth. I was sure they would ignore the significance of the bloody scarf, if they even believed my story of finding it in the first place. I climbed into my car.

Whether or not Devi had killed Scott, I assured myself as I drove down Throckmorton Avenue, she wasn't going to kill me. I wasn't going to lie down on a table and expose the back of my neck. My body must be stronger than hers. And I practiced tai chi. By the time I had reached her house I was convinced that there was no way Devi could be a physical threat to me.

I issued a mental apology to Wayne as I opened Devi's gate

and strode up the bricked walkway to her front door. I kept my eyes and mind averted from her beautifully tended lawn and garden, alive with pansies, Iceland poppies and alyssum, and shaded by an elderly oak tree. No time to fuss over beauty. I rang the doorbell.

Devi answered the door, her stick-thin body clad in white from head to foot. She wore an exquisitely embroidered white-on-white silk kimono, over white stockings and white satin slippers. A white iris was pinned in her wispy blond hair. The only discordant note was the clunky steel-grey revolver she clasped tightly in her right hand. A gun. Damn.

I moved back a step. She raised the gun ever so slightly. That was enough for me. I stopped moving. Then she glanced down at the purple scarf I was carrying.

"Oh, did you find it?" she asked in a hoarse voice. Did she still have a cold? She took a breath. "I thought someone might. Please, come in," She waved her gun airily in my direction. My heart kicked at my rib cage. So much for her physical frailty. I stayed where I was.

"Is that thing loaded?" I asked.

"I think so." She looked down the barrel of the gun as if to check for bullets. "I hope I did it right." She swung it back toward me so I could take a look. With an Olympic spurt, my heart jumped into my throat. "Does it seem right to you?" she asked breathlessly. Her eyes were wide and slightly glazed in her gaunt pale face. Drugs? Or just insanity?

"Fine," I choked out. The lessons I had learned while working in a mental hospital were returning to me quickly. "Just fine," I repeated in a soothing tone. I put out my shaking hand open-palmed, hoping that she might give me the gun. She didn't. Her attention had fluttered elsewhere.

"It's beautiful out here, isn't it?" she asked as she surveyed her yard. "Really beautiful. No more weeds. I made sure. Well, almost no weeds." She looked down at an offending dandelion. "Maybe I should . . . No, no. We have to go in now," she said, straightening up, her voice now that of a schoolmarm.

I took a quick look behind me. The gate was closed. There was no one on the street. Would she shoot me if I ran? I returned my gaze to her glossy eyes and forced my face into a gentle smile. She gestured impatiently with the gun.

"We can't stay out here anymore." Her voice had turned

peevish. She was breathing in short rapid gasps. Just listening to her made my own lungs constrict.

Tai chi versus bullets? Maybe the Master was fast enough to dodge them but I wasn't. Reluctantly, I entered her house.

Her front room was done in soft pastels. The slightest blush of rose in the walls was echoed in the carpets. The scattered sofas were a pale, pale mauve, and the coffee tables were creamy white. A room for gracious living or quiet meditation. I wondered how she kept it clean.

Devi smiled a weak social smile and pointed her gun at one of the low sofas. I sat down carefully on its cushioned edge, heart still thudding, ready to move instantly. Then I smelled something burning. My eyes quickly followed my nose to a low glass table at the other end of the room. Large chunks of crystal and burning incense sticks were arranged in a circle on the table. In the center of the circle stood a single white iris in a fluted glass vase.

I turned back to watch Devi as she sat down across from me on another sofa. She sank into its cushions heavily. The sound of her labored breathing echoed in the peaceful room. I looked into her eyes. They were floating dreamily.

"Thank you for coming," she said finally. "I didn't want to be alone. It'd be okay, but . . . but I get so tired." Her eyes shut for a moment, but reopened before I could even consider running. "And thank you for the scarf. I . . ." A spasm contorted her face for a moment. "I got blood on it."

"I know," I said, keeping my voice gentle.

"When I bent over him . . . he was dead, you know. At least I think he was dead then. I missed his head. I'm not very strong anymore." She was breathing even faster now. Her eyes had lost all focus. I looked at her right hand. It still held the gun, although loosely. "I went to the bathroom to think, but when I came out I heard Wayne." She stopped to breathe.

Wayne? What about Wayne? But before I could pursue that thought another one hit me. I had never seen Devi return from the restroom. Because she had been in Scott's room already when I went down the hall. If only I had kept on with my Scrabble reconstruction . . . Her voice interrupted my "if only," drawing me back to the present reality.

"So I went into Scott's room. Just to talk. At least I thought so. But then I saw him lying there face down. God gave me that opportunity, don't you think?" Her eyes sought mine, briefly focusing. I nodded my head carefully. "Oh, I hope so! It must be. Scott was face down and the metal bar was right there. He must have heard me and he still didn't move. God—it had to be God." Her eyes closed briefly. Then they popped back open.

"Tanya!" she yelped and looked around the room in panic. Then her eyes focused again. She gave me a watery smile.

"I'm sorry Tanya spray-painted your house. She was just trying to shield me. She thought she'd scare you away. She even set my clocks back so I'd miss that meeting." Devi frowned vaguely. "But once she told me about the spray paint—once I knew how far she would go to protect me—I knew I had to end this thing.

"She saw me hide the scarf at Nellie's. I saw the blood . . ." Her face contorted again. "It's okay." She said softly to herself in a child's voice. "I used the scarf to wipe off my fingerprints too."

She straightened up abruptly, her breath coming in erratic gasps. Her hand tightened on the gun, whitening her knuckles. "A decisive act. I was decisive." She looked at me, her eyes now almost clear. I wasn't sure I liked this new decisiveness. But I forced myself to smile.

"Very decisive," I agreed in a warm purr. Her hand relaxed on the gun. She leaned back again.

"Had to, for Tanya."

"But why?" I asked. It came out too sharply. She sat up and looked at me in surprise.

"Because Scott was Tanya's father, of course. He never knew it, though. A long time ago I thought I loved him. But I found out he was cruel, horribly cruel, like my own father." Devi began to wave the gun in the air. I shouldn't have asked her why she killed Scott.

"He told me how he blackmailed a drug dealer once. He set up his kids, humiliated them. Not the evil man himself, but his kids! And he was proud of it!" Devi's eyes became as wild as the gun she was waving around with each word.

"I couldn't let a man like that raise my child. I left town when I got pregnant. All the way to Oregon. Then I sent Scott a letter telling him I had had an abortion. And I raised my child. My beautiful little girl. She'll be okay. My brother Bobbie will take care of her. She's a good child."

I nodded sympathetically. "A lovely girl," I agreed. Devi lowered the gun, but then her face stiffened.

"My father abused me every day of my life after my mother died. He drank. Then he went into rages. With fists and kicks and words. His nickname for me was "whore." He broke my nose once, my ribs three times. But he was rich. So no one did anything. Not a thing." Oh God. I remembered what Eileen had said about Devi's family. I held my hand out to her. But she didn't see it.

"And my poor brothers. My oldest brother killed himself when he was seventeen. But Bobbie and I bided our time for the five years until I was old enough to leave. I left the day I turned eighteen. And I took Bobbie with me." She paused to calm her ragged breathing. "Tanya will never go through that, never!"

"No, she'll be just fine." I said. It would have been useless to mention that fists and kicks wouldn't have been Scott's style of cruelty. In Devi's mind her father and Scott were the same man. Pharmaceuticals, LSD, they both sold drugs. Maybe Ann Rivera could explain why Devi had re-created her relationship with her father.

"Scott would have taken Tanya," Devi said. "As soon as I was gone. He was rich and powerful too. And I heard Wayne. He said Scott liked children and didn't have any of his own."

"But . . ." I began. Then I remembered: Don't argue with a crazy person. Especially one with a gun in her hand.

"You think he couldn't have gotten custody? After I was dead he would have had her." She was glaring at me, not a look I wanted to see in her eyes. Her ragged breathing had an angry edge to it.

"But why would you die?" I asked reasonably, my voice soft and low.

"Why? Ask God why I have lung cancer."

Lung cancer? I felt very cold as the truth hit me. Now I remembered Maggie telling me that Devi was seriously ill. This thin, hoarse, breathless woman didn't have a cold. She was dying. Tears stung my eyes suddenly.

"I'm sorry," I said. Her face softened.

"Don't be. I've come to terms with it. At least I've tried to." She paused for breath, and then went on. "I had rheumatic fever as a child, and a heart murmur. So I thought all the symptoms were related to that. And to my smoking. Which I guess they were, actually." She laughed hoarsely. The sound was unnerving. "So I didn't go to a doctor until it was too late. Oh, well. Now it's busy metastasizing into my other organs.

"Did you know I used to be fat? Layers and layers of lovely fat. Cake and lasagna. Bearnaise sauce. Ice cream." Her eyes glazed over. She lay the gun on her lap. "But now I'm nauseated most of the time. From the cancer. From the pain medication, too. But I can't do without it. I hurt too bad. I get confused sometimes, though." She looked at me blearily. Drugs. I was right the first time.

"I'm not afraid. My brother Bobbie's going to take care of Tanya. That's why I moved back to Marin. She's with him now. And I'm going home. Going towards the light." She gripped the gun again. "Death is always the next step. The transition's the only hard part." I eyed the gun nervously. Was she trying to convince me? "I've given up my life to God. I just couldn't give up my daughter's too."

She straightened up on the couch and grasped the gun. Her eyes looked completely focused for the first time since we'd entered her house.

"I sent a full confession to the police. I hope it's clear. I stayed off the medicine until I finished it. I've said goodbye to Tanya, my little girl." Tears flowed from her eyes. "Thank you for being here. I needed someone to be here. I just hope I can do this right." She put the gun to her temple just as I realized who was to die. My realization came too late. As I jumped up from the couch she pulled the trigger.

The shot exploded into the room, sound and crimson splattering across the pastel landscape. The acrid smell of burnt gunpowder collided with the cloying incense. My legs gave way beneath me. I told myself it was only a dream.

But my nausea was real. The blood was real. The buzzing in my head was real.

And the banging on the door was real too. I rolled my head slowly toward the door, to watch it splinter inward. A booted foot came through and then a hand, turning the knob.

I watched Wayne burst into the room, eyes blazing. "She . . ." I began. I couldn't finish. I felt something wet on my face. I shivered, thinking it was blood. But it was only my own tears.

"It's okay," he said. But tears were running down his face now too.

He knelt on the floor and picked me up. Tears and blood. I closed my eyes until I felt the cool outdoor air on my wet face.

Gently, he eased me down on the lawn, under the branches

of the oak tree, making a pillow of his down jacket for my head. The sky was blue and oddly shimmering through the oak leaves. I could smell the grass, the wet soil and the sweet scent of alyssum. And hear the hum of traffic, saws buzzing and dogs barking. A shrill laugh broke out somewhere nearby.

"It was all right with her," I said finally. "She was ready to die."

"Thank God she didn't think you were," Wayne said.

"I'm not, am I?" I whispered. I sat up to reach for him. He held me until I had finished weeping. Then he went back into the house to call the police.

- Twenty-Five -

AFTER TWO EMOTIONAL weeks of mutually assisted recovery, Wayne and I sat at my kitchen table eating breakfast. I watched him as he silently used his spoon to trace pattern after pattern in his bowl of oatmeal. Nude healthy oatmeal. No butter. No sugar. No milk. His brows hid his eyes as he stared downward. His shoulders were hunched unhappily. Was the honeymoon over so soon? I fixed my eyes on him questioningly until he looked up.

"Appreciate you cooking me breakfast . . ." he began. His voice faded out before he could finish his sentence.

"But," I prompted.

"But, I have a confession to make." His eyes were on mine now, fully visible and loaded with feeling. My shoulders tightened with the old, familiar tension. Was he going to tell me he murdered Scott? No, I reminded myself. That was all in the past.

"So confess," I said impatiently. He had another woman? He was already tired of me? He was really gay? Actually, I doubted that possibility after our two weeks together. He was leaving the country? He had six illegitimate children? What?

"Somewhere along the line I've misled you." He dropped his eyes to his oatmeal again. "Kate, I'm not a vegetarian." His low voice rose. "I don't even like health food!" Then he brought his eyes up to mine, pleading for understanding.

I reached for his hand across the table. As my muscles relaxed I began to laugh. I couldn't help it. The laughter grabbed me by the throat and shook me. The dawning relief in Wayne's eyes made me laugh even louder.

"Maybe I can learn," he said, with a hesitant smile. A gleam came into his eyes suddenly. "Is there such a thing as soy sausage?"

BODY OF EVIDENCE

In Kate Jasper's offbeat, *totally* California lifestyle, there's no such thing as "routine"—a routine visit to her chiropractor, for example, leads to cold-blooded murder when a dead body turns up on the examining table. There are no known motives for the death of Scott Younger—only a handful of possible, and very unlikely, killers seated in the doctor's waiting room.

But Kate suspects that old-fashioned vengeance is behind this thoroughly modern murder. Now Marin County's one and only vegetarian-divorcée-detective finds herself in the midst of a positively bone-chilling crime...

ADJUSTED TO DEATH

00453

0 78252 00399 5

ISBN 1-55773-453-4